Escaping West

Morgan K. Wyatt

Chapter One

"HELLO, KITTY."

Kitty Hamilton turned in response to her best friend yelling her name and waving with both arms, if you could call it waving. It looked more like she was trying to shoo off an annoying nanny goat, spinning her arms like an out of control windmill. Most of the strolling women pulled up their trailing skirts as if to avoid touching the arm-flailing Harriet. A few stopped to stare and actually stepped off the wooden boardwalk to make a wide circle around the petite girl while Dirk, the grizzled barber clad in his apron, felt compelled to comment loudly. "The gal needs a keeper!"

The sight of her friend's moving dimpled arms caused Kitty's lips to tilt upward. Harriet appeared wound up, and she needed to find out why before Harriet did something even more outrageous. Most everyone in Lancaster, Ohio already talked about her as that German orphan girl who worked up at the dairy. Depending on who was doing the talking it could mean different things. It could mean odd if Postmaster Mallory did the talking or beautiful if old man Simmons spoke. If Johnnetta Taylor was exercising her jaw, it meant lazy. She couldn't stand the fact blonde, blue-eyed Harriet worked side by side with her husband, George.

Grabbing her skirt, Kitty stepped off the boardwalk to cross the street. Her eyes focused on her friend, she walked into the path of a team of straining Belgium draft horses pulling a beer wagon. Blocking out the curses of the irate teamster, she stumbled forward to avoid becoming horse slippers. Kitty managed to gain the sidewalk where Harriet waited and stood beside her smaller friend, trying to gain her breath and balance.

"Kitty, you slower than a wagon dog," Harriet commented, wagging her index finger at her.

Kitty didn't have to look to know she'd garnered the townspeople's focus. Wrinkling her nose, she started to say something about it being all Harriet's fault for distracting her, but she stopped before the words were out. Harriet had her share of troubles, and today she was happy. What kind of friend would burst her bubble?

The strident voice of Wilhelmina Parker saying how disappointed Kitty's parents would be in her hoydenish behavior did reach her ears, but Kitty didn't show any sign it had. This wasn't the first time she had heard something along these lines. Early on, she made the mistake of reacting to Wilhelmina's remarks. That's why the malevolent bat continued to chastise Kitty. In the past when she'd felt charitable, she rationalized Wilhelmina's behavior by believing the woman gave her parental advice since Kitty had no parents to do so. They drowned crossing a flooded stream in her twelfth year, leaving her the ward of her Aunt Eugenia and the recipient of unsolicited comments by the town's busybodies. She'd given up on thinking charitable thoughts about Wilhelmina Parker, however, and accepted the fact she was plain mean.

Harriet and she, as two orphans, made easy pickings when it came to gossip. For the most part, the townswomen were married and secure in their lives. They'd fulfilled their duty to marry and procreate. Somehow, it caused them to act superior to everyone who hadn't. The have-nots, which definitely included her and Harriet, received the same dislike and suspicion normally reserved for copperheads, the snake as opposed to scoundrel types. The good thing about Wilhelmina's attention on her was it spared Harriet. Kitty hooked her arm with Harriet's and pulled her away from the watching crowd.

In front of the livery where the men who were too old to fight in the war even when beardless boys fought, loved to talk about it. They met daily there and rehashed the details. Old Mister Johnson had started in on the importance of General Sherman as the girls hurried between buildings.

Popping up unexpectedly behind the hotel, the girls surprised a chambermaid and a guest caught in an amorous embrace. Harriet giggled, while Kitty glanced back over her shoulder trying to determine if the girl was Betsy Lockhart. If it was, maybe she and Joseph Shipley were not sweethearts anymore. In a town almost barren of marriageable men, a girl had to keep herself open to possibilities, especially when each year diminished her choices. Joseph struck her as a decent, quiet man. Betsy had him hogtied by age fourteen, while, Kitty, at nineteen, within kissing distance of twenty, was practically a spinster like her aunt. Definitely not the future, she envisioned for herself.

"Let's walk a little further before you can tell me why you're so excited," Kitty said in what she deemed a low voice. There was no reason to give the townspeople any more gossip fodder. She certainly gave them enough with her past beau fiasco. Even more reason she needed to know if Betsy threw aside Joseph in favor of a hotel guest. They walked a few steps and turned off the main thoroughfare. The noise of the horses and people diminished as they headed across a fallow field.

"The letter, it came." Harriet retrieved a rumpled envelope from her pocket with a flourish.

Kitty stopped, turning to look her friend in the eyes. Harriet quivered with excitement. "What letter?" Kitty didn't remember anything about a letter. Then it hit her, Harriet's mail order bride scheme.

"Harriet, you didn't? I know we talked about it, but I thought that was it." Kitty tried to keep the censure out of her voice. She didn't want to sound like her bitter Aunt Eugenia.

Harriet grabbed both of Kitty's hands. "No, it was over for you. I know you thought it a silly plan, but you have a place to live."

"You do, too." She gave her friend's hand a reassuring squeeze, not knowing what to say to calm her friend's fears.

"Not for long, I am afraid," Harriet muttered looking down.

Kitty looked at her crestfallen friend carefully. "Why?"

"Mr. George Taylor wants the milk without buying the cow." Harriet continued to study the ground.

"What's this about buying cows? George owns the cows already." Why wouldn't her friend look her in the eye? George Taylor owned the dairy where Harriet worked and always acted friendly to her, maybe too friendly.

"You remember Ebenezer Shrout? The one I thought sweet on me." Harriet managed to get one hand free of Kitty's grasp and started worrying her apron trim with it.

"Uh-huh, you never told me what happened with him." The change of topic confused Kitty. Ebenezer was old news.

Harriet broke the other hand free, turned her back to Kitty, and started walking.

"Harriet, whatever it is, you can tell me?" At the same time Kitty caught up with her friend, Harriet spun around, and they collided, bumping heads.

"Ow!" they squealed in unison, grabbed their sore heads and plopped to the ground.

"What were we talking about?" Harriet wondered aloud.

"The free cows, Ebenezer, and Mr. George." Kitty nearly shouted in frustration.

"Oh ya, well Ebenezer tries to milk me like cow." Harriet placed her hands over her large breasts to give Kitty a clue to what she was talking about.

"Like a cow?" Kitty raised one eyebrow in disbelief.

"I told Ebenezer no hands until married. Know what Ebenezer say?"

Kitty shook her head, too busy picturing a man's hands on her breasts to reply. Glancing down at her hands, she flexed them, picturing them as larger and more masculine.

"No one going to marry immigrant orphan girl. All I was good for was a poke," Harriet answered with a telling catch in her voice.

"No, he didn't! I never liked Ebenezer Shrout, anyhow." Kitty's face drew up in a scowl as she denounced the farmhand. "I always thought he looked like a weasel and smelled like a skunk."

Harriet giggled. "You never spoke."

"I didn't say anything because I thought you liked him. Did you slap him after he talked to you like that? I want to slap Ebenezer for treating you in such a horrible manner." Kitty's eyes squinted menacingly as she planned appropriate retribution.

"Oooh, no, I say I could do better.'" Harriet threw back a blond pigtail for emphasis.

"You're right!" She noticed Harriet's grimace. "What is it?"

"Mr. George." She spat the words.

"Not him, too?" Kitty gasped.

Harriet scampered to her feet, shaking out her broadcloth skirt.

"He tries, I hide, and then Mrs. George comes. I figure Mrs. George will let me go even if Mr. George doesn't catch me," Harriet concluded glumly.

The image of Johnnetta, with her constantly pursed mouth, came to Kitty's mind. She always looked like she swallowed a spoonful of vinegar, as if she was indulging in vinegar drinking, the current diet fad. Johnnetta, however, was stick thin, and apparently, Mr. George liked to dally with women carrying a little more weight.

"Sorry as I am to say it, I think you're right about this," Kitty said, shaking her head.

"Now you know why I'm so excited about the letter." Harriet grabbed both of Kitty's hands, lifted her to her feet and spun them in a circle, literally sweeping Kitty off her feet.

"Stop, stop, before I take off like the rock in David's slingshot,"

Kitty shrieked.

They both stopped, although the ground kept spinning.

"Read it to me." Kitty lowered herself to ground while pulling up the back of her skirt to keep it out of the dirt.

"*Dear Harriet*—he called me dear. No man ever called me dear," Harriet gushed while flourishing the letter.

Kitty held her hand out for the letter.

"But Kitty," Harriet complained.

"Harriet, I'm supposed to be returning a library book. I can't be gone all day. Aunt Eugenia will have a fit. You know how she is."

She reluctantly handed the letter over. "Could you read it aloud and start with dear."

Kitty ignored Harriet's heart-felt sigh and read.

Dear Harriet,

I was overjoyed when I read your sweet letter. I know you will make a good wife and mother.

"What did you tell him?"

"I was young enough to bear children and a hard worker. Keep reading." Harriet motioned for her friend to continue reading by circling her hand.

"Okay, let me see. Where was I?" Kitty said and scanned the letter.

"I should tell you about myself. My name is Adam Easton, and I came out west like so many others to strike it rich. When I reached California, the strike was over, so I headed to British Columbia where there was a rush.

Gold mining didn't work out too good for me so I hired on at the dry goods store. The owner wanted to go back east, so he let me buy him out. I've owned the store for the past three years. It is a good business and provides a decent living. You would never have to worry about going hungry. I live in the rooms over the store. There is also a yard for a kitchen garden. If you want, I can get you a cart and mule to go places.

The one thing you might miss is your friends. I realize it will be a change for you. I hope not too hard of one. You did mention you liked change and were ready for an adventure. You will have plenty of change. I will promise you I will do everything in my power to make you happy.

Many men here would like to have wives, too. If you have any friends who would like to be mail order brides, you can bring them. I look forward to the time we meet. The ride out will be long, maybe as long as three weeks. Please come soon since the Columbia road becomes impassable in the winter, and we get snow often as early as October. I have enclosed a train ticket for traveling to Sacramento. From there a stage will bring you to the Washington-Canada border. A freight caravan goes over the Columbia Road once a week to Druthersville, where my store is located. The driver will be expecting you. I wish I could come for you myself, but my store is the only one in town. The trip down and back would take me the better part of two months.

All my best to you,
Adam Easton

Harriet sighed and fell back onto the grass.

"I'll admit Harriet he sounds like a good one. Still, you don't even know what he looks like, he could be older and fatter than Mr. George," Kitty reminded her friend.

"He sent a photograph." Harriet fished out a small piece of cardboard and handed it to her friend.

Kitty squinted at the picture. She held it first at arm's length, slowly bringing it forward. "This is awful. It is such a bad picture I can barely tell it is a man. Well, you do know he has a mouth, a nose, and two eyes. I wonder why he only sent a headshot."

"It doesn't matter. The important thing is I will be his wife.

Paper said you had to be married before you even head out to make it legal. Some towns don't have preachers."

"How do you get married without the groom?" Kitty asked.

"Poxy. It sounds awful." Harriet wrinkled her nose as she said the words.

Kitty laughed. "Proxy, the word is proxy. Someone else stands in and does the groom's part." Looking at the watch pinned to her dress, Kitty stood. "Are you sure this is what you want?"

Harriet scrambled to her feet. "Ya. Why not? I can make this work. I will miss you." Harriet grabbed her hand and pleaded, "Come with me, Kitty."

"Whoa, I didn't think you were heading out to Mormon country. This man only wants one wife." The idea of leaving both the town and her disagreeable aunt did sound tempting, but she wasn't ready to belong to any man unless she could have the type of relationship her parents had. You couldn't pick out a husband like ordering a plow from the Sears and Roebuck catalog.

"Think about it. Adam knows many men who need a wife. You could have your choice." Harriet clutched her letter to her bosom reverently.

Kitty wrinkled her nose at the thought of toothless old men in dirty long underwear, begging her to pick one of them. True, the young men of marrying age were rare in the county, falling into three categories—married, dead, or headed out west lured by the promise of adventure and sudden wealth.

Being a man rather than a woman would be a definite plus. They had control over their lives. While she, on the other hand, merely hoped to find her perfect mate, one who would rescue her from being Aunt Eugenia's personal drudge and whipping girl. That would never happen.

KITTY SLOWLY CLOSED the screen door so it wouldn't make a

betraying squeak. Once inside, she exhaled in relief. Perhaps she really hadn't been gone too long. Then again, maybe she had. A half-turn brought her almost nose to nose with a red-faced Aunt Eugenia. A quick step back allowed her to take in the whole picture. Eugenia scowled at her with hands propped firmly on her black clad hips. She looked like an angry crow ready to peck. A buggy whip served as her beak of choice. Eugenia brought the whip down before Kitty could think. Whistling by her face, it struck her hard on the shoulder, sending a sharp pain through her body.

"I'll teach you to shame me, Katherine Rosemary Hamilton."

Kitty put up her arms to shield her face as her aunt advanced. What could she have done to earn a whipping?

"What were you thinking to prance in front of a beer wagon, swishing your skirts and showing off your ankles?" The whip came down across her hand, drawing blood.

"Aunt Eugenia, stop!" Kitty caught a glance at the gleam in her aunt's eye. Oh dear, she was in for it now. Experience deemed Eugenia wouldn't stop until she broke the whip.

"Jezebel" Eugenia reared back, winding up for the next swing.

Kitty dropped to the floor in self-preservation. Momentum carrying her, Eugenia stumbled over her prone body and flew into the marble-topped pedestal table headfirst. An ominous crack sounded unusually loud.

In the following silence, Kitty peeked through her fingers to see what her Aunt Eugenia would do next. The buggy whip lay useless on the wooden floor beside Eugenia's still body. Blood oozed down the side of her head.

For a moment, Kitty wondered if her Aunt was dead. A tiny tingle started at her heart and worked its way through her body. Freedom. She could finally be free. No more lectures on the irresponsibility of her parents drowning while crossing a too fast stream. No more looks clearly indicating she wished Kitty had been in the buggy with them. No more endless petty errands to satisfy

Aunt Eugenia. She was finally free. The tingle spread to her fingers and toes. Hope returned. Maybe she wouldn't end up as some embittered old spinster like Eugenia. Perhaps she still had a chance at a life. After all, she was only nineteen.

Out of the corner of her eye, she saw it. A flutter, a slight movement, her aunt's hands opening and closing like a spastic spider getting ready to move. The tingle left faster than it came. Kitty pulled herself up and knelt by her aunt to help her up. Her aunt looked at her in horror and pulled away.

"Unhand me, you devil," Eugenia hissed.

Despite the fact, her aunt had never been kind she'd never called her a devil before. Kitty looked over her shoulder to see if someone else had walked into the room. No one had.

Eugenia raised herself to a sitting position under her own steam, though her eyes had a strange glazed look to them. "I know what you are up to, you imp of Satan."

Kitty hesitated, unsure if she should leave Eugenia alone while she ran to get the doctor. She definitely didn't sound right.

"Thought you'd kill me and take the money Daniel left for your dowry." Eugenia reached for a chair and managed to pull herself up.

"What? My father left me a dowry?" Aunt Eugenia never before mentioned money unless she was complaining about not having enough.

Eugenia gave a little cackle as she settled into a chair. "Didn't guess? I never figured you for a clever girl. It was actually your mother's dowry, but they saved it for you, and I am not going to feel guilty. It should have been mine."

"Why didn't I ever hear about this?" Kitty asked, white-faced and shaken.

"Why bother telling you? No one would marry you. No, no, the money was for me to take care of you. Why should you have it to get a good husband when it was taken away from me?"

"I could have married. Why did you do this to me?" Kitty advanced on her, but stopped when Eugenia threw an arm out as if to deflect her approach.

"Would you want a husband who'd only have you for the money you'd bring him? That's what you get with a dowry."

Eugenia's eyes were still glassy, and she wove precariously. Kitty knew she'd been knocked senseless and was spitefully glad. She'd never have known the truth otherwise.

"It was my right if that was the type of husband I wanted," Kitty answered. "Most girls have dowries, even if it is only a mule or a milk cow. Why shouldn't I have something?" She slid into a chair.

"You didn't deserve a dowry. You did nothing to earn one. I had a dowry once." Eugenia faced her niece with one outstretched bony finger as she swayed back and forth. "Your father took it."

"That's a lie! As a man of God, my father wouldn't steal." Kitty's hands balled into fists, her nails cutting into her palms.

"The ministry did it. Your grandfather took my dowry to pay for Daniel, your father, to go to seminary. He told me he would make the money back in no time in a business venture. I had a long-time beau, Robert, so he didn't even worry about scaring off prospective suitors. Father never had a chance to make back the money, he died of a heart attack that week." Her voice faded as her chin dropped to her chest.

Kitty found it hard to believe her Aunt Eugenia ever had a beau. "What happened to Robert?" The question was out before she even knew it.

Eugenia's head snapped, and she fixed Kitty in a basilisk stare. "Robert, who I thought loved me, loved money more. It turns out my late father was a gambler. We had to auction all we had to pay off his debts. No wonder he took my dowry to pay for Daniel's schooling. Therefore, in his own way, your father, my brother, stole my only chance at happiness. He wasted his life and my dowry and left me with his orphan. His ungrateful orphan who tried to kill me for the money left in the clock."

"No, Aunt Eugenia, I didn't try to kill you. You tripped." Kitty worried about her aunt. Her behavior was getting more and more strange. Her sudden spilling of years' old secrets demonstrated how rattled the fall made her.

"Go, run, and get me a constable. I need to make a report." Eugenia straightened her back and fired off the order expecting an immediate response.

Kitty took off, but not for the station house. She stopped first at Doctor Weber's and explained what had happened. He promised to meet her at the house in a quarter of an hour. She ran up the road as fast as she could to Taylor's Dairy.

Harriet was balancing two full pails of milk as she walked to the cheese house.

"Harriet, Harriet, wait up." An extra burst of speed brought her up to her friend's side.

"What is it, Kitty?" Harriet carefully put down the pails.

"When are you leaving?" Kitty watched Harriet's face intently.

"Tuesday or Wednesday. Why?"

"I want to go with you." The words surprised her as much as Harriet.

"You want to be a mail order bride? You called it foolish."

"I have to leave right now. My aunt fell and hit her head. She is going to tell the policeman I tried to kill her over my missing dowry," she managed to explain in a rush.

"What dowry?"

"I'll explain on the way out. We'll have plenty of time then. I have to go back home and pack before she calls for the constable. Meet by the apple tree on Simmons' farm tonight after moorise," Kitty threw over her shoulder as she turned to leave. "She'll probably figure out I didn't obey her. I need to get there before the doctor."

"Okay. Hurry home, Kitty," Harriet called after her.

Kitty settled for a wave instead of goodbye. Thank goodness, the road sloped downhill because her sides ached from all the running.

She'd need to toughen up if she was heading out west into the wilderness.

"HELLO, ANYONE HOME?" Doctor Weber's voice boomed ahead of him as he opened the front door of the house. At the same time, Kitty slipped in through the back.

"Thank you for coming," she called out as she walked slowly to the front room huffing to catch her breath.

"Where is our patient?" Doc looked around inquisitively.

"Oh, I believe she is in her room, resting." Kitty hid her crossed fingers in her skirt. It would be like Eugenia to drag herself to the constable's office.

Her heart hammered with every step she took up the stairs. She tapped lightly, hoping against hope her aunt resided inside.

"Enter," a weak, whispery voice called out.

Gingerly, she pushed the bedroom door open. Eugenia lay across a Rose of Sharon quilt with a perfumed hankie over her face.

"Well, Eugenia, I hear you had a bit of a fall," Doc commented as he opened his bag.

"Foster?" Eugenia pulled the hankie off and struggled to sit up. "You didn't need to come."

"Yes, I did. I wouldn't rest easy until I saw how you were." His weathered face creased into a smile.

"Oh, I'm fine. Nothing really." The flustered woman patted her hair.

Kitty's mouth fell open. Her aunt called it nothing after she practically accused her of murder. There she sat smiling up at old Doc Weber like a smitten fool. She looked at Eugenia and then the doctor. They were both around the same age, and if you could get past the meanness, Aunt Eugenia remained a handsome woman. All the same, she'd eventually remember her threat to turn Kitty over to the law. It was best she'd be out west before her aunt's memory returned.

"No sign of a concussion. The best thing for you, young lady, is rest."

Eugenia giggled slightly. Doc sat beside Eugenia and urged her to drink a sleeping draught to help her wake refreshed. Eugenia refused at first, but agreed when Doc took her hand and asked again. They chatted a little until Eugenia closed her eyes. Doc closed his bag and stood.

"I guess my job is done." He looked at Eugenia.

"How long do you think she'll sleep?" Kitty scampered to open the door for the doctor.

"She should for about ten hours or more. Let her wake naturally. I'll check on her tomorrow."

"Thank you. Let me know what we owe you." Kitty wanted to push the man out the door, but besides being rude, it would be suspicious.

"No charge. Eugenia back on her feet will be payment enough." Foster winked as he pulled the door shut.

Chapter Two

CLOCK. AUNT EUGENIA said her dowry was stored in a clock. There was only a couple in the house. Kitty certainly hoped it wasn't the tiny bedside clock in Eugenia's bedroom. It didn't make any sense because nothing could fit in the small china clock.

The grandfather clock in the front sitting room could store plenty. Kitty never went in there because her aunt had banned her from using the room she kept only for company. Yes, it must be the grandfather clock.

Kitty slipped into the room and pulled the shades. A casual passer-by might remark if she spied her rooting through everything, especially once they found Kitty gone the next day.

The clock stood there like a sentinel, one Kitty approached with trepidation. What if there wasn't any money? What would she do then?

She reached out and pulled open the door. Nothing. There was a pendulum and the chains to set the clock, but nothing else. Her heart fell. Still, who would leave the money in plain sight?

Aunt Eugenia's friends had passed through this room, perhaps noticing the clock or even looking inside. In no way would anything could get past Dorcas Phelps, Eugenia's best and nosiest friend. Therefore, it wouldn't be in clear view. Kitty tapped on the bottom to find a hollow-sounding place. A drawer flew open, revealing a small velvet drawstring bag.

Kitty shook out the gold pieces onto a piecrust table, over six hundred dollars in twenty-dollar gold pieces. Kitty fingered each coin. If not for her aunt, she could have married Teddy Merckely. He'd married Florence Mottsinger, and her dowry measured a mere hundred dollars.

All this time her aunt had been sitting on her birthright, depriving her of a possible marriage and family. Her lips tightened in anger, thinking about what might have been. She counted out the money again. It was all hers, all the same—the hateful crow did take care of her for the last eight years. Kitty placed five gold pieces back in the bag and returned it to its original spot.

Money secured, she tiptoed upstairs to gather the few things she would take with her, including her parents' wedding photograph, her mother's shirt watch, and her father's compass. Kitty stuffed the carpetbag with a nightgown, a change of clothes, and a Colt pistol she found abandoned in an alley. Too bad, she didn't have any ammunition. She could get some on the way to Druthersville. Her appearance might be a problem. She couldn't count on Eugenia's continued memory lapse, especially after she discovered the majority of the dowry missing.

Peering into her mirror, Kitty frowned at the wide-eyed girl. Her naturally curly hair would be a dead giveaway. The hair would have to go. Aunt Eugenia's good sewing shears went into the bag too. If people were on the lookout for her, a girl with short hair might stand out—but not a boy. She needed clothes. How would she obtain boy's clothing without observation? Mentally she reviewed what boy nearby might be her size. A half dozen who attended church came to mind. Most of their clothes would be inaccessible since they would be on their bodies or stored inside. There was no way to slip into the house without anyone noticing. The best she could hope for was laundry on the line.

Tiptoeing back down the stairs, she went through the kitchen stuffing her pockets with biscuits and apples. Even though she wasn't hungry, she knew she would be later. Dusk was close to falling. It would be better to wait a little longer before leaving, except Aunt Eugenia might wake up. Being an ornery woman, Eugenia probably wouldn't sleep for ten hours as Dr. Weber promised.

What meager belongings she took with her were packed, and she was gone before that could happen. She didn't stop for an easy breath until the night sky blazed with stars and a silvery crescent moon illuminated her as she waited beneath the ancient apple tree. She kicked at some rotting fruit with her newly acquired hobnailed boots. They were a little big. She'd relieved the livery owner of his boots, since he made the mistake of leaving them in plain sight on his back porch. Pierre probably left the muddy boots out to dry never realizing a thief lingered nearby. Kitty left a five-dollar gold piece to replace them. Pierre may not have had the smallest feet in town, but her feet were none too small either. An extra pair of socks helped make up the difference.

All the same, she liked the feel of the new Kitty, um, Kit. A white spot growing closer must be Harriet. Just to be safe, Kitty hid behind the tree.

"Kitty, are you here?" Harriet hissed over the bullfrog chorus.

"Here I am!" Kitty dressed in her purloined boy clothes jumped out from behind a tree.

"Eeek!" Harriet jumped back in surprise.

"Harriet, it's me." Kitty took off the hat and ran her fingers through short, curly hair.

"It is you." She circled her friend slowly taking in the pants, shirt, and suspenders.

"I figured I needed a disguise in case the law is after me." Kitty pulled her hat back down over her curls. She grabbed up her knapsack. "We need to get going. We might be able to catch a ride on Jeb Wilson's freight wagon to the train station."

"Should we worry about Jeb seeing us?" Harriet picked up her bag and followed Kitty.

"He's so seldom sober; I doubt he'll know anyone is on the back of his wagon. We need to hurry."

The girls crept across the darkened landscape in the direction of the road. The wagon stood in front of the dry goods store as Jeb staggered to the wagon seat.

"Make sure you get my merchandise on the nine-thirty express this time," the storeowner yelled at Jeb, before walking inside the store.

Jeb fumbled with the reins and located his whiskey bottle as the girls silently slipped under the tarp. He clucked at the mules to go, unaware he'd acquired two extra passengers.

"I come from Alabamy with a banjo on my knee…," the drunken voice warbled.

"Do you think he is going to sing all night?" Harriet whispered.

"Quit complaining. As long as he's singing we know he hasn't fallen off." Kitty poked at the canvas covering them. "I'll be glad when we get there. This wagon stinks."

"I think its Jeb." Harriet tittered a little. "Can he hear us?'

"Not as long as he's singing and we whisper."

"Tell me about the dowry, Kitty"

"Aunt Eugenia got all the money in the will. It was my mother's money for my dowry."

"You never knew?"

"Not a word. She was spending my dowry. She bragged about it. Said I would never get married." Her voice trembled with anger.

"Kitty, you could have married? Your aunt chased all the beaus away?"

"There was Teddy Merckely who I thought was going to propose. Once he talked to my aunt, he stopped coming around. He always looked away from me whenever I saw him in church after that."

"I bet Eugenia said—" Harriet stopped in mid-thought when the wagon halted.

"Whoa, you stupid nag," Jeb called above them.

"That's our cue that our ride is at an end. Harriet, grab your stuff. We need to slip off before he lifts the tarp." The girls tumbled noiselessly to the ground.

Harriet shook out her dress and picked off the straw. "Wonder what he was hauling?"

"We're better off not knowing." Kitty straightened her vest and pulled down her hat. "How do I look?"

"Handsome. Why the boy clothes and hair?"

The girls headed toward the main road, the moon still high in the sky, lighting their way.

"I told you how I had a dowry. I took it—at least part of it." She patted her buttoned pants pocket to reassure herself the money was there.

"How much?" Harriet sidled closer to her friend.

"I counted out six hundred. That's what remained of my dowry. I took five. In reality, it's all my money."

Harriet grabbed her friend's arm, "You could have married Teddy Merckely. Your dowry was bigger than Florence's, and she's already pregnant."

Kitty laughed. "Believe it or not, it was the first thing I thought of when I found out about the money. All the same, I don't know if I want to be Florence. She got the man she wanted, but she doesn't look too happy."

The girls walked in the direction of the nearest town since boarding at Lancaster would cause talk. They used the train tracks as a map. Harried didn't complain, but long hours and hard work were nothing new to her. Kitty felt sure her purloined boots sliding and back forth on her feet were raising blisters.

They took a few breaks to nap and share a biscuit before reaching their destination in the dawn light. Early morning workers and travelers began to fill the gravel and pitch streets. A train whistle helped them to locate the station. A pair of passing men ogled Harriet as she strolled by.

Kitty noted the men's obvious interest. "Harriet, I'm thinking you may not need to go all the way to British Columbia to get a husband."

Harriet clicked her tongue at the idea. "There's the office." She towed Kitty in the direction of a newspaper office, which squatted next to the train station. The bell above the door rang as they entered.

A young, bespectacled man looked up from setting type. "Can I help you?"

Harriet studied the paper in her hand. "Mr. McIntyre?"

"No, I'll go get him." The man went behind the printing press to a glass enclosed office.

A middle-aged gentleman with impressive ginger sideburns stepped out and smiled in their direction. "Good morning, Miss," he nodded at Harriet and turned to Kitty. "Son."

Kitty glanced behind her to see if a boy stood there before she remembered she was masquerading as a boy.

"Mr. McIntyre, I'm Harriet Gruber. I'm here to marry Mr. Easton."

The man blinked a few times, and then squinted at Kit. He held out his hand to her. "And you are?"

"Kit, Kit Gruber, Harriet's brother." She managed a sheepish smile and moderately firm handshake.

McIntyre acted suspicious. "Miss Gruber, I understood from your letter that you were on your own in the world." Mr. McIntyre looked at her intently while his bespectacled helper jockeyed to get a better position to observe the scene.

"I am. We are. Brother and I got separated when we come to 'Merica." Harriet cut her eyes to Kitty.

"Our reunion was fairly recent. I finally tracked my sister down, and she tells me she is leaving to get married. I decided to come along for safety reasons and meet my new brother-in-law."

"Do you still want to marry and travel all the way to British

Columbia?" Mr. McIntyre asked.

"Yes." Harriet answered succinctly and with an emphatic head bob.

McIntyre did a double take. "Did I hear you right?"

Harriet nodded her head again.

"Before you start the trip, you must marry by proxy. The trip is expensive and most men will not finance a woman who might change her mind before she arrives or after. Do you understand, Miss Gruber?" McIntyre watched Harriet carefully for a reaction.

Harriet looked at *her brother*. Kitty nodded slightly.

"When do I get married? I have a train to catch." Harriet interlocked her shaking hands.

Twenty minutes later, they stood before the preacher. "Do you, Adam Easton, take Harriet Gruber for your lawfully wedded wife?"

Kitty felt four pairs of eyes fixed on her. Harriet's were twinkling above the hastily gathered bouquet she used to hide her smile.

"Um, I do," Kitty managed to rasp out, maintaining what she thought to be a manly timber.

The minister herded everyone to the wedding license and pointed where the husband was to sign. *Adam Easton, Proxy*, stood out against the white page. Harriet carefully signed her name adding Easton at the end. Mr. McIntyre signed as a witness before passing the fountain pen to Kitty.

She stood with the pen in her hand, staring at the paper and wondered what to do. If she signed the license as Kit Gruber, would it make the marriage illegal? Maybe it would be good for the marriage to be null, especially since Adam Easton could turn out to be worse than George.

"Son, it's okay to put down an X if you can't write. It all counts the same." McIntyre suggested.

Kitty placed a large bold X by the proxy designation. Not sure if not signing her real name made the marriage legitimate or not, she wanted what was best for Harriet.

Chapter Three

T HE EXCELSIOR, ONE of Cincinnati's best hotels, catered to an elite crowd. The five story stone hotel loomed over the shorter buildings. Inside the gaslights hissed and flickered a bit, throwing shadows on the dark paneled walls. Ornate framed pictures of foxhunts graced two of the walls. The third had a long cherry wood bar with an equally long mirror behind it. The difference between being in the east as opposed to the west, if a mirror made it out west intact, the barkeep placed it above the bar to see if anyone was sneaking up on him, not for decoration.

A thick oriental carpet silenced his boots. Good thing Nick removed his spurs or he would be stuck to the showy rug. Hard to believe a man's domain consisted of this fussy clubroom with its ornate wainscoting and faux Grecian statues. Give him hardwood floors and scarred tables of rustic western bars any day.

"Smoke, sir?"

A uniformed attendant opened the decorated wooden box to display a collection of cigars and cheroots. Nick picked out an aromatic cheroot and lit it. Taking a long pull of the burning tobacco, he sized up the potential players. For a two-bit tip, the attendant had clued him in to them, including a couple of well-heeled merchants and a kid, dressed up in his best gambling gear.

Nick eyed the three players. The kid's flashy jacket with the black on black embroidering looked a great deal like Nick's own jacket. His own followed the strong line of his torso due to custom tailoring. The boy sported a Windsor tie sloppily knotted. He needed a little more work on his wardrobe. His hair looked rough, probably due to his momma cutting it. It would need work, too, before he could be taken seriously.

The boy, noticing Nick close perusal, sent him a squinty eye glare, which almost made Nick laugh. It reminded him of a duckling that once attacked his boot, not having enough sense to know he could crush him with one foot. He saw so much of himself in the boy. Actually, he saw more the way he used to be, about twenty years ago, when he was convinced he had what it took to whip the world.

"You said your name was Kennedy?" One of the merchants, a stout man, peered at him as if questioning his name.

"I didn't, but you have it already." Nick kept his answer short, unsure if the question was more about his heritage than his gambling reputation. He picked the moniker the same time he chose a life as a gambler. Little did he know he would encounter the common belief that all Irishmen were two-fisted drunks? "Your name, sir?"

"Waggoner, Horace Waggoner. I own the Waggoner Wagon Works," the big man barked as he lowered his girth into the waiting club chair. "I'm here to play poker. How about the rest of you?"

Though tempting to make some remark about Waggoner's Wagon Works, Nick controlled his mischievous streak. Good chance Horace had not only heard it before, but also did not find it funny.

A black-suited, thin man, who resembled an undertaker more than anything else, introduced himself, adding he was an importer of fine women's clothing. Nick nodded at the introduction, finding it hard to imagine the man even touching women's clothing, but he guessed someone had to do it. The Cecil Smedleys of the world could import all the women's clothing they wanted. He savored the pleasure of taking them off the fine women's bodies.

Nick signaled the attendant they had a foursome ready to play. A dark-haired man flirting with a fancy girl near the bar turned and walked their way. The red vest identified him as a dealer. His job consisted of keeping things civilized and making sure the house got its cut. The dealer took everyone's buy-in money and laid their chips on the table. He slid the actual money in his front vest pocket. The scar by the dealer's mouth announced he wasn't afraid to throw a punch or pull a knife, not that he would have to with all the hired muscle they had walking around the place.

The dealer announced the game was five-card stud and dealt the initial down card and one up card to each player. Waggoner had the lowest up card.

"Mr. Waggoner, I believe you are the bring-in," Nick quietly reminded the merchant, receiving a scowl for his helpfulness.

The man threw in a chip while grumbling about not needing to be reminded how to play poker. Mr. Smedley, the bespectacled merchant, rearranged his cards with a shaky hand and pushed one chip forward. Bart, the would-be young gambler, smirked and threw in two.

"So, Bart," Nick drew the words out, catching the boy's attention. "How long you've been out of the schoolroom?"

Bart, who picked the same type of cheroot Nick chose, suddenly choked. Coughing violently, he turned an angry face towards Nick before croaking, "Years."

"That long?" Nick pulled his lips straight to look appropriately sober. He'd bet the boy snuck out of the schoolroom mere minutes before the game started. Too bad no one at the table would take it him up on the bet. "Got any plans for the future?"

Bart's eyes shifted to the door as if looking for someone before he spoke. "I'm going to be a gambler and travel the world, fleecing stupid men and seducing pretty women."

Smedley inhaled suddenly at Bart's cavalier remark and fidgeted with his two cards.

"Harrumph, fool-pup," Horace complained, taking another puff on his cigar.

"Hmm," served as the best non-committal answer Nick could

come up with, especially since Waggoner and Smedley took offense at Bart's attempt at worldliness. It probably served as a reminder that they might end up fleeced. He could feel Bart's eyes on him expectant, waiting for an answer. "Good work when you can find it," he finally muttered.

The best thing to do was to trounce the boy soundly. Stomping any dreams he had of being a gambler. He was probably the son of the hotel owner, which would explain his expensive clothes and his presence in the hotel. Even if Bart was no more than the son of a farmer, as Nick had been, it was still a better life than being a rootless gambler. Nick tapped his down card and blinked.

Where did that thought come from? The other players checked their cards, sure Nick would change the game somehow. The overstuffed leather club chair squeaked as he shifted his weight, which startled the bespectacled clothing merchant across from him. Poker was not a game for those who easily startled.

What in tarnation caused these odd thoughts to pop into his head? He lived the life most men envied. He hit all the big cities from east to west, plying his skills in poker and blackjack, although poker was his preferred game. He was in one of the most expensive hotels in Cincy, drinking twenty-five dollar a bottle scotch. Not too much though, he needed to keep his head clear. He would discreetly fleece the other players. Only an amateur would beat them immediately. He let them win a little money, gain confidence, so they would keep playing. When they finally lost, they'd appeared surprised, a ploy that worked well, They would play with him again, convinced the next time they would win.

For reasons he could not explain to himself, he kept feeding chances to the would-be teenaged gambler. He would bet the boy's mama didn't christen him Bart. He held no more claim to his name than Nick did his. His mother probably gave him a Biblical name like Micah or Joel. It could be something even worse, like Uriah or Moses. No wonder he might choose a different moniker. The boy beamed as he raked in his winnings. Nick tried to send him an unspoken message to go home while still happy. Maybe he needed to try verbal since mental messages weren't taking.

"Chips equal dollars. Maybe you might spend some money on entertainment." Nick nodded his head in the direction of the various provocatively clad women lounging about the room.

The women were there for the enjoyment of the patrons, whether it was conversation or otherwise. The fact hadn't registered with the boy, nor did he get the hint. Bart flashed a toothy grin, making him look all of ten. He might want to lose the affectation, too.

"You'd like that. Me leaving the game. Afraid, I might clean you out?" Bart flashed his boyish grin again and practically rubbed his hands together in anticipation of the money he would be winning.

Greed had obviously grabbed young Bart by the hand and was dragging him ruthlessly down the garden path. Nick knew his job was to beat him soundly. Humiliate him so the very thought of gambling made him physically ill. He hated doing it even if were for the best. Professional gamblers didn't play to lose or to make youngsters feel good.

His nod in the direction of the women had no impact on Bart. It did bring a sultry blonde, who'd previously chatted him up, to their table. She said her name was Delilah and was available for after-hours entertainment. Yep, he'd bet she'd be available, and her name wasn't Delilah, either. She slid her arms around Nick from behind giving the men an extra look at her charms.

"Can I get you anything?" Delilah purred into his ear. Anything sounded a great deal like twisted satin sheets and sweat slicked bodies.

"I'm fine, but Bart, who is winning big, might need something," Nick answered, waving a hand in the youngster's direction.

Delilah looked at Bart and stiffened in response. "Oh, him." Her practiced smile fell flat as she turned and headed to greet the men entering the room as if that were her original plan.

Something wasn't right. It was an uncomfortable feeling akin to pulling on a pair of long johns, which had fallen into a poison ivy patch. You didn't notice it at first, but it got you later. Even though he knew he was making a costly mistake, Nick folded, threw in three kings, a jack, and one ace, and picked up his hat. Smedley sucked in his breath. It was hard to tell if Smedley's gasp reflected shock or relief. Bart tried not to show too much excitement but failed as a giggle erupted. He definitely would need to work on that, too.

Why did he do this? Come to this part of the Ohio Valley region. He got sentimental whenever he neared the old homestead. He didn't want to say the word, homesick. He'd sworn he was never going back, the reason he usually stayed west of the Mississippi River. Ironically, playing in the big hotels with the crystal chandeliers was all he aspired to at the grand age of eighteen, back when he found his girl in his brother's arms. He'd sworn to show them all. If Rebecca preferred bad boys, he would be the worst. That was his original plan. Brought up as a staunch Methodist, he couldn't think of anything worse than gambling. Maybe a bank robber, but he preferred to take people's money legally, a lot less messy.

His saddled horse stood outside the main doors. Talk about service. He tipped the stable boy a dollar, much to the boy's delight.

"Tank you, sur," the boy called after him as Nick swung up in his silver-tooled saddle.

The saddle, a souvenir from a game near Mexico, weighed almost as much as a man. With the extra weight it put on Duke, his horse, he should get rid of it. Besides, it was practically an advertisement asking for thieves. Probably take Duke with the saddle. Back as an eighteen year old set out to be a big, bad gambler, he'd failed to consider such mundane things as robbers. Since he'd learned there was always someone bigger and meaner. They usually stole your stuff if they couldn't win it.

Nick dressed as if he was expecting to start a war. He carried an army issued Colt pistol, a small Derringer pistol strapped to his calf, and a stiletto tucked away in a special boot pocket made for that purpose. He usually kept a Sharps rifle on his saddle, just in case. Sometimes it was better to keep the bad guy far away so he didn't have to use the pistols, and a Sharps would do that.

Yep, gambling hadn't turned out to be as easy as he thought it would be. He fared better than most after a more experienced gambler took pity on him and showed him the ropes. If he had any type of compassion, he should have done the same for Bart. Instead, he let him win, but because Bart was a horrible player, it took major work. Oh, well, he hated when he got like this, all maudlin and introspective. What he needed was to leave this part of the country. What he was going to do was the last thing he should. He'd sneak over the state border and check on the remains of his family.

No prodigal son coming home, he was more like a thief in the night. He would watch them from a distance. Rebecca had married his brother, Noah, either because Nick left or it was the plan all along. When their first son arrived less than a year later, not ever returning looked like the best plan. Noah settled down and worked the family farm to support Rebecca and their three kids. His brother turned from a hell raiser to a church going man. At least, it would have made his mother happy.

He wondered if it made Rebecca happy. What made women happy? He'd put a smile on dozens of women's faces, but it was never enough. They were always wanting something else, a new bauble or to go to the opera house. Maybe it was the reason he never settled, or maybe no place ever felt like home.

The wind ruffled the tops of the pine trees, creating a sighing sound. The gurgling of an unseen brook sounded left of the path Nick followed. Cicadas serenaded the darkness in an effort to attract mates. Barely a sliver of moonlight illuminated the road, forcing Nick to keep Duke to a careful walk. Fool that he was he shouldn't ride a valuable animal like Duke at night. He could injure a hoof or break a leg, not to mention sending Nick headfirst to the ground.

After all, this wasn't a matter of life or death, not even close, only his curiosity to see how his family fared.

"Almost there, boy," Nick murmured to his horse. A huge silver maple tree marked the edge of his family's farm. He remembered the tree well. He'd climbed it often to hide from his brother, plopped down under its shade after plowing on many a day, and stole his first kiss from Rebecca there. The tree loomed much bigger than he remembered. It had grown. So had he. Hard to imagine what an incredible naïve boy he had been back when he thought his life was contained in this piece of land and a certain brown-eyed girl. Everything he hoped for was right here. That was when he was Levi Johnson, one of the Johnson brothers.

Something caught in Nick's throat. Probably a bug he'd swallowed. "Duke, the bugs are bad this time of year." Nick coughed out the words.

Smoke curled out of the cabin's chimney, indicating everyone wasn't asleep. Not the first time he'd passed through without bothering to knock on their door. He'd been gone so long he was unsure if his mother still lived. She tended to be on the sickly side.

Suddenly the snick of a rifle being drawn back broke the silence. Ironic his demise would happen on his own family land. His heart skipped a beat until he heard a familiar voice. "Stop right there, stranger. Hands up where I can see them."

Nick slowly raised his hands before calling out. His brother always had a jumpy trigger finger. No need to test it. "Noah, I'd count it a favor if you didn't shoot your only brother."

"Levi?" Noah's voice mirrored his confusion as he lowered his rifle. "What are you doing here?"

"Um, yeah, that's the question. Just passing through," Nick said, unwilling to confess the homestead pulled at him like a nail to a lodestone. He couldn't pass by without coming here. Swinging one leg over the saddle horn, he dismounted and dropped his reins to let Duke graze.

Noah rested the rifle across the back of his shoulders, his arms draped over the barrel and stock. "Most people don't drop by in the middle of the night. What's your story?"

"I was in the area and wondered about ma and Sarah. How is ma? Has Sarah married up?" Nick confessed his voice cracking a little.

Noah peered at his brother as well as he could in the moonlight. "Want to come inside and ask ma yourself?"

"Um, no." Nick was uncomfortable with coming face to face with his past. What could he say to his mother? He'd spent the past twenty years breaking several commandments. Not the type of thing any parent wanted to hear, especially his Bible-toting mother.

"All I want to know is if she is okay?" Nick asked.

Noah's lips tightened into a grimace. "I suppose she is as good as can be considering she spends most of her time praying for her runaway son."

That wasn't too surprising since he had been her favorite before he left.

"She never said so, but I figured she blamed me for you leaving. Didn't matter I was the son who stayed home and kept the farm going," Noah said.

"I'm sure she appreciates you keeping the farm going," Nick said, ignoring the invitation to say more, since his brother was part of the reason, he'd left.

"Maybe. She never says much." Noah's voice was a little rough.

"What about Sarah?"

"Little sister has grown up. She married the youngest Cunningham boy who runs the livery in town. You'd know this if you'd stuck around." Noah lifted an eyebrow. "I'll ask you again, why are you here?

"Wanted to see for myself if things were all right with the family. How are things going with you?" Nick asked, not expecting much of a real answer.

"Not too much to say. Farming is farming. Last year was a hard one, though. Wheat rust wiped out most everything I managed to put aside." Noah kicked at the ground a little.

Opening his wallet, Nick peeled off several bills and pushed them in Noah's direction. "Take this to tide you over to next season."

"Levi, close your wallet. I don't want your money," Noah growled.

"Quit being the bullheaded cuss, you've always been. Take the money for mother and Rebecca and my nephews and niece. No one needs to know, but me and you." Nick shoved the money in Noah's direction again.

"Don't want it. I'll manage." Noah released his hold on his rifle, lowered it, and rolled his shoulders.

Nick removed his hat and ran his hand through his hair. The years did not make his brother any easier to deal with. If anything, he was even more stubborn.

"If I'd stayed, I would be helping you with the farm. This money is me helping."

Holding out his hand for the money, his brother remarked, "I could have used your help, especially before the boys got big enough to be of any use. This will make things easier, but it doesn't make up for all the years you were gone."

Nick put the money in Noah's hand. His free hand bunched the reins, ready to leave. "Well, glad I could help out some." He swung into the saddle.

Noah examined the silver-studded saddle and blooded horse. "It looks like you're not doing too badly for yourself, little brother."

"I do okay. I don't have what you have, though," Nick admitted.

"What might that be, a pair of worn out mules and a played out farm?" Noah asked, while running his hand down Duke's muscled flank.

"A home and someone to love. You did well, brother," Nick

flicked Duke's reins to get him walking.

"Do you want me to tell them you stopped by?" Noah asked.

"No, it's better if you don't." Nick rode off in the direction of the road, but stopped and turned for one last look at the farm.

A woman stood at the door and called out. "Noah, is there someone out there? Who are you talking to?"

"The wind, there's no one out here." Noah walked back to the house to his wife, illuminated by the fire behind her.

Kicking Duke into a trot, Nick knew it was past time to be gone. He made it to the train station by riding most of the night. The trip west guaranteed plenty of time to sleep.

After tipping the attendant in the stable car to keep an eye on Duke, Nick boarded the train. The mystique of riding horseback to the west coast had long lost its appeal. Besides being damnably long, it left a man fairly saddle sore. One blistered butt is all he wanted in a lifetime. Of course, that happened before he and his mount could ride in style. If Duke could talk, he'd probably agree he liked heading to Sacramento via the train rather than his own hoofs.

After scratching his old pal between the eyes, Nick sought out his own railroad car. Why delay? The best seats went fast. He always liked to sit in the back where he could observe everyone who boarded the train. The habit saved his life once when he noticed would be train robbers boarding with so much weaponry they could hardly walk upright.

In a civilized Cincinnati, he didn't expect train robbers. He didn't have to worry about it until he hit the Indiana border where the Reno Gang staged the first daylight peacetime train robbery back in 1866.

Working his way down the aisle, he spotted two empty seats in the back. He placed his carpetbag on the aisle seat and slid into the window seat. He canted his hat forward so no one could tell if he was awake.

A hefty woman dressed in a sensible brown travel dress whacked a few unwary travelers with her oversized basket. Her minute sized husband apologized profusely to the victims as he hurried behind her.

"There's the reason I'm never getting married," a salesman in a checkered suit announced in a booming voice. Nick was the nearest person, which meant he must have been talking to him. As much as Nick wanted to ignore Davy Caruthers, seller of men's fine hair pomade, according to his valise lettering, he figured he'd better answer. Davy struck him as someone who would talk louder when he didn't get a response. The salesman nodded at his bag in the seat next to him. Sighing, Nick moved his bag, allowing the Caruthers to sit down.

"Lucky me," Nick mumbled under his breath. He could only hope Davy's next stop was Louisville, Kentucky. Nick grunted, which was as much of a reply as the man needed.

A young mother herded three small children onto the train while balancing a baby on her hip. She struggled with a suitcase she pulled behind her.

"There's the other reason I am never getting leg-shackled. Children." Davy shuddered dramatically, but Nick ignored the man's theatrics, more concerned by the young mother who had no one to help her with the children or her oversized suitcase. Getting up, Nick went forward to help the still struggling woman.

"Let me help you," Nick said, taking hold of the suitcase. The woman let go of the handle more in surprise than willingness. Perhaps no one ever helped her. He swung the heavy suitcase up on the rack over the seats.

"There you go, ma'am. Where you headed?" he asked the still silent woman.

She herded the three children into seats before answering. "Leavenworth, Fort Leavenworth. Husband's there. Thank you for helping." Once she delivered her brief say, she sat and began to fuss with the baby, not meeting Nick's eyes.

Walking back to his seat, he thought it odd the way the woman acted almost afraid of him. For a moment, she looked like she thought he would steal her bag, and she didn't have enough energy to fight him.

"Woo-hee, she didn't care for you. I'm not sure why you'd go after one with a passel of young'uns." Davy chortled, delighted as if he'd cracked a great joke.

Nick glared at the stupid fool, hoping he'd shut up. It looked like it was going to be a very long trip, especially with his self-appointed bosom buddy in Davy Caruthers.

Nick puzzled over the woman's reaction to him, which was peculiar. The woman made sure to let him know she had a husband as if he was planning to abduct her from the train. Fort Leavenworth most likely meant her husband was a military man. Still, he'd frightened her. He had good manners. Women liked him, at least working girls did. Society ladies who wanted a little spice in their lives always came looking for him. In addition, there were the madams, the chambermaids, and the occasional cooks he came across, but it had been a long time since he'd conversed with an ordinary woman. Was he doing it wrong?

"Lookee there," Davy hissed through a space in his teeth.

Nick worked hard not to roll his eyes, but roll them he did. Great Scott, now he had a hissing drummer beside him. What could have Ol' Davy so excited? Did a farmer get on with a live piglet under each arm? He'd seen it happen. Davy was about as annoying as the piglets.

Nick spotted a pretty, blonde woman with pigtails and a huge smile, looking to be straight from the farm, as innocent as they come. No wonder Davy's eyes lit up. Behind the corn-fed beauty, was a slight young man wrestling with a carpetbag. The way the girl turned and talked to the young man indicated they were together.

The boy struggled to toss the carpetbag up on the rack without success. Just pitiful. Nick got up to help the scrawny lad. About the time, he'd reached the pair, the girl had swung the bag in place, proving she was the stronger of the two, even though she was shorter. Nick drew close enough to see the boy's face half shadowed by a faded newsboy cap. The sight of strangely beautiful wide set green eyes and high cheekbones shocked Nick. Definitely unexpected. The boy must be much younger than he originally thought.

"Hello, Nick Kennedy at your service," he said and gave a half bow in the crowded area. He saw a British man do it and thought it appeared debonair. Women liked it or the least gave the impression that they did. The blonde giggled, while the boy looked away.

"Hello, I'm Harriet. This is my brother…" The blonde stopped as if she couldn't remember her brother's name.

"Kit, like Kit Carson," the boy interjected in a husky voice that didn't match up with his slight frame.

"Pleased to meet you, Kit and Harriet. I'll be sitting in the back of the car if you need any assistance." Nick nodded and headed back to his seat to keep the aisle clear for incoming travelers. The trip had just become interesting. The two of them were obviously lying. The girl had a German accent. The boy didn't. The girl looked German. The boy didn't. He was an awfully delicate boy. His size and lack of muscle probably merited him his share of teasing. Nick decided to keep his eyes on the two, a project of sorts.

"I see you, city slicker, trying to chat up my girl. I saw her first," Davy grumbled, arranging his face into a menacing scowl, resembling indigestion more than anything else.

"I was not chatting up your girl. I'd advise you to leave the farm girl alone. She's as green as they come. Besides, you might get her brother riled up," Nick said, before pulling his hat back over his eyes.

"I can handle the pup," Davy said.

"Pups have teeth." Nick simulated a snore to indicate the end of the conversation. Glancing at the peddler from the shadow of his hat, he thought if that puppy doesn't bite you, I certainly will.

Chapter Four

THE TRAIN PULLED out, encompassing the station in smoke. The gentleman across from Kitty and Harriet pushed up the window. Kitty glanced at the stogie hanging out of the man's mouth. Did the man really think he ejected the smelly smoke outside when he continued to puff away? He attempted to grin around the cigar in Harriet's direction. In response, Harriet pulled Kitty closer.

"We could say we are married." Harriet nodded in the direction of cigar-smoking man.

"Well, we could, but you already said I look about twelve years old. What would that make you?"

"It would make me desperado."

Kitty glanced out the window to hide her smile and watched the scenery chug by before commenting. "Harriet, I think you mean desperate."

"Desperate, desperado, why do they make so many words same?" Harriet shrugged her shoulder as if the matter carried little importance.

Her friend could be so amazingly contradictory at times. Willing to travel across the county to meet a husband she'd never met, and yet she had an amazingly slim grasp of English vocabulary to accomplish the trip. "Promise me, *sister*," she emphasized the last word, "you will not refer to yourself as a desperado."

"I will." She nodded in agreement. "What will you do when I am not desperado?"

Kitty straightened her hat to cover her curls, fiddled a little with the buttons on her vest. "Can't say I gave it much thought. It looked like a good time to skedaddle from Lancaster."

"You come with me because we're friends?" Harriet grabbed Kitty's hand and gave it a squeeze.

"You know I had to leave. I might have ended up in jail depending on Aunt Eugenia's mood. Still, I'm glad I came. It makes me feel better knowing you aren't heading out west alone." Kitty squeezed Harriet's hand back, but let go when the conductor entered the car, passing back the punched tickets.

Kitty wiggled on the hard, wooden seat, fantasizing about luxurious padded train seats. Their train served mainly as a freight hauler with a couple of passenger cars hooked on as an afterthought. Her shoulders tighten at the thought of spending days trapped inside the stuffy car, while having her bones jarred twenty-hours of the day. All the same, still better than jail, she reminded herself.

Harriet elbowed her to get her attention. "Did ya think on gold mining? I might try it." Harriet mused aloud.

"That would be up to your husband. You can't do whatever you please. You're not a man like me."

Harriet laughed, attracting the cigar man's attention. Kitty sure hoped he wasn't heading up to Cariboo.

"Bruder männlich, what are you going to be?"

"What did you call me?" Kitty asked.

Harriet smiled, flexing an arm and patting a bicep. "Manly brother."

"Okay, sassy sister, maybe I could work in a business. If nothing else, I can always play the piano." Sad to say, at the advanced age of almost twenty, her only legacy was she could play the piano, thanks to her church pianist mother.

"Where do you get a playing piano job?" Harriet asked while twisting the plain wedding band Mr. McIntyre had provided, courtesy of Adam Easton. A glimmer of a smile graced her face.

"You're not smiling at the thought of my one skill, are you?" Kitty joked at her own expense.

"Nein. It is nice to be married, to belong somewhere."

Good for Harriet to belong somewhere, but she needed a place, too. She cast about for possible topics, remembering a newspaper article.

"I read in the paper all kinds of entertainers are heading west." Kitty tried to cheer herself up about going west by thinking even famous actresses made the trip. She stroked her chin thoughtfully the way she saw the postmaster do whenever he was thinking something over, a masculine move she'd do well to adopt.

"Who is going west?" Harriet raised one curious eyebrow.

"Maude Adams."

"Is she from Ohio?"

Kitty laughed and ended it with a cough when she realized it was too high pitched. "Well, maybe not Ohio, I think Utah."

Harriet's brow wrinkled up. "Utah? Is that near Druthersville?"

"No, not really, but she is heading to California to perform. Miss Adams is a famous thespian. She might come to British Columbia." Kitty highly doubted Maude Adams would come to the small mining town, but the thought might make Harriet feel better.

Harriet pulled out the letter with the trip itinerary. "Are you sure? Is thespa-um-ian like a seamstress?"

"No. She's an actress, and she sings too. Miss Adams probably won't go to Canada, but there's still the Hurley Gurley Girls. They must need a piano player."

"You say Hurley Burley? Ya, must be some big women." Harriet chuckled.

"Very funny." Kitty managed to swallow a giggle. A deep chortle might work, but that was too much work. "I know you've heard of the girls. They go to the mining towns to dance with the lonely miners."

"Maybe a job for you." Harriet wiggled both eyebrows with

comic effect.

"No thanks. I'd rather be gold mining. First, I have to figure out what to do. Do you know how to mine?"

"Huh?" Harriet tried to focus her attention on Kitty. "Mine? No. How about marrying up? Adam mentioned many men need wives. Even with your chopped off hair, you could marry."

"Thanks, I think. I guess that can be my last option once I've exhausted everything else." Kitty knew it would never happen, but somehow the idea soothed Harriet. The day wore on with the monotonous whine of the train wheels lulling her into a half-doze into the next station.

Stiff from sitting so long, Kitty and Harriet descended the train steps. Once on stationary ground, they both stood for a few minutes to adjust, then, hurried off to find the facilities. Kit pushed in after Harriet, but Harriet held the door half-closed against her.

"Bruder Kit, this is for ladies. Men's has a sun instead of crescent moon."

Kit stopped, realizing her mistake. Thank goodness, the station-master hadn't spotted her in her male disguise trying to enter the Ladies' Room.

"Oh," was the only response Kit could come up with as her demanding bladder screamed for relief. She stumbled around not knowing where to go until she saw the peddler. She watched him enter a room and waited until he came out. She hurried to the necessary only to have the outhouse smell assault her. Kit attempted to get her business done while holding the door close. Luckily, no one tried to enter.

"Phew." She shuddered, thinking about the times were still coming for repeating the odorous experience.

"Get used to it." Harriet came up behind Kitty while she still shook.

"Mercy—how?" Kitty wrinkled her nose. "There wasn't even a catalog to wipe with?"

"Kit, you act like a girl." Harriet gave her skirts a swish and headed toward a pushcart.

"Uhm, yeah, wait." She took long strides to catch up with her friend who stood by a vendor. A woman dressed in a faded calico dress and oversized poke bonnet carried a steaming coffee pot up to the pushcart.

"Coffee, mam, sir?" she inquired. "Only two cents for a hot cup of coffee?"

Harriet carefully counted out four cents to the woman who immediately pocketed it. The coffee was strong and bitter without sugar or cream. Such commodities were luxuries. Kitty and Harriet both gulped the coffee, almost burning their tongues. The vendor's small son took the empty metal cups with one hand and held up a slightly grubby hand clutching a brown egg.

"Egg, sir, hardboiled egg?"

Kitty was ready to refuse. They still had some hard biscuits they bought at the last stop, only the woman looked at them imploringly. Her facial skin stretched over prominent bones, emphasizing her gauntness. Before she even knew what she was doing, Kitty fished a nickel out of her pocket to hand the boy. The train's warning whistle hastened their steps.

They both went back to their original seats where Kit peeled the egg, offering it to Harriet first. She took a bite and made a face.

"Need salt."

"Aren't we the picky one, Miss I'm Going Out West and Roughing it," Kitty teased.

Harriet sighed. "Ya, you right. I thought on cream and sugar, too."

"Oooh how awful! I was thinking about a hot bath with French milled soap, apple pie, and chicken with fluffy dumplings."

"You make me hungry," Harriet grumbled, rubbing her stomach.

Kit peered out the window at their well-attired fellow passenger.

Harriet leaned over her shoulder to see what caught her interest. "Look, Nick Kennedy." She started to point, but Kitty grabbed her hand.

"It isn't nice to point," Kitty murmured, hating how much she sounded like Aunt Eugenia. The hurt expression on her friend's face made her feel lower than a snake's belly. How could she explain to her friend that she didn't want Nick to look up and notice them? Notice Harriet is more like it. Not likely, a man would notice a slender boy who couldn't even swing a carpetbag up on the luggage rack.

"Coffee lady is smiling," Harriet announced as she continued her observation.

Kitty leaned around Harriet to take in the tableau.

"I bet Mr. Kennedy spoke nice to her," Harriet concluded.

"He probably gave her money, being a show-off and all. They're always doing things to act important."

Harriet turned and gave her measuring look. "Does it matter? The woman is happy."

Nick had a champion in Harriet. Odd really, since Harriet spent all her time avoiding troublesome men. Kitty had better things to think about than Nick, like food.

She began to paw through the carpetbag in search of something to eat. Her hand slid over the smooth barrel of the pistol. She really needed to get bullets. An unloaded gun wasn't much use. Still, she wanted to put distance between herself and her aunt before walking into a city, in case there was someone following her. Perhaps it would have been better if she could have dyed her hair, but she wasn't sure how. Unfortunately, she didn't know any fancy women who could teach her. Her fingers found the lumpy handkerchief of the remaining biscuit she carefully unwrapped and divided.

Harriet attempted to bite into the biscuit, but her teeth slid off. "Coffee would be good now."

"I guess they're even harder than they were yesterday. Try breaking off a piece and sucking on it. Maybe then, it might get soft enough to chew."

Harriet managed to break a small bit off the main biscuit. She mimicked gagging before placing the biscuit piece in her mouth.

Kitty pocketed her biscuit. She wasn't that hungry yet. Placing her hands behind her head, in a gesture she saw many of the men on the train use; she crossed her ankles and looked out the window. The woman with the coffee pot was earnestly asking each traveler if he or she wanted coffee. Most hurried past her with barely a nod. One man yelled something at the woman, which caused her to look at the ground. What a hard life, putting up with abuse from chance met travelers for a few pennies. What was her story? Was she a widow? Perhaps, a farmer's wife trying to earn a little extra money? Maybe a mail-order bride whose marriage didn't take? Kit had heard a few stories of men who didn't turn out to be the paragon their letters painted them to be. She didn't bother bringing up the stories. With no other options for her friend, there was no purpose. Harriet's hand was deep in her dress pocket, fingering Adam's letter like a talisman.

A man swung on the train at the last minute, his long duster caught on the door, revealing a six-gun strapped to his leg. He muttered a curse while unhooking his coat. Kit slid down in her seat to avoid his gaze. She tugged on Harriet's arm to get her to do likewise. Unfortunately, her friend shook her hand off intent on re-reading her letter. How could kit expect her to know about the James-Younger gang and train robberies when she barely understood the constrained community life in Ohio?

Kit listened to the boot heels beat a tattoo to the rear of the train. She was over-reacting, wasn't she? They *were* in Missouri, not only the home of the James-Younger gang, but an unsettled state where the Civil War had settled little and stirred up more. It probably wasn't unusual for a man to pack a gun in such a place.

"Do you think Adam is thinking about me?" Harriet turned to look at Kit.

"Yes, all the time." She reassured her friend, or would especially if he knew a shady character just stepped on the train.

IN THE FOLLOWING week, the train ride morphed into an endurance contest as opposed to an adventure. Giving the impression Harriet was under male protection no matter how thin that protection might look, Kitty did her best to look dangerous which involved scowling. Most of the men nodded at the grimacing boy, maybe remembering when they attempted to act tough, back before life coarsened them up, and they had no need to act menacing because they were.

Harriet and Kitty had worked out a makeshift system for sleeping, where they sat opposite of one another and braced the soles of their feet against each other. This way they could sleep without sliding down in their uncomfortable seats. Huddled in such an attempt, Kitty opened her eyes to a chuckling Harriet.

"Hey, what's so funny?"

"Nothing." Harriet managed to choke out before smirking.

Kitty rubbed her face vigorously with the heels of her hand. "Okay, out with it. Seven days of being inside this rolling wooden box, I might enjoy a joke or two."

"It's you."

"Me?" Kitty reached back to scratch her neck. Her hand came back dirty. "Eyuk. Is it because I am disgustingly filthy?"

"No, it's because you make a pretty boy. I bet Mr. Nick thinks so, too." Harriet reached over to ruffle Kitty's already tousled curls. Kitty looked around to see if anyone was awake to notice.

About three stops ago, a newlywed couple boarded, holding hands and cooing endearments at each other. The conductor asked them to put some distance between themselves since the other passengers complained. Kitty felt a little pang looking at the two nestled like puppies in sleep. No one else had awakened yet. The car was mostly empty except for a peddler who slept with head thrown back and his mouth open. His impressive belly vibrated with each snore. Oh, and of course, Mr. Nick, as Harriet called him, slumped silently in the back with his hat pulled down. The farther west they went, more travelers disembarked, and fewer boarded to replace them.

Kitty crammed the hat back on her head, turned up her collar to hide the grimy neck, and tucked her slender hands into her pockets. A glowering frown completed her transformation. "Pretty boy, ha!"

"Yes and a pretty girl, too."

Kitty glanced back to the snoring man to make sure he was still asleep. "You think I'm pretty?

"Yes, I want to look like you." Harriet patted her rounded hips.

"Me! I want to look like you, blonde and beautiful."

Harriet and Kitty began to exchange animated comments on which feature they wished they had that the other possessed.

"Your eyes are so blue," Kitty said.

"I want to be taller." Harriet stood, pulling Kitty up beside her. She put her hand right at Kit's bottom lip even with the top of her head.

"You might change your mind if you were." Kitty patted her shorter friend on the head. "At five foot four, some folks consider me tall, even too tall to wed. Of course, that just might be an excuse." She flattened her hands over her bound breasts. "How I wish I had your figure all full and rounded."

A loud guffaw announced the peddler was awake. Both girls sat down in a hurry.

"What'd he see?" Harriet hissed through clenched teeth.

"Don't look at him. In fact, let's pretend we're asleep so he will think he was having a dream."

Kitty immediately let her chin drop to her chest, while her friend slumped boneless against the window. The peddler rubbed his eyes twice before closing them again. His snore filled the car once again.

Harriet and Kitty lay like so much dropped firewood in the

throes of pretend sleep, gradually falling asleep until the conductor came through.

"Next stop, St. Louis," The conductor barked as he passed sleeping and almost asleep passengers alike.

Kitty came alert immediately checking her hat. In the short time since leaving home, she'd gone from waking slowly to instantly awake. Anyone could walk by and notice her pale skin or long lashes. Still, she'd found people only see what they expect to see.

Harriet woke up slower, stretching, bringing her rounded breasts to the attention of the lecherous peddler who leaned forward to enjoy the show. Kit stood up blocking the man's view. The train jerked a little as it slowed coming into the station, causing Kit to stumble.

The view outside the window hadn't changed too much. A few trees, some grass, a skinny looking cow or two. In the distance, weathered unpainted buildings sprouted out of the ground. It didn't look like much, but the promise of a break as coal, mail, and merchandise was loaded on the train tantalized.

"St. Louis. Two hour stop for those continuing west," the conductor said in warning to the departing passengers.

Harriet looked down at the watch Kitty gave her pinned to her dress. "Long enough for a bath?"

"You could have one if you hurry. I have something else to do." Kit's hand slid into her jacket pocket to touch the smooth gun barrel.

"You do not take a bath; I do not." Harriet placed both hands on her hips for emphasis.

"What?" Kitty tilted her head to stare at her friend.

"Without your help, I can't get undressed." She hissed the words.

"How did you manage at the farm?" Kit asked incredulously. Personally, she gave up on wearing a corset after her beau fiasco. No real reason to cinch in her already small waist or push up her equally modest breasts if her lack of dowry negated any marriage possibilities.

"There are other milk maids at the farm, but most of the time I don't wear a corset." Harriet put a hand on her tightly cinched middle.

"I told you not to wear one. You mean you had that thing on since we started the trip?"

"Ya, you were right! I feel like my middle is squeezed between bear claws."

Kitty's hands landed on Harriet's shoulders, stopping her in mid-stride. "We have to get your corset off somehow."

Harriet smiled while looking over Kitty's shoulder.

Nick slowed as he passed the arguing couple. He winked as Kitty turned to see what had caught her friend's attention.

"You think he heard?" Harriet wondered as he passed from view.

"I know he did." She thought about the wink—a form of *atta, boy* because she was going to relieve Harriet of her corset. Her face flushed when another meaning for corset removal occurred to her. His handsome form faded into the crowd giving no indication what he really thought.

"Bath, no bath?" Harriet asked.

"Well, we can see how long the baths will take. Maybe you can get a private bath, and I will sneak in and help untie the corset, or there may be an attendant to help."

"What?" Harriet looked puzzled.

"A woman or a girl who hands you towels or gets more hot water is an attendant." Kitty explained.

"Men have male attender-ant?" Harriet asked.

Kitty shrugged, her friend wondered about the oddest things.

"I guess you find out," Harriet replied with a rather matter of fact attitude.

"Oh no, I never thought." Kitty pulled her hat lower to strengthen her disguise.

"Attender-ant will see many other things, besides hair." Harriet covered her mouth with her hand as she laughed.

"What am I going to do?" Kit saw the promise of a bath slipping away, and Lord knew she needed one.

"Tell them you do not want attender-ant, less work for them."

They walked past the bathhouse initially. Maybe because they both expected something a little more house-like. It was near the train station to accommodate travelers. The bathhouse was little more than a glorified stable, except instead of stalls, there were small rooms crammed with hip tubs and oaken buckets. The aroma of soap laced water called out to Kitty. The idea of bathing in a public house was unsettling, especially since her aunt insisted only riffraff frequented bathhouses. Still, after a whole week of coal soot and plain old dirt, even a cold creek looked inviting. Since there were no nearby creeks, a bathhouse would have to serve.

Harriet was able to secure a private room and an attendant to help her dress for a few more coins. Kitty managed to reserve a bath and attempted to shake off the helpful attendant who happened to be female. The skinny, partially damp girl looked Kitty over carefully, too carefully.

"Name's Lolly. All the gentlemen likes how I scrub their backs," she bragged while giving Kitty a promising smile, which would have been more inviting if she had a full set of teeth.

"I'm sure you do a wonderful job, Lolly. I can scrub my own back. Thank you." Kit tried to take the towel from Lolly, but she resisted.

"Sir, I can do other things for you. Like hand you soap or light your cheroot." Lolly had a determined grip on the towel.

Who knew it was so hard being a man? Kitty gave the towel a tenacious tug and managed to loosen the mulish attendant's grip when Lolly slipped in a water puddle and fell.

"Have it your way,' Lolly grumbled, rubbing her abused backside as she walked away.

The way the girl's eyes caressed Kitty when she first entered made her afraid she would do more than wash her back. After two trips with full buckets to fill a steaming tub, the sullen attendant left. Shucking her clothes off as fast as she could, Kitty stepped into the bath. Heaven, absolute bliss, who would have known hot water, could be so wonderful. Grabbing the bar of lye soap, she started scrubbing her feet working her way up to her legs. Having worked up a bit of lather, Kitty sunk down to her neck in suds. She contemplated shampooing her hair when Lolly lumbered back in toting two steaming pails of water. Nick followed close behind.

"Hey—this is a private bath." Kitty grumbled as loud as she dared. She couldn't very well jump up in agitation.

"Not anymore." The girl gave her an arched look and proceeded to pour the water in a nearby tub. "Out of rooms and the train will be leaving soon."

Pulling a cheroot out his mouth, Nick turned in Kitty's direction. "Don't mind me." He stopped in mid-speech, eyeing Kitty's curly hair. "Hey, it's you, Kit—the corset removal boy."

"Do you mind?" Kitty huffed with indignation and fear. What was she going to do? How would she get out in time to catch the train?

Lolly slopped in two more buckets. "Need me to wash your back, sir?" Lolly leaned forward and repeated the question as if he missed it the first time.

"No, I can handle this." Nick removed his superfine coat and started unbuttoning his vest, but stopped when Lolly placed her hand on his shirt.

"I said I could handle this," he said with a pointed look at the hand on his sleeve, causing Lolly to swish out of the room.

Raising one eyebrow at the exit of the rejected attendant, Nick stepped toward Kit's tub holding out his right hand. "No hard feelings, Kit?" He held out his hand to shake.

"Um, no," she mumbled while attempting to rise the two inches she needed to shake his hand. Kitty's hand emerged from the bubbles only to disappear inside his powerful grasp. She gave him a quick handshake.

Kitty wondered if Nick thought it odd that she hadn't even looked into his face when they shook hands. Maybe it made her look shifty. Still, being dressed in bubbles made it difficult to be cordial. Worse, Nick continued to undress while she pondered the situation. Pulling off his boots, he cut his eyes to her, which only made her do her best to whip a bunch of bubbles. Nick shook his head. What did it mean?

"Son, what are you doing?" Nick lifted an inquiring eyebrow as he unbuckled his belt.

Kitty turned in the direction of his voice, her reply caught in her throat as he dropped his pants.

"Son?" Nick tried again.

"I'm taking a bath." Startled by his dropped drawers, Kit ducked under the water, covering her head, but forcing her knees up.

Sputtering, Kitty shot up with a gasp, forgetting her need to shield her feminine attributes in a need for oxygen. Taking a deep breath, she made sure to sink back into lather. Cutting her eyes toward Nick, she noticed an odd expression cross his face. It reminded her a little of her old dog, Roscoe, when he got caught stealing eggs. The only thing Roscoe wanted to do was get clear of the hen house.

Nick scrubbed in record time and dressed as she discreetly looked away.

"It's been fun, Kit, but I have a train to board," Nick called out as he grasped the door handle. He waved as he left.

Kit counted to one hundred before jumping out of her icy water where soap scum clumped on top. It would be her luck that he'd forget something and come back. Pretending to be a man was more involved than she originally thought. Ducking under water hadn't made Nick disappear, nor did it erase the image of his naked body.

No siree, she was afraid she would carry that picture to her grave. Nature played an unfair hand making a man with wide shoulders, defined muscles, and powerful horseman's legs. No fat on that torso—not that she looked. When she'd finally came up out of the water, gasping like someone who had been lung shot, he was still there.

It would never do for Nick to discover she was a female. Not that it would matter too much. She never expected to see him again once the trip ended. Still, she wondered what would have happened if she stood and showed Nick that *son* did not apply.

Would it matter? Would he become a ravening beast that men turned into according to her aunt? Would she mind if he did? Such thoughts for a pastor's daughter? Her parents would be shocked, or would they? The thought bounced around in her head as she ran in her ill-fitting boots.

A small blonde woman argued with the conductor as Kit jogged to the train platform. As she drew closer, she recognized Harriet and could hear parts of the conversation.

"You must wait on brother." Harriet insisted with a stomp of boot-clad foot. The conductor shook his head and turned to go, causing Harriet to grab his arm and wilt into a swoon, looking fake even from far away. The ploy did stop the conductor. Burdened with an unresponsive woman, the railroad employee cast his eyes about for some type of assistance and spotted Kit.

"Could you help me, son?" he asked as Kit trotted toward the train.

"Glad to," Kitty replied, causing Harriet's eyes to flicker a little. Slinging one of Harriet's slack arms around her neck, she bent her knees and tried to straighten to a standing position. "Jumping Jesophat, how much does she weigh?"

"I heard that," Harriet muttered with her eyes still closed. Kit staggered with the additional weight. The freed conductor scurried away to alert the engineer to depart.

Kitty heard the final toot of the train whistle. "As good as your fainting act was, we'll miss the train, sister, if you don't wake up and climb aboard."

Harriet's eyes popped open, as she yelped and scurried for the steps of the slow moving train. Kit ran after her barely catching the train as it chugged to life. The two of them stumbled into the passenger car to hear a single handclap.

Nick finished his applause and touched his hat. "Great show, Gruber family. I've not seen professional troupes do as good of a job."

"Really?" Harriet beamed under his praise.

"No, he's joshing us. Let's go find our seats." Kit grabbed onto the seatbacks to hold her balance on the moving train as she walked.

Harriet voice carried a little, maybe because she yelled over the sounds of the departing train. "Why late, bruder?"

Kit half-looked over shoulder at her and noticed a pair of very interested eyes belonging to Nick staring back. "Varmint trouble. I ran into a smelly pole cat in the bathhouse." She watched as Nick made a distressed face before holding his hand to his heart as if wounded.

"Good you made it back in time." Harriet said, nudging her in the direction of two empty seats.

The rest of the day, they spent with two old maid sisters named Joyce and Jillian. The women joined them for a couple of hands of whist. They provided a dog-eared pack of cards, which demonstrated their love and expertise of the game. Card playing turned out to be an activity Harriet excelled at, but because of her staunch Methodist upbringing, Kitty didn't fare as well. Before she knew it, Nick managed to work himself into the seat behind her.

"I could give you some tips," he offered, causing the competitive sisters to fuss about rules and fairness. He smiled at the women, introduced himself with a tip of his hat, and called them by name. Suddenly they were fine with his helping out, as long as he stayed close by. He had that effect on all women, including her, if she were honest.

Nick helped her and Harriet to win the next two hands and in turn killed the sisters' desire to play with them anymore. Harriet was absurdly pleased with winning, but Nick looked after the two sisters as they return to their seats, placing a finger beside his nose.

"What's wrong?" she turned and asked, wondering when she became so aware of his moods and gestures.

"Those two old ladies ran a good con. I wouldn't even have suspected it if I hadn't been looking for it." He grinned a little at the backs of the departing women.

Kitty eyebrows lifted into her forehead. "Cheat? Why would two little old ladies cheat? Why would you look for it?"

Nick pushed his hat up with his index finger, perhaps so she could see his whole face as he stared at her with an incredulous expression. "I'm a professional gambler. I expect people to cheat. I have to look for it and see how good a cheat they are. If I can outsmart them, I will without calling their bluff."

It made sense. "So how did those dear sweet old ladies cheat?" The thought of elderly spinsters tricking her confused her. She'd never expected them to know how to play cards, let alone have a well-used deck with them.

"Marked cards, I noticed it right away. Although, sometimes you made it hard for them the way you palmed the cards. Most ladies hold cards by the corners. I noticed they spread their fingers wide to try to hide the markings. It was a trial to outsmart them, but then I managed with seeing your cards."

"Oh, thank you. I guess it was nice of you to help. It wasn't like we were playing for money." She tried to make small of his help, wondering if it might offend him. A woman pretending to be a man would definitely not attract him. No real reason to want him around. Besides the way he tended to make her heart speed up couldn't be good for her health.

"If the two of you played long enough, they'd make sure you won a few games before they'd suggest playing for money. As it was, once I joined in they knew the game basically ended."

"Good thing you joined." Kitty still had her doubts about those two sweet, old ladies being card sharks.

"They saw the two of you, greener than spring grass, and knew you were ripe for the picking." Nick pulled off his hat and speared his fingers through his hair.

She watched his long fingered hands plow through his thick wavy locks. The diamond pinky ring winked at her. Then she realized what he said. "Green, green! Harriet and I can take care of ourselves."

Nick rubbed his palm over his face as if rubbing off the train soot or hiding a smile. Kitty suspected the latter.

"Of course, you can," he muttered behind the hand. "Didn't mean to imply otherwise."

Somehow, Kitty didn't believe him, not a word of it.

Chapter Five

"ONE MORE DAY to go and we'll be at the end of the train line." Kit muttered as she looked at the makeshift map she'd sketched out for herself.

Harriet ignored her friend and stared out at the passing terrain. "Look!"

Instead of looking, Kitty inspected her nails, pushing back the cuticles with her thumbnail.

"Kit," Harriet hissed, managing to grab her friend's attention.

Kit stared in the direction of her frantic finger pointing. The scene outside the window remained more compelling than Kit's non-masculine grooming habits. On the other side of the grimy train window, a bedraggled caravan of people made their way. Some walked, while a few rode horses and a few lay in a sort of a stretcher pulled by a horse. Someone behind her called it a travois. She did remember reading it was a device used by the Plains Indians for transporting teepees and household goods.

"Who are they?" Harriet wondered aloud.

"I don't know, but it makes me sad." Kit commented.

Nick's deep voice commented behind them, startling Kitty. "They're Indians, and they are sad. You would be too if people kept taking your land and kicking you out of your home."

Kitty turned to see the nattily dressed man standing next to her seat. Nick resembled a weed in some ways, always popping up where he wasn't wanted. As if reading her thoughts, he grinned at her.

"No, not Indians. They do not look like them." Harriet concluded.

"One of them has a Rebel uniform jacket. Another one has on a Mexican serape. You're right." Kit was glad to champion Harriet, especially if it meant proving the annoying Nick wrong.

Kit continued eager to prove her point. "I remember when my aunt took me to Cincinnati because she wanted to attend an event at the museum. They had an art show by Alfred Jacob Miller, all scenes from the west and American Indian life. I remember one picture in particular of a French trapper marrying an Indian maiden. The trapper was beautiful, almost like one of those pictures of the angels, Gabriel or Michael. The Indian girl was in a pure white dress and shyly looking away. No, those people don't look like anybody Mr. Miller painted."

"In the painting you're describing, Mr. Gruber is referred to as romanticism or part of the Romantic Movement. The artist idealized a subject—making it perfect, an example of what people might think something is like instead what it is." Nick raised a challenging eyebrow.

Cocking her head to stare up at him, she knew this game. "Um, so you're saying Mr. Miller is a fraud, a painter of lies." Kit crossed her arms defiantly, wondering how ol' slick would work himself out of this one. He probably would. He always had before, but it was a pleasure to watch him work.

The emotions flashed across Nick's sculpted face. He ran a restless hand through his thick hair and shuffled his pointy-toed boots. "Not a lie. More of a fish story." Nick started to explain until Harriet broke in.

"I know. Man goes fishing and catches a little fish and throws it back. When he gets home, he talks about the big one, which got away."

"You're right, Miss Harriet. In Miller's case, he may have witnessed a wedding between a trapper and a squaw. They both could have been young, but ugly as sin. People don't usually buy ugly pictures or even go to museums to see them so he fixed them up some. In fact, I've heard tell the Indians liked for him to paint their pictures because he did such a good job."

Nick flushed after his long explanation, shoved his hands in his pockets, and contemplated his boots until Kit commented.

"I'd sure like Mr. Miller to paint me. You imagine he could romanticize me, and people wouldn't recognize me?"

Nick answered without thinking. "You don't need Alfred Miller making you into something you're not. You're fine the way you are."

The statement was rather gruff, sounding like it had unexpectedly popped out of Nick. Kit gave a small nod acknowledging that maybe Nick did know something. Yep, he guessed it, or he was in the market for slight, beardless boys. Kitty was betting it was the first. However, she didn't want to be right. She like being a fellow and having the freedom men took for granted. Kitty even liked it when Nick called her son. Then there was the remark he made. Fine—what in the world did that mean? Was she fine as an undersized boy trying to act like a man? Was she fine as a woman pretending to be a man? On the other hand, had he actually seen her feminine charms in the bathhouse and thought they were fine? Couldn't be. She took care he saw nothing. He was probably talking to hear himself talk.

Kit turned away from the discerning hazel eyes, which had a tendency to see too much. Outside the window, she saw the last of the stragglers from the group pass behind the hill. The Indians did look sad, hopeless, unlike the proud, noble savages portrayed in art or the bloodthirsty barbarians, which caused Aunt Eugenia to fret. No, these were people long past tired, and every expectation they might have had dried up like the morning dew on a summer day. Here she was thinking she had it bad. At least she could start a new life in a new place, definitely better than the one she left behind.

THE TRAIN WHEEZED in a sighing whistle as it lumbered into its final station in Sacramento. Goodness, it sounded as weary as she felt, and the trip wasn't over by a long shot. They might be able to stay overnight at a boarding house and catch the stage in the morning. The squealing train brakes set Kitty into action. She shook Harriet awake and then reached for their traveling bag. It was gone! Everything, the food, her gun, their money were in the bag. What were they going to do? Kitty looked again until a definite throat clearing caught her attention.

Nick stood behind her holding both his bag and theirs.

"Looking for these?" he inquired silkily.

"Damn right," she said, angry and relieved at the same time. Nick popped up everywhere, and that bothered her. Maybe Nick didn't bother her as much as being dressed like a boy when Nick sauntered by or stopped to chat. It was hard to flirt with a man when you both wore pants. As for her hair, it looked like a demented monkey had taken a blade to it. What a shame because she knew Nick would be a world-class flirt. A person didn't get much experience flirting with Aunt Eugenia around, and the early tragedy with her sweetheart had soured her on about everything. Aunt Eugenia didn't want anyone happy since she lost her own beau.

Their arguing woke Harriet who yawned, blinked, and then shook her head. "Kitty—uh, Kit, watch your tongue!"

"What?" Kit looked over at her agitated friend. What was wrong now? Something odd about her tongue?

"She's referring to your cursing," Nick cheerfully pointed out.

"I don't curse." What in the world was wrong with the man?

Harriet confirmed his spurious claim. "You swore at Mr. Kennedy."

"Well, the man would make a preacher cuss. Give me some slack, sister," she snarled in frustration.

"You'll be glad to know, Kit, once I help the two of you off the train, I will trouble you no more."

Harriet tried to reassure him. "Mr. Kennedy, I'll tell my husband Adam of your kindness."

Kitty rolled her eyes at the both of them. Harriet managed to work Adam's name in almost every conversation as if the man were traveling with the two of them.

"Adam?" Nick's eyebrows shot up, as his forehead furrowed in thought. "That wouldn't be Adam Easton, who owns the dry goods store?"

Harriet bobbed her head with vigor. "Ya, ya, you know him?"

Kitty sidled closer, curious about her friend's husband. Would Nick give them information that would send them off in the other direction? Harriet's expectant face mirrored her interest and anxiety.

"I do." Nick's lips tipped up, displaying a wide smile. "Adam's a good man and a hard worker. The two of you will deal well together. I feel better knowing he's your husband."

Harriet placed her clasped hands over her heart. "Thanks you."

Touching a finger to his hat brim, Nick replied, "You're welcome, ma'am. I appreciate your gratitude. I have a younger sister. I hope she married up as well as you."

Kit snorted at the thought of him having siblings. Harriet shot a warning look at Kit before Nick, unperturbed, continued. "And I would like to think someone would look after her if she were on a long trip."

Nick helped Harriet down the railroad car steps, passing the bag to Kit to carry. The combined weight of the meager posessions still stretched her arm a couple of inches. It would have been like him to give her all both bags to carry to get her goat. She stumbled after Harriet and Nick. Even when she lost sight of them, they weren't too hard to track. Women whispered behind their gloves or fans as their eyes cut in the direction of the handsome gambler. Anyone who cast a spell over women like Nick did would never look twice at an almost on the shelf spinster from Ohio.

"I don't know why I rub your *brother* the wrong way," Nick

commented in a carrying voice Kitty could hear.

"Do not worry. Kit is no good at travel." Harriet patted Nick's hand as if to comfort him.

"No good at travel," Kitty mimicked the words as she stumbled behind them. "No good at putting up with men's nonsense would be a better explanation." She ignored some of the sideways glances the other travelers gave her as she talked to herself. She increased her pace so she'd hear what Nick's response was.

"He's a little rough around the edges, but I like Kit. In fact, I'd like to get know your brother better. I'd love to travel on up to Cariboo, but there is a high stakes poker game here with my name on it."

"Good fortune," Harriet said with enthusiasm, smiling up at him.

Ick, even Harriet reacted to his charm. It made Kit want to be sick right there in the public street.

"If I win big this time, it will be all I need to leave the gambling life and retire to a farm," Nick confided.

What! Did she hear right? Big, flashy gambler with his fancy boots wanted to play in the dirt? He was probably making up stuff so Harriet would feel sorry for him, but Nick did sound almost wistful when he said the last part. Maybe a career in the theatre would suit him better than farming.

Nick stopped at Mrs. Bakersfield's Boarding House. She usually didn't like single young men as boarders, but once Nick explained, they were brother and sister, she agreed to let them stay the night. Harriet thought it was proof of Nick's goodness while Kit figured it meant Nick was friendly with the Widow Bakersfield. She wasn't exactly ancient or hard to look at, although she did have a passel of rules.

Kit imagined the widow would have Nick ask for romantic favors in full sentences since she used to be the local schoolmarm. The woman prefaced her introduction with "as a former school teacher," before reading through the rules. Kit preferred not to think about Nick asking any woman for a kiss.

"Kitty, what is it?" Harriet asked, hearing her friend's sigh.

"Nothing, I'm tired. I'm ready for a bath," she answered, unwilling to explain the wayward direction her thoughts had taken lately.

"Oh ya, I remember your last bath," she teased.

Kitty could feel her face turning July tomato red. Of all the things Harriet could have mentioned, she chose that, especially after she explained Nick played the part of the polecat. Harriet had to effrontery to ask what Gambler Nick looked like without clothes. When she said she didn't look, Harriet had snorted her disbelief.

"Ah-ha, I know what you think." Harriet rubbed her index fingers in a shaming motion at her friend. She leaned forward to whisper so she wouldn't be overheard. "Thinking about Gambler Nick in the bath?"

"Harriet!" Kit flushed even redder since a bare chested Nick did fill her thoughts.

"Handsome and not married. He might get a farm," Harriet commented.

"How do you know he's not married?" Kit had wondered.

"I asked," Harriet, answered with a twinkle in her eye.

Kitty grabbed Harriet's shoulders and shook her. "Tell me you didn't."

Mrs. Bakersfield stood at the corner of the stairs and watched them, maybe wondering how the two tenderfoots could ever make it out west.

"I did, because I am married woman." Harriet held her be-ringed hand out as proof.

"I know I was the proxy groom. I want to know why you did it." Aggravated, she threw down her hat.

Harriet handed her hat back to her. "I did it to see if he was good husband for you."

"Ha, ha," Kitty managed to force out. "Hey, Mr. Gorgeous

Kennedy—who can get any girl he wants—would you be interested in my skinny brother over there with the bad haircut?"

"I didn't say anything. He knows you're not a male." Harriet nodded knowingly.

If she dares to say anything about knowing because she's a married woman I'll scream, Kitty silently promised herself. "It doesn't matter either way because we'll never see him again."

Harriet turned to go into her room. "Think what you like, brother. I know different."

Kitty settled for snorting her disbelief as she entered her room. Already she had picked up two male habits, cursing and snorting. Before she knew it, she'd start scratching herself in public. Tomorrow would bring the next stagecoach leg of the trip, bringing her closer to who knows what. Unlike Harriet, she didn't have anything waiting for her in Cariboo. She wasn't totally sure if she'd stay there, but it was a start.

THE NEXT MORNING came before she was ready to welcome it with Harriet banging on her door and warning her they'd missed their ride if she didn't get a move on it. Clutching her bag, she managed to trot down the stairs to meet Harriet, who was finishing her breakfast. When Kit tried to sit, Harriet reminded her there was no time. The coffee smelled genuine, and the biscuits steamed a little. Kitty gave the fluffy scrambled eggs a lingering look before turning to leave and hurrying to follow Harriet.

A portly woman dressed in no-nonsense brown calico climbed into the coach helped by the driver and an outrider. An intense young man, with thinning hair and supercilious manner, crawled in after her, while a tired looking woman prodded her two rambunctious sons in the direction of the stagecoach door.

"Do you think there is actually room for us inside?" Kit wondered aloud as she watched the parade of people climb into the coach.

"There's plenty of room for you and the missus inside. We usually carry eight to ten passengers." The stagecoach driver scratched underneath his sweat-stained hat. "But that one female might count for three, so that means." He held out his fingers to count. "Not ten, but it still might be tight."

Kit helped Harriet into the stage and took a deep breath, mentally preparing to follow.

"You're welcome to ride up top with me, young feller," the stagecoach driver offered as if anxious for company.

Harriet shot her a *don't you dare* look from her position wedged between a toy waving tot and haughty young man.

"Um, thanks, but I think I'll ride inside at first."

"You'll change your mind."

The driver guffawed and climbed to his seat. Kit stood hunched in the middle of the coach waiting for everyone to settle before she'd be able to squeeze in beside Harriet. A crack of the whip started the horses out with a lurch.

Kit to hit the floor with a thump, allowing her an excellent view of everyone's footwear. The brown calico dress woman was wearing a pair of men's hobnail boots. The young man's polished boots were developing holes on the bottom. The young mother's boots were mud encrusted, and her youngest son's were—"ouch"—in her face.

"Johnny, no!" The distressed mother pulled her son back into her lap. Harriet covered her mouth with a cotton-gloved hand to hide her smile.

The calico dress woman leaned forward and grabbed Kit's arm to haul her into the seat. "Mercy, you don't weigh more than a wet hen. The name's Agatha Rigsby, and I'm headed up north to be with my husband," the large woman declared with pride.

Kit settled back into the seat with an exhausted sigh and muttered thanks. Her eyes closed. Smells assaulted her. Horse manure on someone's boots, apparently Agatha enjoyed a cigar recently, and someone must have doused himself or herself in lilac water. Underneath it all, body odor clung to the stagecoach inhabitants. Kit wondered if she smelled that bad.

Feeling obligated to reply, Kit opened one eye. "Kit Gruber and my sister, Harriet."

"Easton, Harriet Easton. I am on the way to see my husband in Cariboo," Harriet cheerfully confided.

The young man with the shiny shoes caressed a worn Bible as he declared, "I'm Eugene Hutchinson. I'm traveling as far as Morgan's Creek to lead the faithful and save the sinners,"

"Nora Saegasser, my sons, Johnny and Billy." The bedraggled woman paused as if she was trying to catch her breath or center her thoughts. "We're going home."

Kit could tell by the soft, rounded vowels her home wasn't anywhere near. She wondered if Nora was meeting her husband somewhere farther north. Just in case she was a war widow, she wouldn't ask.

The first couple of hours of the trip was pure misery. Little Billy flailed his little legs until they encountered Kit's. The boy must be wearing steel-toed boots. Nora apologized and scolded Billy, causing him to stop for five minutes before he started again. She'd be black and blue before they got to the next town. Then a miracle happened. Billy fell asleep. His brother already snored, slumped up against the side of the coach giving their mother a much needed break.

"I'd thought those two would never fall asleep," Agatha whispered loudly.

"Me, too," Kit added.

Agatha swiveled her head to take in the whole group. "Now we adults can get down to the good stuff, any news?"

"The bridge went out over McCormick's creek," Nora said.

"Bad thing." Agatha's eyes twinkled as she looked around. "Anything else? A new song or story? Out here it takes forever to hear anything."

"Well, um, I did hear a story," Eugene stammered. "I don't know if it is fit for the ladies." He glanced at Harriet and Nora.

"Go ahead, preacher, tell your tale. Anybody who has traveled this far west is no delicate miss. Am I right, Harriet?" Agatha asked.

"Ya, Agatha."

"Well, I'll tell you first it's a ghost story." Eugene paused, waiting for objections. "Not that I hold with ghost stories, except for entertainment."

"I love ghost stories," Nora girlishly gushed.

Eugene started his tale, surprising Kit with his resonant voice and storyteller skill. "It was during the Civil War that a young Union Officer was in love with the prettiest girl in New York. She was also the daughter of a Southern sympathizer. Her father refused to let them marry unless the officer quit the Union army. He refused and promised his lady love he would return to waltz the *Blue Danube* with her."

"As soon as he left for battle, her father forced her to cast off her true love and get engaged to a man of his choice. She wrote a letter renouncing her true love. The nurse who read the letter to the dying soldier changed the words to give the man comfort. She read of the girl's love for the officer and how she was waiting for his return. The man died with a smile on his face."

"Is that it?" Agatha demanded, crossing her arm and giving the man a stare, daring him to be done with the tale.

Eugene shook his head and smiled, maybe feeling his hold on his audience. "No, I was getting to the good part. While her true love lay dying, the girl was getting married in a big, expensive New York wedding. The reception was at her father's mansion. Everyone was standing around, ready to watch the married couple dance their first waltz when the orchestra started playing the *Blue Danube*, the song she last danced with her true love. She didn't want to dance, but her husband and father made her. It was a beautiful, summer day, but when her new husband drew her into an embrace to dance a storm rushed in. It blew out all the candles and lamps.

"The sky, heavy with dark clouds, and the occasional lightning bolt could be seen through the open doors. When the lightning struck, she saw a man in a Union uniform walking toward her. Most everyone else was running around in a panic, but the orchestra still played on. The man bowed and asked for the dance. That was their signal, you see."

Eugene looked around making sure all eyes were on him before he went into the finale. "At first the girl was scared and wanted to scream. Then she realized her own sweet love had come for her. She went into his arms and danced the waltz up and down the ballroom. By then, they'd re-lit the candles, and people could see the bride whirling around in her bridal finery alone. Smiling up at no one, she continued to dance despite her new husband's pleas to stop."

"What happened to her?" Kit asked.

"They put her away in an insane asylum because she kept talking about her dead lover coming back for her."

"Wonderful story," Harriet cooed as she brought her hands together in delight.

"Harriet, it was a ghost story," Kit said, surprised at her friend's enthusiasm. Maybe Germans were different.

"It was a love story. I hope Adam loves me as much."

Kit shook her head in disgust. She hoped Adam would love her. If not, they didn't have to stay. She held onto enough money to go somewhere though she had no idea where.

Chapter Six

"HOW LONG CAN it possibly take her to get here?" Adam Easton queried.

The freight driver, Jacob Johansen acted as if didn't understand Adam's agitation. "Adam, iffin she wore at the station, I'da brought her. A woman is a woman. Knowing women, she'll take her own sweet time to get here."

"A month ago, she said she was coming right away." Adam ran an impatient hand through his hair.

"Well, now." The freight driver paused to spit a wad of tobacco juice onto the dirt street. "How long did it take ya to get out here?"

His brow wrinkled in thought. "Indirectly, it took me about two years. I hauled freight for old Cosmo for a few months. Then I tried my hand at gold panning, but it was already played out. Between the river flooding and the Indian attack, I almost never got here."

"So now young feller, you're complaining about a month. Wait until she sinks her claws into ya. Be liken those poor souls ramblin' to the ends of the world to escape." Jacob laughed so hard at his own wit he had to lean against the freight wagon.

"Mr. Johansen, do not speak about my wife in such a manner." Adam's eyes narrowed meaningfully.

"Don't get ya bloomers in a wad."

"I will not stand here and listen to you demean my Harriet. She is a good and pure woman. I understand people like you don't understand people like my Harriet. You'll see when she gets here."

Jacob snorted once before he started to unload the freight Adam ordered. "Don't mind me. I knows that women be scarce in these parts. You'd be lucky with a buck-toothed hag."

The routine work of putting away supplies couldn't keep Adam's mind off all the things that might hurt his Harriet. It was unbelievable someone as sweet and honest as she would travel all the way to Cariboo to marry him. He knew the men around here didn't believe the sepia photograph he carried next to his heart could be his Harriet. The picture looked a little fuzzy, but he could still see a rounded face with a shy smile and blonde hair. It was enough for him, a woman who would be his alone. Someone who promised to love and care for him. He hoped she'd love him. Before he headed out west, he was never very clever around the girls. The only kiss he ever had was from Eloise, one of the girls down at the Gilded Lily. He had to steal that one. Eloise didn't kiss despite the fact she did everything else. Adam didn't understand, but he figured it was her choice. He hoped Harriet wouldn't mind the marital act too much. Some women did. He hefted one of the hogsheads of molasses onto his broad shoulder and grabbed a keg of nails with his free hand. His body shook at the thought of his Harriet.

"Whoo-whee, Adam, you carry dat hogshead likum it was a bale of cotton. Most shop owners roll their supplies." Jacob shook his head and whistled in appreciation.

"What is the point in being a big galoot if I can't throw things around some?" Adam joked. People were always amazed at his size. Sure, he stood well over six feet tall with hands the size of Virginia hams. He'd always been big as long as he could remember.

The dry goods business appealed to him. He'd never go hungry. He clasped his hands together and stretched them until his knuckles popped. Maybe he should have gone and picked up Harriet personally. He would make sure nothing bad happened to her. Besides not being able to afford to shut up the store for so long, he was afraid. Some women didn't care for big men, and he certainly was one. He'd sent her a photograph of his head. Maybe he misled her, but he knew they'd have a proxy wedding. He hoped their married status would keep her from running off before she got to know him.

"Ye don't think Indians gone and got your gal? Maybe she's some chief's third wife-squaw. Most of 'em Indians like the yeller haired gals." Jacob pursed his lips sagely as he delivered his latest insight.

Adam straining under a load of horse harnesses merely grunted, before he threw the whole mess on the ground. "Enough," he roared. The last thing he needed was to think of his wife as some chief's squaw.

THE RIVER RACED by pushing uprooted trees in front of it. The stage driver shook his head and spat a stream of tobacco. Kit's curiosity initiated by lack of movement, caused her to stick her head out to see what was happening. A stream of warm tobacco spit dampened her inquisitiveness.

"Arghh." Kit pulled her head in quickly while wiping at her face.

"Kit, what happened?" Harriet handed over her handkerchief.

Kit remarked, as she covered her besieged face with the cotton square, "I can hear you laughing."

Harriet attempted to explain. "No, I smiled. You end up in so many accidents."

Kit grunted her disbelief as she scoured the spittle off her face. The spit might be gone, but the smell and memory remained.

"So why are we stopped?" Agatha asked.

Eugene peered out of the opposite window at the turbulent water. "I think it may be the river."

Nora stood to peer around Eugene. "Last time I went this way a bridge spanned this section."

The stagecoach door swung open to reveal their bewhiskered

driver. "Well, folks, we got us a slowdown. Bridge is out. Twenty miles to our next bridge—a hard twenty miles."

Nora sighed when her two boys woke up with a whine. Twenty more hard miles and another extra day of traveling, but not much could be done about it. The harried mother shepherded her boys outside to answer nature's call. Agatha and Eugene followed their example, leaving Kitty and Harriet alone in the stagecoach.

Harriet turned to Kitty and whispered. "It will be another day before I can see my Adam."

"I know you want to see your husband, but there isn't much we can do about it. My parents died crossing water like that." Kitty looked away from the river. The swirling torrent brought back the pain of being an orphaned child.

"I think only of myself." Harriet grabbed Kitty's hands. "Please forgive me."

Kitty tried to summon a weak smile to reassure her friend. "Why don't you tell me what's on your mind? It will help me to think about something else."

Harriet nodded her head. "You did not want me to be a mail order bride. Now, I wonder if you were right."

"Oh, Harriet." Kitty pulled her friend in for a tight hug. "I thought this was what you wanted. Adam sounds like a nice man." She patted her friend on the back.

"He is nice," Harriet sobbed. "I am lucky woman." She sobbed a bit more and then started hiccupping.

"Honey, if Adam is such a good man, why are you crying?" Kitty continued to pat Harriet on the back.

Harriet pulled out of Kitty's hug to backhand her nose. "What if he not like me? He send me back?"

Recognizing her degree of stress by her difficulty in remembering English, Kitty took her friend by the shoulders, turning her, so she could look into her eyes. "Harriet, listen to me. This man advertised for a wife. Many women probably applied, but he picked you. You,

Harriet. Of course, he'll like you. If he doesn't, I will have to whack him upside the head with a manure shovel."

"Kitty," Harriet smiled through her tears, "you are silly."

"I mean it. I still have most of my dowry money. You and I could start a business." Kitty tried to reassure herself and her friend. She didn't know what type of business they might start.

The mingled voice of fellow travelers reached the stagecoach before they did, especially the high pitch childish whine.

Kitty looked at Harriet. "We better hightail it and make our call to nature before the driver starts up again."

Everyone piled back into the coach. Two unhappy children, a young pastor who alternately tried to save their souls and told ghost stories, not to mention the seat with the wayward spring made the extra day difficult, especially the spring. A good jolt set it in motion and usually picked Kit as its victim. Her entire lower body played host to a number of bruises. Who knew the stagecoach would be the hardest part of the trip? Sleep offered the only reprieve to the discomfort. When it became dark, the driver slowed the coach and advised everyone to make camp. Thank goodness for Agatha, the only one who had a clue how to make camp. She shifted into a military mode and began giving orders. Eugene gathered firewood. Nora's boys picked up river stones for the fire circle. Kitty and Harriet worked their way down to the river to bring water.

"Oh my, what an adventure," Harriet exclaimed.

Kitty grinned and wondered if they bore any resemblance to Jack and Jill of nursery rhyme fame as they carried their pails. "I imagine we will have many more adventures."

"You will. I will have a quiet life with my Adam." Harriet kneeled to lower her bucket in the murky water.

Kitty imagined her friend would have a settled life with her husband. That's all she could wish for her. Jealousy lurked around the edges of her consciousness, but she managed to tamp it down. They took the water back to Agatha who made soup by throwing in everyone's food supplies, including the driver's jerky. Surprisingly, it wasn't too bad, but it might have been because they were all so hungry.

The next morning the stagecoach pulled into where they were to have met the freight wagon driver the day before. Kit didn't expect the driver to be there since so no one knew when Harriet would arrive. A wiry man holding a whip watched the stagecoach unload. He studied each passenger carefully with his mouth pulled into a mulish line. When Nora descended, he rushed forward and demanded.

"Are you Adam Easton's mail order bride?"

"Gracious, no." Nora took a step back and looked around wildly with her eyes alighting on Harriet.

The man's switched his glare to the blonde woman behind the skinny woman. "Are you Adam Easton's bride?"

"Ya," Harriet answered and looked for Kitty.

"Let's go. I've been cooling my heels long enough. Adam will be fit to be tied if I show up again without his bride." The man turned and started walking toward a loaded wagon.

"Sir," Kitty called out. "A minute, please, I need to get our bag."

The bewhiskered driver continued to walk, towing a reluctant Harriet with him. She struggled in his grasp, looking back over at her shoulder. "Sir, we must wait on bruder."

"Wait for what?" Reaching up under his battered hat, he scratched his head.

Running with luggage bumping against her legs was getting old. Luckily the driver stopped, to look around confused, while scratching what Kitty seriously hoped weren't lice.

"Brew her? What's a brew her? Do you want a beer? Gonna have to wait. Germans," the driver complained.

Harriet stood her ground, digging in her heels, refusing to move, despite the determined pull of the driver.

"Dang blamed woman. Why a man would send off for one baffles me." He complained, pulling on Harriet's arm while regarding her with the same caution as man might regard a coiled rattlesnake.

As soon as Kitty caught up, Harriet relented and turned toward the wagon almost tumbling the driver into the dirt. He caught sight of Kitty heading toward the wagon.

"Hey. Where ya going?" he called out as she wedged the carpetbag among the freight.

"Cariboo, with my sister." Kitty answered, taking a seat on the back of the wagon beside Harriet.

"Adam never sed nothing about no brother. If'n you can manage your sistah, then you're welcome to come," the man threw back as he climbed onto his seat and picked up the whip.

The mules huffed as they pulled the heavy wagon up the steep incline. The driver lashed the mules to motivate them. Kit and Harriet huddled between two barrels in the back of the wagon holding onto each other.

"So far we traveled only to die miles away from my Adam," Harriet pushed out through chattering teeth.

"Almost there, we'll be okay." Kitty reassured her friend and herself. Harriet was worried about surviving the ride into Cariboo, while she was worried about what she would do once she got there.

The hardened ruts and rocks the size of small boulders made the ride rough. The driver must have veered to hit each rock. A few black-eyed Susans peeked out between boulders. Large pine trees stood shoulder to shoulder, and the vegetation that ran out to the road was lush and green from the rain. The Pacific Northwest was as hardy and untamed as the people who chose to settle the land.

The teamster wasn't the talkative sort. He neither talked to them, nor sang like their first driver. The only words to pass his lips were all colorful instructions for the mules straining in their traces. Kit thought about getting out and walking to give the mules a bit of a weight reduction, but she was afraid she'd get left behind. There was no sign of civilization as far as the eye could see. If she dropped off the wagon, she'd probably die of starvation or be eaten by a bear. Maybe one of those wild mountain men might see through her manly disguise and carry her back to his shack. None of the options sounded pleasant. She shivered.

"You cold, Kit?" Harriet asked and huddled a little closer.

"A little, but I was thinking about how different it is here. I don't know what to expect or do once we arrive at Cariboo," she admitted.

"I'm scared, too," Harriet shyly confessed. She laced fingers with Kit's offered hand. "All the trip, I talk about how great my Adam is. He must be a good man to write such sweet letters, but all of the sudden, boom, I'm the wife."

"I wondered if you were putting on a brave front," Kitty replied while giving her friend's hand a reassuring squeeze.

"What if my Adam meets me and is disappointed?" Harriet questioned.

"As far as I can tell, women are like gold out here. Agatha mentioned some of the women who moved out west saw they could do better so they divorced their husbands. They had their pick of any man. The women here are like queens with the various men telling them what they would do for her if she marries them. If Adam doesn't work out, you could go elsewhere. The parson we were riding with looked at you with less concern about your soul and more about your form."

"Oh, Kitty, I would not leave Adam. We arrive today. Maybe he wants me to cook dinner tonight." Harriet wrinkled her nose.

"You'd do it. You know how to cook. Besides, he has a dry goods store. It would be a luxury to cook with all the right ingredients instead of using substitutions," Kitty commented. "Maybe he has real coffee. All we ever had was that chicory stuff during the war, and my aunt got used to it, or she was too cheap to buy the real stuff. Will you invite me over for coffee?"

"Invite you over? You'll live with us, as my brother, of course,"

Harriet patted her arm reassuringly.

"Um, Harriet, I don't know if that would be such a good idea. Being a newly married couple, you'll need your privacy and all." Kit flushed talking about the subject. She also didn't know how long she wanted to pretend to be a man.

"You mean the baby-making," she commented matter-of-fact. "I do not think we would share the same room."

"Um, yeah, that's what I was talking about. Maybe there is a boardinghouse in town. Adam ordered a bride—not a bride and brother. I don't want to start things out bad for you," Kit said.

The cursing grew louder and more vigorous as the mules strained up another rise. In the distant buildings flocked together like a group of setting hens.

"Thar's Cariboo," the driver yelled, then spat a huge stream of tobacco juice.

"Eyuk!" Kit pulled her legs up to avoid the spit.

"I hope my Adam doesn't chew," Harriet said before turning to look at the buildings. The sound of a heavy wagon and a team brought people to the windows and some into the street. Almost all of the onlookers were male. One woman attired in a blue calico dress continued to sweep her porch. She stopped and waved when she saw Harriet and Kit on the back of the cart. They both waved back.

Comments were swirling around them as the driver pulled the team to a stop in front of a two-story building where a hand painted sign read EASTONS.

"Whoo boy, ya think dat's Easton's mail order bride?" one slightly disheveled man asked another.

"Can't think of anyone else who ordered one. Must be," his friend replied.

Harriet looked down at her hands in embarrassment.

The men continue to discuss the merits of Harriet as if discussing a cow or a horse. The sound of footsteps thundering down the staircase coming from the store's second floor caught everyone's attention. A giant of a man came galloping down the stairs so fast he almost fell.

When he came closer, the comb tracks in his damp hair were obvious. The half-buttoned shirt demonstrated his rush.

The man turned bashfully to Harriet and held out his hands. "Harriet?"

She took his hands and let him help her out of the wagon. "Adam, I need to…"

"Oh, oh," he stuttered, suddenly aware of what she might need after traveling so long. "Come inside, I'll show you where everything is," Adam offered while he tucked his new bride's hand in the crook of his arm. His wide grin announced to the lingering crowd how he felt about his new wife.

Harriet looked over her shoulder at Kitty. Adam glanced back as well.

"Adam, I want you to meet my brother, Kit." Harriet beamed up at her new husband.

Adam's open face expressed surprise as Harriet looked up with a tight smile and her hand still on his forearm.

"Good afternoon, Mr. Easton," Kit stepped forward and held out her hand.

Adam's giant paw swallowed up her hand as he pumped his arm in a hearty welcome. "Well, I didn't expect a brother, but I can always use another man around to help me out."

The crowd laughed. Adam stared the crowd down until every titter faded. His towering height intimidated the crowd into silence.

Inside the building, Harriet turned in a slow circle, taking in the rolls of canvas sheeting, the animal harnesses, the casks of turpentine, vinegar, and molasses. Behind the counter was a coffee grinder. Somehow, Kitty reached it before Harriet or Adam to inhale the scent of actual coffee.

"Mrs. Easton," Adam rolled the words around on his tongue. "Let me show you your new home. The first floor is the store. When you get used to things, I was hoping you might help me in here." Adam looked at Harriet. Kit elbowed her.

"Yah, I want to help," she said in a pronounced accent.

Harriet's accent worsened when nervous or scared. Kitty mentally predicted by nightfall, she would not be able to speak a word of English. It probably wouldn't matter to Adam. Talking was probably not, what he was planning to do to consummate the marriage.

The new husband opened the back door and pointed to two outhouses in the distance. "I built one for you when I knew you were coming."

Kit looked at the new raw lumber outhouse with a crescent cutout in the door. She'd heard about a new inside flush water closet. That would be a real way for a man to show his love for his new bride. She never met anyone who had one, but it did sound nice. Judging by her smile, the idea of an outhouse created for her own use pleased Harriet. Who was Kit to complain?

Kit watched Adam's eyes track his bride's every move. He held his breath when Harriet talked. He only let it out when she found favor with his efforts to please her. She wondered if such behavior was normal between a man and a woman. She never saw it before, but meeting your spouse, you've never seen before might make a person act a bit odd. Adam was so lost in Harriet, he wasn't even aware Kit existed or so she thought.

"Um, Kit, that's not a German nickname. I believe it is short for…"

"Keidrich, it is the name of dead uncle," Harriet hurried to explain despite Kit making a choking face.

"Keidrich, hum, not a name I've heard before, but I guess there are many German names I don't know. Anyhow, I was going to say it is short for Christopher or even Catherine in English." Adam shrugged his shoulders indicating the end of the subject.

A stack of dress material bolts lured Harriet to the other side of the store. "Look at all the colors."

"Pick out what colors you like. You can have as many dresses as you can make," Adam offered.

Silence greeted his pronouncement. Adam looked at Harriet, who held the sturdy broadcloth material in her right hand and was fingering a colorful blue calico with her left. Tears streamed down her face. Adam tenderly wiped away the tears with his hand. Taking her small hand, he placed it on his arm and guided her in the direction of the stairs.

They climbed the steps together. Kitty followed slowly, unsure if she should. There was a small kitchen, a living room modestly furnished, a bedroom with an oversized bed to fit Adam's large frame, and another room with a traveling trunk and a cradle. Adam blushed when Harriet caught sight of the cradle.

"A cradle," she cooed and rushed forward to smooth her hands over the finished wood. "It's beautiful."

"I made it myself when you wrote and said you would marry me," Adam quietly confessed.

Harriet looked up all soft and melting at Adam. Kit knew it was time to vacate the scene.

THE BACK DOOR was propped open to capture the breeze or maybe to air the place out. Kit thought as she caught a whiff of stale sweat and spilled beer. Inside were scarred floorboards, a few tables with chairs, and a bar stretching the length of the room. Kitty couldn't see the piano or its mystery player. In fact, she didn't see anyone. It might not be a pianist, but a pre-punched roll, which they loaded in the piano to play. Still a roll wouldn't include all those sour notes. The song was supposed to be *Sweet Betsy from Pike*. She vaguely recognized it.

A peek to see who was playing the piano was all she was going to do. Her aunt would be horrified that she would even think of stepping into a saloon. In the far corner, an upright piano stood. At the keyboard sat a thin woman, picking out notes one handedly. She wore a tired-looking shiny red dress hemmed short to reveal her stockings. Kit moved a little closer and watched for a second. Before she even thought of it, she placed her hand on the piano and played the harmony with her left hand. Startled, the woman looked up.

Instead of a woman, Kit realized she was looking at a girl, perhaps younger than herself. It was hard to tell from her vacant eyes—as if the owner had left. The girl giggled nervously.

"You play the piano?" the girl asked.

"Some," Kitty answered. Her fingers danced across the keys playing the opening notes to Beethoven's *Moonlight Sonata* and stopped.

"That's beautiful. Could you play some more?" The girl got up and offered the stool to Kitty so she could finish the song.

The tone of the piano sounded good, and she soon found herself doing a medley of Stephen Foster's songs. When she looked up a large bald man with a handlebar mustache and a woman with unusually bright red hair and a low-cut black dress were standing with the girl.

The redheaded woman looked Kit over thoroughly before speaking. "You're a little on the scrawny side, but it might be good. Last piano player we had was sweet on Daisy here." She nodded in the direction of the girl. "Didn't take it well when Paul Henry wanted a little companionship."

The bald man added, "He didn't stand up well against Paul Henry's knife."

"You can have the job if you don't chase after any of my girls," the woman offered.

"Um, well." Kitty didn't know what to say. True, she did need a job. This might be her only opportunity. "Ma'am, what would the pay be?"

"Did you hear that, Otis? The little city slicker called me ma'am like I was a real lady." The woman beamed. "Just call me Stella. Your name?"

"Kit," she said, remembering the hat and yanking it off her head in deference to Stella.

"See that, Otis, he took his hat off for me. I like him more and more all the time. Okay Kit-boy, the pay isn't great. The best I can do is two dollars a week, but room and board are free. Iffin someone wants you to play a special song and gives you money for it, it's yours, but don't play any of those war songs. I don't need any Civil Warring in my saloon. You understand?

"Yes, ma'am. Stella, I mean."

"He's as cute as a bug," Stella cooed. "Don't you think so, Daisy?"

"Cuter than a bug, seeing as I don't like bugs overly much," she said. A small spark twinkled in her eyes, making her almost attractive.

Stella grabbed Kitty's arm and pulled. "If we're going to put you to work we need to outfit you. I can't have you bringing the tone of the place down."

Kitty felt caught in one of those ocean currents she read about in her geography book. It said you couldn't fight against them. You had to go with the flow until the tide swept you ashore somewhere. The last thing she was going to question was the tone of the place or lack of it.

Twenty minutes later, outfitted in shiny black pants, a white shirt, a colorful vest, and a bow tie, Kit looked more like an organ grinder's monkey than a musician. Fortunately, Stella left and allowed her to dress in peace only to return with a sleepy-looking brunette in tow. The brunette introduced herself as Rose, which probably wasn't her name. Stella informed her she went with a flower theme to set her establishment, The Gilded Lily, above the others. Of course, some of the other places Kit had seen included the Bucket of Blood and The Hanged Man, which made her wonder what names their workers used.

Rose trimmed her hacked up hair cut so it fell into curls instead of sticking out like hay gone to seed. Stella surveyed the finished product with a frown.

"What's wrong? I did a good job. I know I did," Rose insisted with both hands on her hips.

"Yes, you did. You made him too pretty. I don't want the girls to make sheep eyes at him," Stella answered.

"Don't worry. He's too young. He wouldn't know what to do with a female," Rose said.

Stella asked, while cocking her head inquiringly, "Kit, you ever poked a female?"

Kit stopped her first reaction to scream, "Lord, no!" but instead she dissolved into a coughing fit, which left her red faced and wheezing.

"I guess that means no," Rose concluded with a grin.

Kit nodded her head up and down in agreement. She didn't trust herself to speak.

"That's good. Keep it that way. We don't want your business here. If you get a hankering, there is Widow McHenry, who might be up to teach you a lesson or two. She's young, newly widowed, but not real anxious to marry again. Word is she is up for a bit of fun," Stella said.

Rose mumbled, "That's probably the reason Ben Townsend hasn't been here in over three weeks," as she swept up the hair clippings and tidied up the room.

"Don't get your bloomers in a knot. It's not like he's a great lover. The widow will decide she can do better, and he'll come crawling back."

"I'll take him back, of course," Rose said with a sigh.

"That's what we do here, Rose. Remember that." Stella bit off the words to Rose, then told Kit, "We won't need you until eight o'clock. Plan on working until three in the morning or a little later. I want you to help Otis clean up after closing. Make sure you keep your new clothes clean." She shooed Kitty out of the room.

Chapter Seven

KIT SHOVED HER hands in her new pants testing the fit. Only weeks ago she would've been horrified to wear pants. Now she wanted them to fit right. Too big and the material ballooned out in unflattering ways. Good thing, Stella had a couple sizes in stock. "Wonder what the life span of an average piano player is?" she whispered to herself.

The room and board would be a good deal too. Harriet would fuss, but she'd smooth it over by saying it was only for a short time so she and Adam could honeymoon. The way those two were looking at each other, they'd scarcely notice she was gone. It was no wonder Kitty was standing on the back step of the dry goods store not certain if she should knock. Could be they already started consummating their marriage. She definitely didn't want to walk in on marital wooing. The knocking dilemma ended when Harriet opened the door to toss a pan of dishwater.

"Bruder, I wondered where you went." Harriet stood back so Kitty could enter.

"I've been busy finding a job and a place to live." Kit answered not making eye contact.

Harriet eyed her flashy attire. "They have a circus in Cariboo?"

"Very funny. I am the piano player over at the saloon. I can't remember the name of it." Kit hoped she could find her way back by eight tonight.

"A saloon, Kitty? Adam needs your help." Harriet fussed with straightening the canisters on the counter.

Kitty walked around the counter and grabbed both of Harriet's hands. "Everyone laughed when he said that. Adam was only being polite. I only work at night, so if Adam did need help during the day I would be available."

"This isn't the way I thought it would be." Harriet scampered across the room to rearrange the rockers by the potbellied stove.

Kit followed slower. "How did you think it would be?"

"I figured I would have my Adam, and you would meet a nice man like Nick, get married, and move next door to us. Our babies would play together."

Kitty chuckled, then snorted, but finally brought herself under control. "Harriet, you're a dreamer. There's a few things wrong with the dream. Nick is not a nice man. He's a gambler and a womanizer. I am betting he does not want to settle down in Cariboo and have a passel of kids, not to mention the fact I am masquerading as a male." She propped her hands on her hips, wondering how her friend was going to react to the bald truth.

"Kitty, I saw the way he looked at you." Harriet shook her head as if mystified by her friend's obtuseness.

"How did he look at me?" Kitty asked as she picked up a wool horse blanket and studied the pattern of the weave as if she could care less what Harriet might say.

"That Nick, he is sly, when I pretend to be asleep, he stares at you. Then, he smiled, maybe a smile of a man in love."

"You go too far now, unless you think Nick likes boys!" Kit stalked around the room. Harriet had her going with the thoughtful look and sweet smile stuff.

"Kit, stop pacing. It is dizzy making. Come, sit." She motioned to the pair of rocking chairs. Once Kitty settled, she continued. "The boy disguise was good for a little bit, but Nick knows."

"Wait a minute. It wasn't like that, and we were in tubs. He didn't see any of my female parts," Kit insisted.

"What about this smooth face?" Harriet rubbed the back of her hand across her Kit's cheek. "Or how about these?" She reached forward to grab Kitty's elegant, long fingered hands.

She held her hands out in front of her and tried to see them as a stranger would. "Piano player hands, that's all."

"I bet he saw your feet. Too little to be a man's." Harriet continued.

Kitty looked down at the worn boots she left a gold piece behind for as payment. They were too big, even though they were for a small man. She stuck cotton in the toes for a better fit.

"Sometimes when you woke up or were surprised, you used your normal voice."

"Oh my, I didn't know. What am I going to do? My disguise isn't as good as I thought it was."

"I could make you dress," Harriet offered.

"Harriet, you know I can't. I don't know if there is a notice out for my arrest. I need to do a better job being a male. Any suggestions?" Kit rocked back in the chair, wondering if her paltry disguise fooled Stella and Rose.

"You could talk less and stick a rolled sock down your pants," Harriet advised with a wink.

"I'll talk less, but what's with the sock?"

"You're manly parts. You might even want to move it now and then." The blonde chuckled at her friend's horrified expression.

"Stick my hands down my pants and start scratching away?"

"No." She had difficulty in stopping her laughter, but Harriet managed to draw in a breath before continuing. "You do the scratching on the outside. Haven't you watched men at all?"

"Well, I never saw Nick do that."

"Ah-ha, you did pay attention. Nick has manners."

Kitty quit rocking and stared at her friend. "I am supposed to act like a rude fellow?"

"You are supposed to be a male. No one doubts Nick is a man."

She exhaled a hearty sigh. Harriet was definitely right about that. Even without his bathhouse striptease, she never doubted Nick was a one hundred percent male.

"Still going to play piano?" Harriet asked with an arched look.

"You know I am. It is something I have to do. It will give you and Adam time alone."

"I don't mind you here."

"I believe you, Harriet, but I would be uncomfortable, knowing what you two were doing in the next room. Truthfully—a little jealous because I don't have a big, handsome husband, too."

They both rose from the rocking chairs at the same time. Harriet, wrapped in a canvas apron, hustled behind the counter. "Is there anything I can do to help?"

"You could sell me some bullets. I've been meaning to get some the whole trip." Kit grabbed the carpetbag by the door, pulled out the pistol, and laid it on the counter.

"No bullets," Harriet shook her head to underscore her words.

Adam walked down the stairs, hearing the tail end of the conversation. "I'll sell you bullets."

"Adam," Harriet protested.

"Now, dear, things are different out here. A man does carry a gun. Doesn't mean he'll ever use it. The possibility he could will protect him. You do want your brother protected?"

"Yes," Harriet murmured in a chastened voice.

Adam picked up the gun. "I see you have an army issued Colt. Too young to have fought in the war. Where did you get it?"

"I found it in an alley." Kitty told him truthfully.

Adam rotated the chamber before going to look for bullets among the various boxes he had lined up on the shelf.

"How many did you think you'll need?" Adam asked.

"About twenty-five," Kit guessed.

"Twenty-five! Are you going to shoot twenty-five men?" Harriet directed her glare at Kit, but Adam felt the sting of it, too.

Kit explained to her irate friend. "No, I need to do some target practice."

"Then, I'll give you a hundred." Adam started counting out the bullets while Harriet simmered.

"Go on out, Kit Gruber, with your gun and bullets. Go to your piano playing job. See if I care." She turned with a twirl of skirts and stomped up the stairs.

"You got a job already?" Adam asked as he put the bullets in a small brown sack.

Kit hurried to explain to the big man that she wouldn't be underfoot. "Yep, playing piano down at Stella's saloon. She's giving me room and board, too."

"Stella's place is much better than any of the others. You did well. I understand a young man wanting to get out on his own." Adam handed the bullets to his new brother-in-law.

A snort came from the area of the stairs.

"I'm glad someone understands," Kit grumbled more to herself than Adam.

"Give her time. You are the little brother. Once I put a baby in her belly, she'll have someone else to fuss over." The sound of something breaking drew the big man's attention. "I think maybe my bride needs some help." He grinned and trotted up the stairs.

Kit slipped her gun in the carpetbag and headed to the saloon to check out her new accommodations. One of the saloon girls had offered to show her around. She couldn't remember her name, but it had something to do with a flower.

ROSE SWUNG THE door open to a small room that could have easily doubled as a linen closet. "Here's your room. It's not fancy, but it was never used for entertaining purposes."

Kit's eyes passed over the narrow bunk, the cheap muslin curtains at the lone window, a faded rag rug, and a small dresser topped by a chipped pitcher and bowl. "It looks fine. I'm not sure why a person would use a bedroom for entertaining." She stopped at Rose's snort. Kitty nervously assured Rose before she could explain the entertainment concept more fully. "Oh, okay, I see."

"Well, I thought you might. Just in case, someone used the room because we were short on rooms, I'd changed the sheets," Rose explained with a grin.

"Um, that's very good of you." Kit thanked her effusively, not even wanting to think of the sheets unchanged.

The saloon girl whipped up the bed cover to expose a chamber pot. "We have the jakes out back, but sometimes it's too cold or dark to make the trip. It's much more convenient to drop a load in the privacy of your own room." Rose winked before she turned to leave. "See ya. Supper is at six downstairs. Be on time."

Kit bounced on the bed, causing the abused springs to moan. A sudden shout and pounding startled her.

"Quiet down in there. I need my beauty sleep," an irritated woman's voice came through the wall.

Instead of answering, Kit clutched her carpetbag. She knew things would be different once she left home. She never had a clue how different.

The double picture frame of her parents took a special place on the windowsill. This way she would see them, first thing in the morning. It made her feel as if they watched over her. Her pair of pants hung on a hook beside her shirt. She wasn't sure what to do with the gun and ended up sticking it underneath the mattress. It didn't take long to unpack her meager belongings. Last, she pulled a ruffled nightgown out and stuffed it in an empty dresser drawer. All the way here, all she slept in were her second hand boy's clothes. The nightgown would be a luxury.

Kit walked to the door and examined it. It had a lock. Where was the key? She would make a point of asking Stella about it at dinnertime.

Kit toed off her boots and stretched out on the bed. It was heaven. Despite the fact, the mattress sagged in the middle and smelled of cigar smoke. It had been weeks since she stretched out. Napping seated or leaning against the wall grew old fast.

She crossed her feet and put her hands behind her head. Imagine if her aunt could see her now, footloose and fancy free. She wouldn't even recognize her niece, which was a good thing since she would probably throw her in jail for assault. There would also be a trumped-up story about how she devoted herself to Kit's wellbeing after the tragic death of her brother and his wife. Never mind, she used Kitty's dowry money to do it.

The water spot on the ceiling looked a bit like a ship under full sail, Kit mused as she closed her eyes.

The creak and groan of the ship's timbers and the flap of the sails was the first thing she heard. The wood felt warm under her feet. She looked down at her bare feet peeking out from the lace edged hem of a skirt. She had on a dress, but not one she owned. The light and gauzy shift skimmed over her body without the aid of a corset. The bodice was low, and the tiny cap sleeves barely rode on her shoulders. She wanted a mirror to check out the scandalous dress she never owned when boot steps headed her way. A tall figure silhouetted by the sun stood over her, a pirate, possibly. Her eyes started at his tall black boots, slid quickly over his tight pants, and a heavy belt complete with a sword—definitely a pirate. His hands were on his hips. On his hands were rings with twinkling gems. She continued to look past the lace edged shirt opened to expose a muscular chest, up past the disarming grin to a pair of familiar eyes. Nick Kennedy—it was Nick.

"Hello, darling, I've been waiting for you to wake up," he murmured before taking her hand and pulling her closer.

"Nick, you're a pirate," she exclaimed in surprise as he tucked her hand firmly in the crook of his arm.

"Pirate is such an ugly word. I specialize in relocation of goods. I find someone undeserving of the goods they possess and reward someone

else with them, like I did with you, my sweet." He flashed his devastating grin before swooping down to press a quick kiss on her lips.

"Tell me again, how it happened?" Kitty turned imploring eyes on her pirate king.

"You minx," he said, before delivering a pinch to her bottom with his free hand.

"Nick," she squealed in surprise.

"Don't play the innocent with me. You know you like it. You want me to tell you again how I rescued you from the clutches of your depraved fiancé."

"Oh." Kit sighed a bit, wondering when she'd acquired a depraved fiancé.

"I saw your ship, a fat merchantman riding low in the water flying the Union Jack. That was all the invitation I needed. Once we boarded, your aunt placed herself in front of your door like a holy martyr. I figured I wanted whatever was inside. It had to be something special. How right I was."

"Go on," she encouraged.

Nick pushed a strand of her wind tossed hair behind her ear. "Well, I broke down the door despite the old battle axe's threats of divine retribution. I figure listening to her howl was punishment enough."

Imagining her Aunt Eugenia, Kit giggled and covered her mouth. She didn't want to give Nick any reason to stop.

Instead of a chest of gold, there you sat on your bed, brushing your hair, as calm and collected as you please. Your first words were 'You've come to rescue me.'"

"I remember. Go on," she urged, nudging his side with her elbow.

"I got you on my ship without too much trouble. The sailors feared for their lives and didn't lift a finger to protect you."

"Cowards," she chortled. "Thank goodness they were. I hate to think I caused any bloodshed."

"Probably the most bloodless encounter I've ever had. Once I got you to my cabin you went on about how your aunt was selling you to the most depraved man in England because no one there would marry him."

Nick pivoted on one heel to gather Kit into his arms, "Do you remember what happened then?"

"No, what? Tell me," she gasped with her heart racing.

Nick gave her a considering look. "You mean you forgot this." His lips came closer for a kiss, when a sudden hammering sound jarred her.

"Kit, Kit Gruber, is you in there?"

Kit blinked a few times. Damn it was a dream, and it was just getting interesting.

"Um, yeah, what do you want?" she called out to the unknown knocker.

"Dinner, better get a move on it. Stella doesn't like slugabeds."

Not wanting to make her new boss angry for any reason, Kit hurried. A large scarred table dominated the dining room. A small man dressed in pajamas placed plates on the table. Kit thought he was a man until he turned she stared at a pigtail trailing down his back.

"Never seen a Chinaman before?" Otis asked as he noticed Kit's intense scrutiny.

"So, he is a man, then?" Kitty asked. She heard laughter as Rose entered the room.

"Cookie wouldn't like it if he knew you were questioning his masculinity. Well, that would be like," Rose drawled as she ruffled Kit's curls, "Me questioning your masculinity."

Kit's breath caught. Rose knew.

"Now, I wouldn't do that, of course. I've seen plenty of pretty boys grow into handsome young men. Same thing with old cookies. Things are different in China."

"You aren't talking about Cookie's pigtail, are you?" Daisy drifted into the room.

"In a way of speaking, we are," Kit confessed shyly.

"Cookie can't ever cut it off because it is forbidden. He told me they wouldn't let him in China without the pigtail. I don't understand why. I guess men over thar all have pigtails. I wonder what the women have."

"Maybe they're all bald like me," Otis joked as he rubbed a hand over his slick pate.

"If that's the case, maybe I should go to China. I'd have more business than I can handle," a petite brunette announced as she shook back her wavy, waist-length hair.

"Iris, you got more business than you can handle now. That sounds like you to want more," Rose said with a distinctive snarl in her tone.

"Girls, let's be on our best behavior tonight. We have a newcomer." Stella nodded in the direction of Kit. "No reason to scare him the first night, he's here."

A young boy hurried in to take his place behind a chair, "Sorry, I'm late, Stella. I finished taking care of Madeline. She threw a shoe, so I had to take her to the smithy."

"No matter, Jimmy. You tried to be on time, which is more than I can say for some people." The loudness of Stella's voice increased until she reached the final word. Almost on cue, a tall blonde glided into the dining room.

"Am I late?" She acted flustered, while her eyes announced she didn't care who she inconvenienced.

"Yes, you are late, Lily. If you were hoping to make your grand entrance, you're out of luck. We have more important things on our minds than you," Stella declared in a no-nonsense voice as she pulled out the head chair to sit down.

Lily raised one eyebrow in disbelief as if she doubted anything was more important than her. She pulled her chair out slowly and made the process of sitting down into a one-act play. Sweeping out her blue lace trimmed skirt, she lowered herself grandly as if she were a duchess in an English drawing room. Lily didn't see Rose behind her, mocking her.

Kit knew she wasn't going to like Lily. She made a mental note to avoid her. It probably wouldn't be necessary. Women like Lily only interacted with people they could use. She didn't have anything Lily could want, or so she thought.

The others pulled out their chairs and sat down as Cookie brought in a large tureen. He ladled out a rice mixture with vegetables and small chunks of meat. Kit eyed the food wondering what it was, but noticed the others were eating with great gusto. She took a bite. It was different, a little spicy, and she recognized the texture of chicken. Daisy winked at her across the table.

"Wha'd ya think?" Daisy asked with food falling out of her mouth.

Aghast, Kit was tempted to tell Daisy not to talk with her mouth full, but quickly suppressed the urge, remembering a man wouldn't bother. Manners were at a premium the farther out west she traveled, and she honestly didn't think she could go more out west without falling into the ocean. "About what?"

"The food," Daisy interjected, luckily with less food in her mouth.

"Oh, it's good. What's it called?" Kit wondered.

Daisy looked puzzled. Stella interrupted before Daisy could reply.

"Chinese food is what we call it. Cookie doesn't speak a great deal of English. He cooks for us, as he did for the railroad workers. He followed a Chinese girl up here who worked at the Silver Bucket. I'm not sure if she was a relative or what. He came round and asked for a job. All he could say was *good cook* and *railroad*. It worked out since our old cook, Mary Malone, had been sweet talked into marriage at the grand age of forty-three."

"Women are as scarce out here as gold, but Mary could cook," Rose said as she reached for a piece of bread.

"She was as ugly as mud and mean as sin," Lily added.

"That's not nice, besides, I heard sin was sweet, not mean," Daisy added shyly.

"Daisy, my friend, it was a misplaced bet that landed you in a saloon," Iris added with a sly grin.

Rose needled a little. "So, Iris, how did you end up the Gilded Lily?"

Iris opened her mouth to reply, but thought better of it.

Kit took a sip from a glass and sputtered. What she thought was weak tea was beer. Daisy, who was closest, noticed her response.

"We only get beer with supper. It helps us loosen up and be more social. During the night, while we're working we get tea." Daisy took a healthy swig of her beer to demonstrate enthusiasm for her subject.

Stella looked concerned. "Will beer be a problem, Kit?" she asked.

Kit knew the only man who refused a drink in Lancaster was her father, the local minister.

"No, ma'am. I mean Stella, but I'll stick with tea like the girls while I'm working." She picked up the glass and took a healthy mouthful. It wasn't sweet, and she was unsure if she liked it. Kit swallowed since spewing it out in the bowl would be even too rude for a saloon, especially since Stella explained the Gilded Lily had a high tone.

Cookie brought out a sweet pastry dessert that quickly disappeared. The girls immediately left the table with dirty dishes left on it. Jimmy started scraping the dishes and stacking them.

"Tonight," Stella turned to look directly at Kit, "you can warm up on the piano. Normally, you would help Otis, set up the room, but since you're new, it is more important you play. Don't forget you can put a jar on the piano for requests. No war songs."

Kit nodded and headed for the piano. Playing the piano shouldn't be too hard. The hard part would be ignoring the smelly miners asking for songs that reminded them of home. The thought frightened her, and she wondered briefly if she should get her gun. She decided against it, especially since she hadn't practiced. More likely, she'd end up hurting herself. Kit started by playing the scales to warm up. There were a couple of sheets of music. One was entitled *Far From Home*. She picked the melody with one hand, adding the left. The last lyric consisted of—

And once on shore, we never more
Will roam through all our lives
A home we'll find, to our mind,
And call our sweethearts wives

The words made her think longing of Ohio. Realistically, her life departed from the warm, loving memories when her parents died. Aunt Eugenia's household existed as austere, regulated, and cold. No love or comfort resided within those four walls. If she had stayed, and hadn't ended up in jail, it would have been endless years of the same. She wasn't missing anything. The only good thing about home was her friendship with Harriet. Since Harriet was in Cariboo with her, there wasn't anything to regret.

"Don't start out with a sad song or we'll have them crying in their beer. We need somethin' happy. How about *Camptown Races*?" Rose suggested as she sashayed into the room.

Kit broke into the peppy song as she glanced at Rose. She worked hard not to do a double take. Rose had added more make-up and pulled her dress neckline down. Her penned up skirts exposed her stockings. Kit understood that all the flowers would flirt with any man who walked through the door. Her problem wasn't the why, but the how. It was their job just as much playing piano was hers, but how could they pretend to enjoy the attentions of grizzled miners?

The first man who came in was a uniformed officer. It wasn't a military uniform, she recognized. Kit played on, watching Rose casually flirt with the man. She called him by name, proving she knew him.

Stella walked into the room and noticed the man. "Otis, bring our friend, Police Officer McCarkin, a drink on the house."

Kit's fingers fumbled on the word police. She managed to recover without too much fanfare and segued into *Jeannie with the Light Brown Hair.*

Daisy leaned against the piano and eyed Kit. "Don't worry about him. The police are only here to keep the miners from stealing each other's claim or killing each other trying."

"Hmm," Kit murmured as acknowledgement and kept on playing.

"Stella gives all the off-duty officers free drinks. It keeps them coming around, which keeps the bad ones at the other saloons. It also gives Stella a pass with the hangin' judge Sir Matthew Baillie Begbie. Ya' know if something bad ever happened, like a knife fight." Daisy stopped to wipe away a tear. "Things go easier for us, because they know we're an upright establishment."

Kit continued to play, the thought of a saloon being an upright establishment overshadowed by the words, hanging judge. True, Eugenia was alive, so she wouldn't hang.

"So, huh, what happens to people who maybe steal?" Kit asked as she went into the folk ballad *Barbara Allen.*

"Oh, I heard one miner stole another miner's gold dust, and Judge Begbie put him on the chain gang for two or three years."

"Hey, Daisy," a bearded miner called out.

"Business," Daisy commented as she headed toward the miner with an extra wiggle in her walk.

Kit could figure out the chain part simple enough, even if she'd never heard of it before. It sounded like something she wanted to avoid.

The night went quickly with a few miners flushed with newfound funds requesting songs. Some of them she never heard of but found out if she played a fast version of *Roll out the Barrel,* they were happy. Luckily, her mother didn't stick to strictly hymns, although, her mother told her many hymn melodies were former drinking songs since people already knew them. Katrina Hamilton loved all kinds of music from weepy ballads to rambunctious drinking songs. She passed her love and musical ear onto her daughter.

From the corner of her eye, Kit could see Rose and Iris taking miners up the stairs. They trotted down a short time later, looking about the same. Daisy spent most of the night talking to the same miner. Iris held court with three well-dressed gentlemen. Otis and Stella stood not far from the piano talking.

"I'm givin' Daisy a pass because she was sweet on the boy who got knifed." Stella commented.

Otis grunted his approval.

"I am going to talk to Lily tonight. She's shopping for a husband. I'm not feeding and housing debutantes."

"Do you think that's a good idea? She might go over to the Silver Bucket," Otis said.

"She could, but she would find much harder working conditions. Lily is not stupid. She wants to move up, not down. She either takes them upstairs or she packs her bag," Stella stated.

"I don't know if any man would want a woman who worked in a saloon." Otis commented.

"I don't know, Otis. We lost a cook that way. Look, there's someone at the bar." Stella nodded her head in the direction of the bar.

Otis cut his eyes to the bar. "Jimmy has him."

"Lily should have a chance at marriage," Stella commented.

"She had a chance yesterday, but today, when everyone saw the beautiful mail order wife Adam Easton got. Well, I imagine there are men composing letters right now."

"I doubt the women who become mail order brides are all pure as the driven snow," Stella commented caustically.

"It don't matter what they did in their past as long as their past don't follow them," Otis growled.

They drifted out of Kit's hearing range. You could start anew as long as your past didn't follow you. That's exactly what Kit wanted to do, but the presence of police officers was worrisome. She would make a point of talking to Harriet about it.

Chapter Eight

NICK SCRAPED HIS winnings toward him. He used his expensive felt hat to carry all the assorted silver, gold pieces, and folding money.

"Hey, Kennedy, you aren't leaving without giving me a chance to win back my money." a beefy man with an elaborate handlebar mustache called out.

"Sorry, Dabney, maybe next time. I'm on my way to see a lady, and I'm already late." Nick said, knowing it was the only acceptable excuse.

"Go ahead, Nick. You'll be back before I can finish the next hand with an empty hat, stripped clean by your latest soiled dove."

"Easy for you, Dabney, you weren't robbed blind by the slick bastard," the man with a silver trimmed hat complained.

"Oh, I wouldn't worry overly much about it, Walt. There's probably a couple of hundred in the silver on your hat. Are you in or out?" Dabney shuffled the cards waiting for a reply.

"Out, I have business to take care of." Walt shuffled off, leaving the rest of the group speculating the type of business he might have.

Nick flashed his grin again; glad he managed to get out of the smoky room with his hide intact. He heard the angry rancher, but didn't pay too much attention to him. He wasn't planning to stay in the area. Leaving with a wad of money while everyone was losing was always tricky. Of course, it was the only way to get a wad of money. There was the usual grumbling about being a poor sport or scared to play another hand or worse yet—called a cheat. If things went badly, there could be a fool with a one-shot Derringer hidden in his boot ready to take a shot at him.

Over the years, he'd learned a few things. Never gloat or make the mistake of counting your winnings in public. Often gambling involved drinking, which made it difficult for players to keep track of how much money they were losing. A fool, who counted his winnings at the table, reminded the men at the table how much money they'd wasted. The losers never rejoiced in the winner's good fortune. Escaping from the table was always a delicate dance. Only the excuse of a beautiful woman waiting on him would allow him to leave with dignity. Food and drink were easy to bring to the table. They'd hold the play for men to go out to the john, or sometimes they'd use a chamber pot to save time. The nicer establishments had flush toilets, which were even quicker. Players managed to delay sleep with huge quantities of coffee. A woman would do only as a sure-fire excuse.

With Nick, it was a believable. He never made any secret of the fact he loved women, all women. He flirted with barmaids and society matrons alike. He could turn a female sweet with a compliment and a kiss on the hand. In some ways, women were like gambling, with the exception, he always won with women, except the one time it'd really mattered.

The groom brought him his horse. He swung his leg over the cantle, noticing Mr. Sore Loser kept watching him through the plate glass window. He'd better make a stop before he left town. Luckily, his banker didn't mind him making late night deposits, even if he had to go to his house. Tonight felt like a late night deposit time.

Half an hour later, with his money secure, he hit the trail, but not for long. He didn't like to push Duke in the dark. He trotted the horse while still in the city limits and the gas streetlights illuminated their way, but he slowed to the walk when they had only the moonlight. No sense in taking chances.

His wayward mind went back to the reason he originally left the farm. Before the war, he'd had his heart set on Rebecca. The only child of the town's banker was a pretty thing with heavily fringed hazel eyes and a heart shaped face. Rebecca had a high opinion of herself, which suited Nick fine. He thought highly of her too. He courted her with chance meetings, bouquets of wild flowers, and shy requests to walk her home from church. At seventeen, it was the most he knew to do.

He might have expected to lose out to a successful businessman, but not his brother. Noah came back from the war sullen, bitter, and angry at the world. People tended to forgive him since the war proved a hard road to maturity. Maybe Rebecca, drawn to the broken veteran, tried to offer comfort, and that comfort turned to love. He might have been able to accept it if they'd told him. Instead, they'd met behind his back, while he'd continued to believe there was a future for him and Rebecca.

In his hurt, he'd managed to corner Rebecca to demand answers. He'd wanted to know about their courtship. Didn't she love him? Rebecca gave a scornful laugh. What courtship? There wasn't any understanding between them. He was too young and too boring. She wanted a mature man, someone who had lived. Rebecca flounced out of the room, missing the tear in Nick's eye. He vowed if he couldn't have Rebecca, then, he would stop being boring, young, and immature. No sod busting for him. He'd be the man the farmers' sons would look at and wish to be. The women would look too.

The only skill he had to get him there was his ability to manipulate the cards. He could remember what cards were in play and calculate probability of what cards would turn up. He wasn't always a hundred percent right, but he learned to read faces, and his luck increased. Add whiskey to the mix and his luck increased tenfold. He never drank more than one when he played, but the other players didn't notice.

Before working a game, he put time in on working the help. He had one barmaid exclusively serve him. He might start out with a real drink, but the rest of the game he sipped the same weak tea the working girls drank. He always paid the girls well.

That part of his life ended tonight. The fact he sensed someone following him reaffirmed his decision to give up his gambling ways. Good thing he chose not to stay in town. No reason to bother anyone else with his problems. He'd settle this one last issue before he checked out the mystery of Kit Gruber.

The girl who pretended to be a boy kept sneaking back into his mind. Sometimes when almost asleep, her slightly damp, curling hair would come to mind. He could picture her soaping her slender leg. Then there was the mulish expression she'd get whenever he confounded her, which he tried to do at every turn. Maybe, he would do well to leave her alone. Then he decided not to—after all the *sister* was on his side.

Harriet made sure to let him know they were traveling to Cariboo. Despite the heavy accent, there wasn't too much Harriet Easton didn't see. She caught him a few times looking at Kit in less than appropriate manner, especially considering Kit's male disguise. She grinned whenever he'd get Kit so flustered she would blush, stammer, and sometimes curse. Something sparked between him and Kit. Make no doubt about it.

He wanted to know what would make a young woman travel across the country disguised as a male. He might not like the answers he'd find, but he was willing to look. He knew the way to Cariboo and was a frequent enough visitor that they knew him too. He wondered if he had a clue what he was doing. Nope. He knew he didn't. The good thing about being independent, all your arguments occurred inside your head. No matter which way the argument fell, you always won.

A WAGON GOING by underneath the window was the first thing Kitty heard upon wakening. Disoriented at first, she stared at the muslin curtains flapping in the slight breeze, and then her gaze fell on the photographs of her parents. At least they remained familiar. The big water spot above her head reminded her of her location, the saloon. She finished her first night playing piano and now it was morning—well, afternoon.

Kit stretched, wondering what she should do in the few hours before she started work again. Harriet, she needed to go see her and ask about the police officer. Harriet could ask Adam and not attract attention. Surely, Harriet would be up by now. The mental picture of big Adam Easton saying he would put a baby in Harriet's belly for her to fuss over came to mind. How long could baby making last? She pushed open the window curtains to gauge the sun. It hung high in the sky.

Dressed in her boy clothes, she slipped down the back staircase. Things were quiet in the saloon. Kit figured she was the only one up so far. Maybe Harriet would have a pot of coffee on. She placed her hat on her head before stepping out the door.

A matronly woman and her teen-age daughter were coming down the boardwalk toward Kit. Without thinking, Kit reached up and touched the brim of her hat to acknowledge them. She smiled as they passed, thinking how she automatically reacted as a male now. Kit cast a glance over her shoulder only to catch the notice of the blushing teen-age daughter. The daughter gave Kit a considering look before turning back to her mother. Wait until she told Harriet.

People were coming in and out of Eastons. Obviously the newlyweds were awake and doing business. Kit mounted the steps and followed a few other men inside the store where the sun cast a dappled light over all the merchandise. A high window on the back wall let in even more light, making the room warm and inviting. Kit liked it better than the stores back home, which had almost no windows or often covered the windows with curtains.

Most of the men called out their orders while Adam scurried to pull them together. A few teased him about working instead of staying abed with his young bride. Kit noticed Harriet's large husband blush at the miners' meddling. She wondered where Harriet was. She scanned the store again and noticed a clutch of women gathered by the bolts of material.

"Ya, you are right, this material would make a sturdy dress," a familiar voice spoke.

Three women, taller than Harriet surrounded Kit's friend as she extolled the virtues of a broadcloth material. The women listened politely as Harriet sold the cloth. Kit wondered if the women were more interested in the material or the new woman in their midst. The women encouraged Harriet to join the church sewing circle, which answered Kit's question.

"My seams aren't too straight," Harriet shyly confessed as she replaced a bolt of cloth.

The broomstick thin blonde confessed, "No matter, it's an excuse to get together and gossip, nibble on some sweets, and possibly sew a stitch or two. By the way, my name is Eula Mae Perkins."

Harriet nodded her head before adding, "Pleased to meet you."

"Oh, I forgot to introduce myself," the middle-aged brunette said with an apologetic smile. "I'm Honoria Hortensia Hutchens. Lots of folks call me Triple H behind my back and my friends to my face." She added the last with a chuckle.

The ladies managed to gain a soft-spoken acceptance from Harriet to the next sewing circle before they left the store.

"I thought they'd never leave," Kit complained, stepping closer to Harriet.

"Kit," Harriet sang out joyfully.

She raised one eyebrow at her friend's exuberance. "You act like you haven't seen me in twelve years instead of twelve hours."

The young bride grabbed her friend's arm and pulled her behind the counter. She grinned when she noticed her husband staring.

"Hello, Kit," Adam shouted across the store. He handed the two miners their supplies before turning back to the women. "How goes the piano playing business?"

"So far, so good. I got a whole dollar tip for playing Danny Boy," Kit proudly informed both. "I could have earned another tip for playing Dixie, but it's against house rules to play war songs."

"Those are good rules. For some the war never ends. All it takes is a word or a song to bring it back. Suddenly you got men fighting again." Adam shook his head. "One time I saw a knife fight over a man whistling The Battle Hymn of the Republic."

Kit watched her new brother-in-law's face. Concern washed over it for a moment, followed by sadness. He was an easy one to read, which should make it even easier to get information out of him.

"Is that why there are so many police all the way up here in Canada because of the fights between former soldiers?" Kit asked as she accepted a cup of genuine coffee from Harriet. The aroma almost made her miss Adam's reply, so caught up in the smell of coffee beans instead of chicory.

Adam hooked his thumbs behind his suspender as if he was getting ready to make a major pronouncement. "If you needed police to settle things between every old soldier, well, there would have to be police in every state, city, and town. There wouldn't be enough to accommodate every unkind word spoken."

"You're so smart, Adam." Harriet cooed.

Kit wrinkled her nose at the tone of Harriet's voice. A close look at her friend revealed she was looking at her husband in a rather besotted way. Better besotted, than disgusted. She'd do her best to deal with it, although she wasn't too sure about Adam being so all fired smart.

"The police are here to prevent claim jumping and to enforce boundaries. The gold mines are basically all claimed." Adam continued, warming up to his subject under Harriet's scrutiny. "Yep, sometimes they'll steal the claim paper from their partner while he's asleep. Others might jump their neighbor's claim when he's gone to town for supplies. Some will actually kill a man for his claim, especially if gold has been found on it."

Taking a sip of coffee, Kit held it in her mouth, savoring it. What she needed was to find out if the police got regular information from the states, perhaps wanted posters.

"Outside of claim jumping and such, do you have much other crime in town?" Kitty asked in what she hoped sounded casual.

Harriet reacted to the comment by jerking her head in a guilty fashion. Adam didn't notice. In fact, he wasn't even looking at his wife's face, but was staring a bit lower.

"Um," Adam hemmed and hawed, trying to gather his thoughts. "The police can handle what needs to be done, but there isn't too much for them to do. Last month the Johnson family thought someone stole their milk cow. Turned out she got loose. Then there was a fight between two soiled doves at the Bucket of Blood." Adam glanced at Harriet and stopped before revealing the details of the fight. "Well, um, there isn't too much crime to speak of."

"Do they get wanted posters of outlaws?" Harriet asked.

Adam took the opportunity to wrap a brawny arm around Harriet. Snuggling her up to his side, he told Kit, "No need for you to worry. I'll protect your sister from any outlaws. Don't need to worry about them being here in the first place. It's too cold for everyone, except for those who have gold fever and those who make a living selling to the miners."

Adam grinned as if he'd said something clever. It was hard for Kit not to grimace. All this talk and she hadn't found out anything she wanted to know. Maybe she'd be better off asking someone at the saloon, but she didn't want to tip her hand.

"You eat yet?" Harriet asked as she moved in the direction of the staircase.

"Are you offering?" Kitty followed, knowing breakfast would give them a chance to talk privately.

"Got biscuits and bacon left, if you want," Harriet offered already at home in her role.

Adam fell into step behind them. "You got more biscuits!" He exclaimed happily over Harriet's biscuits, missing the shared eye roll between the two women. The doorbell jingled before Adam could place his large boot on the first step.

"Customer," he murmured before turning away. "Save me a biscuit or two," he yelled over his shoulder.

"Whoo-wee, that man is on you like fleas on a dog," Kitty commented as she took off her cap to scratch her head.

Harriet blushed as she bustled around the small kitchen fixing a breakfast plate. Kitty reared the chair back on two legs, looking like a cocky boy all too sure of himself even with her sun-streaked brown curls falling across her forehead.

"Men are dumb," the pretty blonde commented as she placed the plate in front of her friend.

"Are you talking about Adam? Or men in general?" Kit asked as she bit into a fluffy biscuit.

"All. None of them see you as a woman." She sniffed contemptuously.

"Works out fine for me. The way I figure it, if any man starts looking at me for a long time other men will start to look at him and wonder. Do you know what I mean?"

"No," Harriet answered and reached for the coffee pot to refill her cup.

"No man will spend much time looking at me because he won't want men to think he likes boys."

"Are you saying all men hate boys?" Harriet cocked her head as if concentrating on Kit's convoluted reasoning.

"Look here." Kit held both her hands up. She held the right hand higher.

"Men." Then she held the left hand up. "Boys." Then she interlocked the fingers of both hands together to demonstrate her point.

"You mean some men and boys do that together?" Harriet asked red-faced.

"Well, it's what I heard, when I was in the livery one time. I understood it was something men didn't want other men to think about them. I don't worry about men seeing through my disguise. It's the females that are the problem."

Harriet choked on her coffee. "What?"

"It doesn't bother them overly much if they stare. Today, I passed a woman and her teenage daughter and long after I went past, the girl was still staring at me. It was unnerving." Kit shuddered, much to Harriet's amusement.

"Kit, Kit, Kit, you make a very pretty boy. The girl looked because you're young, clean, and pretty." Harriet teased.

"I think you mean handsome," the miffed friend corrected.

"I mean pretty. Nick is handsome, ya?"

"No, I'm not talking about Mr. Kennedy. Tell me about Adam?" Kit held up her intertwined fingers and wiggled them to make her point.

"You bad, Katherine Hamilton!" Harriet slapped her playfully with a dishtowel.

"Watch it," Kitty warned, looking around to see if Adam was close.

"Oh, sorry, I forgot. No."

"No, what?" Kit was a bit confused.

"Adam did not sleep in the same bed with me. He is kind. He wants us to be friends first. We held hands. Maybe today, he might kiss me." Harriet threw her hands up in front of her face and peeked out between the fingers.

"Oh, I see. Just in case, maybe I should head on out so the kissing can start." Kit stood up and brushed the crumbs off her vest.

"No, you don't have to go." Harriet put a restraining hand on Kit's arm.

"I do. I need to get some information. I believe you have some biscuits to deliver to your husband."

Harriet wrapped two biscuits with bacon in a cloth napkin and hurried down the stairs to Adam. Kit smiled at her departing friend. She'd never fetch and carry for a man. She did enough of that for Aunt Eugenia. Still, she slipped out the back door and caught a glimpse of Adam staring at Harriet when she wasn't looking. On the other hand, she wouldn't mind a man looking at her in a similar fashion.

Hands in her pockets, Kit took a calculated walk, sauntering past the building with the Police Department sign nailed to the front. When she looked over her shoulder, she could view the attached jail with a shudder. It would be a simple matter to look inside to see to if any wanted posters decorated the walls. She could even make up an excuse she was looking for a lost dog or something. If she did someone might waste time looking for her pretend dog. She would hate that. Worse yet, she could walk in and they recognized her and threw her in jail.

"Wild West, my foot," she snorted in disgust and looked for something to kick when she noticed purple skirts. Her eyes traveled upward to encounter Rose's shrewd gaze. Did Rose guess why she loitered in front of the police office?

"Kit Gruber, don't you have anything better to do and hang around the police station?" Rose questioned casually. Her eyes told a different story. She knew. Kit couldn't get away from the whole Aunt Eugenia disaster. John Wilkes Booth eluded his captors for weeks and left an obvious trail. He also assassinated the President, which meant everyone looked for him. All the same, he escaped detection better than she did. Two days in town and Rose already saw through her disguise.

"Hey, checking out the sights, new in town and all. I could say the same about you too, Rose. What are you doing here?" Kit joked.

"I'm drumming up business. The policemen get paid regularly so they make good repeat customers," Rose commented matter-offactly.

Kitty's skin warmed. Dang it, she had to stop blushing. People didn't blush. How could she stop her face from turning red every time someone made an off-color remark? Better yet, how could she get rid of curious Rose?

"I know," Rose said, pulling Kit from the front window of the police station.

Kit was stunned. How could the news travel faster than she did? Telegraph, but she didn't see any telegraph lines when they rode into town.

Rose tucked her hand into the crook of Kit's arm. "Let's walk."

Kit walked slowly leery of what Rose was going to do next. If she was going to turn her in, they really shouldn't be walking away from the station. They passed the barber/dentist shop, a two-story restaurant and hotel, and a placard advertising laundry and hot baths. The image of a naked Nick popped into her mind. The man had all the right muscles in all the right places. Then there was the bewitching trail of hair that led down to—Get a hold of yourself, girl, Kitty mentally chastised herself. This was it. Rose knew.

"I am surprised no one else noticed," Rose as they walked past the surveyor's window. A bespectacled man inside waved shyly at Rose. "It's good for Herman to see me with someone new to whet his appetite—even if you are a female. He'll never know."

"What!" Kit exclaimed, and spun to look at Rose.

"Come on, keep walking, we don't want to attract the wrong kind of attention," Rose cautioned. "Besides, I already told you I knew. First time I saw you and you wouldn't look at me in my negligee, I knew."

"I might have been a good Methodist," Kit hissed between gritted teeth. Rose's laughter grated on her nerves.

"Oh, honey, I've had Baptists, Methodists, Lutherans, Catholics, Congregationalists, and even a Jew, and they all looked at me because they were men, and that's what men do—among other things." They kept walking with the buildings getting fewer and the sidewalk less reliable with warped and an occasional missing plank.

"What gave me away?" Kit worked hard on her disguise, obviously, she fooled some folks. Why not Rose?

The saloon girl laughed, before replying. "You're not real big. I don't just mean tall. Everything is small and delicate on ya. You being a piano player is odd for a fellow. Then there's your smell."

Kit's lips twisted to one side as she considered her observations. "What's wrong with my smell? I wash up regular."

"Exactly," Rose agreed, as if that explained everything. "Men smell like a variety of things depending on the man from sweat to tobaccy, but almost never soap. Fellows like Nick sometimes smell clean, but he's an exception"

She felt her head nodding in agreement concerning Nick's lack of odor. Inhaling deeply, she tried to decide if she smelled somewhat foul. Nope and she had no intention of adding that to her disguise. Still, what is her disguise wasn't working. "So, um, Rose, what are you going to do now that you know I am female?"

Mentally she reviewed everything she had done to get to this point, stealing her dowry money, cutting her hair, walking around with an itchy wool sock stuck in her drawers, all for nothing.

"Why should I do anything? I thought at first you were so innocent it wasn't right, you worked in a saloon, but Stella changed my mind."

"Stella knows too? Does everyone know?" She shook her head in disgust. Here she'd thought she was doing such a good job snorting, scratching, and tipping her hat to the ladies.

"Just me and Stella. We're the only ones who know. Stella was the one who told me to leave it because any female who was passing herself off as a man had reasons, and they definitely weren't innocent ones. I did, but then I got thinking that maybe you need a friend and all. It must be hard pretending to be a man all the time." Rose patted her hand reassuringly.

"Trust me, it has its moments. I was telling Harriet today, there might be a young lady with a crush on my manly form."

"Oh my." Rose chortled. "It would have to be a young girl because a woman would be able to spot the difference right away."

"I do try. I keep adding to my male disguise," Kit insisted, a little hurt her efforts had failed.

"You do a nice job. The padding in front was an inspired touch. Did you think that up yourself?"

"Harriet did."

"An experienced woman will want you to look at her with a spark in your eye. It tells her you're all male open to private demonstrations," Rose said.

"I, ah, I don't think I can manage that," Kit admitted glumly.

"I'm glad. Otherwise, I don't know if I would want to room so close to you." Rose noted the blank look on Kit's face. "Never mind. I wonder how someone like you ended up here."

"What do you mean someone like me?" Kit touched her hat as they passed two strolling matrons.

"You don't touch your hat when you're with me," Rose hissed. "Before you ask, once you tipped your hat, and they smiled and acknowledged you, then, they have to acknowledge me, which they won't because I'm a whore. When you're with me, they will pretend not to see either one of us."

"Strange. I work at the saloon now. Should they ignore me too?" Kit wondered aloud.

"No, you're a man or so they think." Rose snorted indelicately at the thought.

"It's not right." Kit angled her head to the matrons. "Them ignoring me because I'm with you. Oh, tell me what kind of person you think I am. I want to know." She grimaced a little having a good idea what Rose might say.

"It's not hard. You're an innocent. You've lived in a small town, probably went to church every Sunday. I wouldn't be surprised if your grandfather wasn't a minister."

"It was my father," Kit interrupted. "Go on, I like to know more about myself."

"You act smart, so you must have finished school, and you can play the piano, but something happened to prevent you from marrying. A pretty girl like you should be married with a baby or two. Oddly enough, you don't know much about men, which makes me wonder if you ever had a serious beau?"

"I almost did, but my aunt put a stop to it," Kitty answered without thinking.

"Why?" Rose asked as they reached the end of the sidewalk. They simply turned and began to promenade back the way they'd come.

"I thought she did it to be mean at the time. Then I wondered if she did it so she wouldn't be alone. I was her unpaid servant in a way."

"It doesn't matter why she did it—it was still mean!" Rose huffed as if she was the one cheated out of a betrothal. "You could have run away and got married if you really loved him."

"I could have. Teddy even suggested it, but that was probably back when he thought I had a dowry. His desertion broke my heart. All I wanted was a husband and children. Does that sound stupid to you?" Kit blushed wondering if it was unkind to ask Rose such a question. Marriage didn't exist as an option for a saloon girl.

Rose shook her head sadly. "It probably sounds stupid to everybody else in this town, but I am a sucker for love, a hopeless romantic. I keep waiting for my prince, who isn't coming. What did you do when your aunt told him no?" Rose asked out of curiosity.

"I didn't do anything. After that, I kept waiting for something to hit me so I would know this was the right man. Maybe a falling star, his name in the wind, magic in his kiss, but nothing happened."

"Did Teddy kiss you?" Rose asked.

"He did, actually more than once, wet, sloppy kisses, which were more like being licked by a dog or having a fish attached to your face," Kit said, wrinkling her nose remembering Teddy's suckerfish kisses. "I felt like he was trying to inhale my face. I can't see why females get so excited about kissing."

"No magic there," Rose added with a chuckle. "So did you know then he wasn't the one?"

"Yes and no. The magic didn't exist. I wasn't in love, but he did have beautiful blonde hair and wide shoulders. He married one of my classmates, which made me jealous, not of Teddy, but because she had what I would never have—a husband and family."

"I don't understand. You are attractive. Why couldn't you marry?"

Kit looked around to see if anyone was close enough to hear their unusual conversation before speaking. "The war took most of the young men, some more headed for the gold fields, and the few who survived the war stayed in the army and went west to deal with the Indians. Pickings were slim in our town."

She continued. Rose appeared genuinely interested "There were war widows too, eager to remarry. My aunt would scare off any suitor who showed any interest. I'm not sure what she said, but it worked. Maybe she was telling them I was a man disguised as a woman." Kitty laughed at her own joke.

"So you are out in the middle of nowhere because of your aunt?" Rose questioned.

"In a way." Kitty noticed they were going to pass the police station again.

"Anything I could do for you in there?" Rose tilted her head toward the station.

Kitty was about to ask her to go inside and check for new wanted posters, but Rose would want to know why, and she would have to tell her. What if there was a reward for her capture? She couldn't trust Rose, at least not yet. "No, I'm fine. In fact, I need to get back to the saloon and start practicing."

Kitty dropped Rose's arm and started walking fast. She knew she was being rude, but she felt unsafe. She'd said too much and had to get away.

Chapter Nine

T HE TREES WERE rather sparse, and there wasn't a likely looking cave or overhang anywhere in sight. Nick swore. Lack of cover was one of the things he hated about being on the trail. He pulled his foot from the stirrup and slid off his horse. Loosening Duke's cinch, he heard a coyote yip in the distance or was it a wolf—another thing he hated about the trail. He made a mental note to build up a big fire to keep all the varmints away.

Since he'd left San Francisco, he'd had an uneasy feeling he was being followed. Some of the boys back at the poker game might think he traveled with a big wad of money, but they'd be wrong. Nick made it a practice not to carry large sums of money after damn near being killed in Denver. The way he saw it, he could still be beaten black and blue no matter what, but at least his money would be safe in a bank. He didn't make it a secret he kept his money in the bank, but some were unbelievers. They thought the claim was a smoke screen to fool the stupid ones, not them.

He touched the handle of his boot stiletto to reassure himself it was still there. Patting his waistcoat, he felt the bulge of a single shot Derringer, a gambler's best friend. The tiny firearm had held off many an angry cowboy. It wasn't the size of the gun that mattered. Pointed straight at your opponent's heart mattered more. After checking his personal arsenal, Nick kicked at the sandy ground. He hated being outside like this.

The hard ground, bugs, and total lack of a good steak tended to irritate him, but being out in the open did more. He felt vulnerable on open ground. A room had corners where you could always have your back against a wall. It also had doors so you knew what direction trouble might be coming from, but the outdoors had nothing. Thieving, discontented card players wasn't all he had to worry about, although he worried about them too. There were snakes, mountain lions, maybe even a renegade Indian round about. Nope, the outdoors lost its charm about twenty years ago.

Wood was a little sparse, but he found enough for a meager fire. He used his sulfur matches to get the fire started and lit a cheroot. Leaning back against a large boulder, he blew smoke rings up toward the clouds. The ominous clouds hovered dark and fat above him. A raindrop hit Nick straight in the eye. Then another. Nick cursed. Another thing he hated about camping on the trail. Rain.

Soaking wet, huddled under a wool blanket—which offered no protection and emitted a vaguely wet sheep smell—Nick muttered under his breath, "What fool idea put me outside in the middle of nowhere in miserable weather?" Damp tendrils around laughing eyes, a shapely leg, and a tempting mouth came to mind. Damn it, there were women in San Francisco, beautiful, inviting women who lived inside of luxurious homes. They would invite him in with a smile.

So why was he on the trail of some cussed ornery female who dressed up like a man? It wasn't as if she was overly fond of him. Of course, not, she was too busy pretending to be a man to give him a second thought. He thought about Kit's choked gasp when he dropped his pants in the bathhouse. One thing was for sure, Kit definitely knew he was a man. All the same, he was taking off after the girl as if he was one of those heroic crusader knights.

Kit and the blonde Harriet were an odd pair, but he'd seen stranger things. No reason to go chasing after the two, assuming they needed his help somehow, especially Kit. Then again, he didn't have anything better to do. The life of the professional gambler was wearing thin. Sitting in poker games night after night was something he didn't relish for the rest of his life. It was especially wearing when incompetent players accused him of cheating. They had no business sitting down at the table if they couldn't play. Yep, it was all getting old. He brushed his hands over the wet, but still expensive tailored shirt. Even the fine clothes had lost their charm. It was time for a change. There was no reason the change couldn't involve solving the mystery of Kit.

A twig broke behind him. Nick whirled, pulling out his gun and pointing it in the direction of the sound. The fire had long since gone out. Whoever was out there could see as much as he could—nada. He peered into the darkness, hoping to discern a shadowy shape. Two large yellowish eyes looked back at him, and then there was a soft nicker.

"Duke! You fool horse. I might have shot you," Nick complained as he pocketed his gun. Kneeling, he felt for the hobble, he placed on the horse's front hooves. The ragged leather strips explained why Duke was walking around free. The moon slipped out from the clouds briefly illuminating the landscape behind. A man shaped shadow merged with the other shadows. Nick blinked. Had he seen a man? Probably didn't. He was turning into a nervous Nellie seeing villains everywhere.

"Betcha, you're wondering why two prime males like us are out in the weather when we should be tucked away somewhere dry and warm." Nick said as he draped an arm around his horse's neck. "Well, friend, it's because of a woman."

Nick realized he had his arm companionably wrapped around Duke's neck and was conversing with him as if he were a drinking buddy. He immediately removed his arm. "That's another thing I hate being on the trail alone, you start talking to your horse."

Duke neighed long and vigorous in response.

THE WATER SPOT grew larger, looking less like a ship under sail, more rounded and lumbering like a hippopotamus. Kitty smiled up at the ceiling, thinking of the large beast she'd seen once in a traveling show. It took a specially made wagon to transport it with a team of ten draft horses to pull it. The behemoth looked so unhappy in the wagon. The handlers would throw water on it since it was used to being in the water. It was out of place there in the middle of the arid town. Dogs ran around the wagon barking as if they were announcing the presence of a stranger. On one level, she was tempted to sneak out at night and break open the hippopotamus' door. She doubted the animal could even stand, since it looked like the wagon was built around its prone body. If the hippo did escape, what would it do in a land where everything was so foreign?

Kitty sat up slowly on the bed, realizing she was the hippopotamus. True, she didn't arrive via a traveling show, but arrive she did in a world totally foreign to her. The bustling mining town played host to men from all over. Texans rubbed shoulders with soft-spoken Cajuns. There were even a few kilted Scotts among the multitude of mud-covered miners. She only knew about them because Rose remarked on their knees and was on a personal mission to find out what they wore underneath their kilts. A muddle of accents added to the chaos of a town being born.

The streets continually lengthened as each new business went up. It was a good thing, all this confusion. No one really knew each other that well. Kit would be another person passing through town forgotten before nightfall. Moving on was the only option. She did what she came to do, escort Harriet to her bridegroom. Of course, before they arrived in her imagination, Adam was a smelly, doddering old man without any teeth. She'd tried to imagine what would disturb Harriet the most about her mail order husband enough to make her leave. The softhearted immigrant wouldn't tolerate a man who abused any animal, especially cows.

She'd been sure she and Harriet would hit the road, but where they would go had been the question. Once they met Adam, there would be no possibility of Harriet not staying around and being his mail order bride. After that Kit's potential plans stopped. Now it was just her. It might be safest to leave the country if she were a wanted man, well, woman. Kitty tried to imagine sailing to England. It was difficult to get a mental picture of it since the only boat she'd been on so far was a ferry.

Voices in the hall caught her attention. "Give me back my purple ribbons!" an angry female shouted.

"I don't have your ribbons, you stupid cow," another female snarled.

A sudden weight fell against Kitty's door as the two women wrestled. There were shrieks, and scuffling noises. What was that? Snorting?

"Girls, girls, stop it!" Stella's voice carried down the hall, stopping the scuffling noise and the snorting.

Kitty opened the door a crack to peek.

"You get yourself scratched up or bruised and you're no good to me," Stella warned. "I run a high-class place here."

Kitty smiled, looking at the growing water spot, wondering what low-class would look like. She grimaced, thinking she was better off not knowing.

"Go get cleaned up. If I hear about you fighting again, you're both out. You'll probably end up at The Bucket of Blood, a place I'm sure wouldn't suit your sophisticated tastes, Iris. How about you, Daisy?

"No, ma'am," a subdued Daisy replied.

Kitty noted the chagrined girl's head hung low as she stared at the scuffed toes on her shoes. Iris' eyes were wide, and her chin quivered as if she were trying not to cry. Stella sent her a telling look that caused her head to droop like Daisy's. The three women shuffled past Kitty's door. No question about it, she didn't want to stay here a long time. What she needed was a plan, since she had money.

The image of Adam staring longingly at Harriet flashed through her mind. It would be nice if someone lit up like that when she came into a room, but it wasn't likely. Harriet was probably the one mail order bride in history who ended up with a man who was as he described himself.

Oh, she'd heard tales back in Lancaster how to translate the advertisements in the Matrimonial News, the magazine men used to advertise for brides. Young meant this side of sixty. Healthy meant he hadn't died yet. Strapping and robust could mean fat or nothing at all. It definitely didn't mean muscular. Attractive or handsome always depended on who was making the call. Many mules found their owners attractive, especially around feeding time.

Yep, no doubt about it, Harriet was the lucky one. A little jealousy started showing itself, but Kitty squelched it. Harriet deserved a little goodness in her life. Realistically, there would be no romance for Kitty until she lost the sock. It might be a while.

Might as well go tickle the ivories, she thought as she pulled on her too big boots. That's the first thing she was getting, well-fitting boots. Luckily, she had a friend in the dried goods business. She wouldn't have to go through the whole boot sizing process with a stranger. Harriet would let her try on boots until she found the right size.

Clomping down the raw lumber stairwell, she tried to imagine it as high class. It was difficult, especially with the smell of sausage and sauerkraut drifting up the stairs. Kit actually liked kraut and sausage, but it didn't fit with her idea of what folks at a high-class establishment would eat. They would probably go for less smelly foods. The smell didn't even fit with what Cookie would cook.

Otis stopped wiping bottles and yelled. "Cookie's day off, I fixed dinner." Kit managed a grin and a wave, but stayed focused on her path to the piano. This pretending to be a male wore on her. Otis was a decent fellow. She hated tricking him. Most of the people she met were decent, a little rough around the edges, but good-hearted people all the same. If she stayed back in Lancaster with Aunt Eugenia, she would not be consorting with saloon girls and barkeeps. The thought caused her to snort. She'd probably work a sampler with some pithy saying about idle hands—when she wasn't running errands for her aunt. Of course, the probability rested on not being in jail. Chances were she would be since Eugenia held a grudge with a vengeance.

Limbering up with a few scale runs, Kitty launched into *The Old Folks at Home*, it was a favorite of soldiers, who often played it on harmonicas by the campfire. Yep, it was a bit maudlin, thinking about the folks back home when you're far away. Her fingers danced lightly over the keys as she reflected on her life in Lancaster. Aunt Eugenia being such a mean old biddy worked in her favor. It gave her nothing to miss with the exception of her parents' graves.

A sudden choked back sob had Kitty looking around to spot a teary-eyed Daisy. Obviously, some people had better memories of the old folks at home. Without commenting, Kit switched to a familiar song. A rousing drinking round would be better, but she slid into *Barbara Allen*, as if her fingers had a mind of their own.

"Supper," Otis barked interrupting her reverie and piano playing.

Kitty turned to go into the dining room, and Daisy slid up beside her.

"It was wonderful," she cooed softly.

"Um, thanks," Kitty managed to mutter, embarrassed at the gushing praise. She never had anyone compliment her piano playing in such a sultry voice.

"I wish I could play the piano," Daisy said wistfully as they strolled past the bar.

"I'll teach you if you want," Kit found herself offering before she even thought about it.

"Really," Daisy shrieked and grabbed Kitty's arm. Her face fell suddenly as she mumbled, "I guess it would cost, huh?"

"No, it doesn't cost anything. You could teach me something. How about it?" Kitty offered.

Overhearing the last sentence, Rose chuckled, before adding, "Do you really want Daisy teaching you what she knows?"

"Rose, I know more than you think. I can show Kit how to throw down the papers," Daisy declared with a toss of her head and a gimlet glare directed right at Rose.

"What's throwing down the papers?" Kitty didn't think it sounded like anything she would use.

"It's playing cards. Haven't you ever played cards?" Daisy asked in surprise.

"Well, actually," Kitty stuck a finger inside her collar to loosen the mighty tight feeling with everyone looking at her. "I never played because my aunt was a strict Methodist. No card playing allowed."

The group gathered around the table guffawed long and hard. Stella wiped her teary eyes and managed to ask with a gasp, "How would your aunt feel about you working in a saloon?"

"Well," Kitty stalled knowing it was a trick question. All the same, she didn't know what the right answer might be so she went with the truth. "I figure she'd say I was going to hell in a hand basket."

This caused another round of laughter. Kitty figured it must have been an okay answer. Everyone grinned. Iris gave her an arch look before asking, "Are you going to hell in a hand basket, Mr. Gruber?"

"I don't know. I haven't got there yet," Kitty replied, noticing the pout on Iris' face, but the rest of the group immediately dissolved into laughter. How unusual. She couldn't ever remember being funny in Lancaster. Maybe the farther west you went the more things changed.

"Okay, I'll teach you to play cards, and you'll teach me to play the piano. Let's shake on it." Daisy held out her small hand.

Kitty grabbed it, noticing her hand was only slightly larger. She squeezed it hard and pumped the arm the way she thought a man might do.

"Woo-whee," Daisy squealed. "You about broke my hand with your manly grip." Her comment sent Rose and Stella into peals of laughter. "I might even teach you to gamble. Then you can win some money."

The prospect of raking in money appealed to her. More money would certainly make her getaway much easier. Kitty could see herself with an unlit cheroot clamped in the corner of her mouth as she gathered up her winnings.

"You don't know anything about gambling?" Iris pointed out.

"You don't know everything, Miss Hoity Toity. My papa was a gambler. How do you think I ended up working in a saloon," Daisy said, with a pointed sniff in Iris' direction.

"He must not have been a very good one then," Iris added cattily.

Everyone else gasped, while Kitty grabbed Daisy arm as she lunged toward Iris.

"Stop it, both of you!" Stella hissed before heaving herself up from her chair to stand by Iris. "For your show of venom, you can go without supper." The madam pointed in the direction of the stairs. Iris slinked away under Stella's watchful eye.

Daisy watched her go, before adding, "My daddy was a pretty good card player. Sometimes Lady Luck isn't on your side. My daddy didn't wager me. No, my own bad choices did that by trusting a gambler not as nice as Nick."

The idea a man would wager his daughter flummoxed Kitty. His actions made Aunt Eugenia appear saint like. A muffled sob and gulp confirmed Daisy might be missing her misfit father.

"Nick Kennedy?"

Rose shook her head. "Everybody knows Nick Kennedy. Gorgeous gambler and his horse, Duke. You met him?"

"Yep, on the train here, but I didn't see a horse." Her nose crinkled as she debated the intelligence of mentioning she'd encountered Nick on the train. No reason to mention the bathhouse, nor did she have to admit to some vivid dreams about him. The dreams baffled her because she certainly didn't want to dream about the pompous horse's rear end, but she did. When she awoke, her heart beat so fast, she had to place her hand between her breasts to keep it from popping out. Well, it felt like it might.

Nick became the conversational topic.

"Trust me, he never goes anywhere without Duke. The horse was probably in a baggage car," Rose confided. "Nick actually comes up here two or three times a year to relieve the miners of their excess gold. Whadya say to that?" Rose winked, indicating something secretive, but what?

"Small world," Kitty muttered. Her heart leapt inside at the thought of seeing Nick again. What good would it do to see the charismatic gambler wearing her garishly striped piano player vest? She doubted he'd notice the piano player anyhow. If things go well, no one notices the piano player.

Later a melancholy drunk leaned against the piano blowing whiskey fumes onto Kitty as he warbled the lyrics to *I Dream of Jeannie with the Light Brown Hair*. It was the fifth time she played it, but the man kept putting money in her cup to hear the song, not paper money, but gold pieces. Kitty sure could use more money, but she wasn't too sure if the denizens of the saloon would tolerate one more rendition of Jeannie, especially with a drunken miner murdering the verses.

Kitty bet none of the original lyrics included references to long toes and a broad behind. If so, Jeannie must have finished off the composer with a rolling pin. The drunk continued to list Jeannie's attributes as he belted out the last line. Money passed hands behind her, probably a wager on the life expectancy of the piano player. The drunk, a large man, would do some damage on impact. Muscles tensed, she made ready to leap out of the way if he fell.

The atmosphere changed suddenly. Formerly contentious card players called out a warm greeting to a newcomer. Iris's sultry greeting indicated someone special had arrived. A sneaking suspicion crept up and whispered in her ear. It might be someone she didn't want to see, especially in her ridiculous piano player outfit. Oh, he wouldn't say anything, but he'd probably grin—his own superior, amused smirk. The last thing she needed. Liquored up, he might blabber how they'd bathed together. No chance of it happening, but even if it did, who would care? Men bathed together all the time in public bathhouses. It was a rare man who had the privacy of his own bathroom. Before she could mentally debate anymore, the drunken man made a sudden move, causing Kitty to flinch.

The man swept the hat off his head and placed it over his heart. "Nick Kennedy," he called out, "as I live and breathe. Nevah thought to see you, again."

The man ambled away from her to greet Nick with much back-slapping and noise. Kitty picked out another tune with one hand while trying to follow the low rumble of Nick's voice. A few miners grumbled about her piss-poor playing, forcing her to use both hands. It made it difficult to hear. Everyone liked him. Which to her way of thinking ought not to be if he took the miners' money. His evocative laughter washed over her, reminding her of steam-filled bath they shared.

The night lasted forever. Thirty-two songs ago—not that she was counting—Nick Kennedy walked through the saloon doors. Men, both young and old, gathered around him asking for news of the outside world. He talked of floods and political scandals. He had the whole group howling as he acted out two wealthy matrons fighting over him at the San Francisco Opera House. The story ended with him slipping out before either matron noticed. Kit wrinkled her nose at the idea of two women fighting over Nick. It could have happened, or he could be making it all up to be entertaining. No matter the results were alike, the same taciturn men who trod the weathered boards only hours before were guffawing and slapping each other on the back. Nick was a breath of fresh air in the sweat soaked room.

Iris's invitations for Nick to accompany her upstairs became peevish and strained as the night wore on. Nick turned away each invitation by pretending not to hear and moving on to the next person or a softly murmured, "Not now, sweetheart."

Stella grabbed the pouting Iris and hissed loud enough for most people to hear. "You better leave Nick alone and get your sorry butt in gear. I'm not paying you to moon over some man who could have any decent woman with a snap of his fingers."

Iris grabbed the nearest man and hauled the half-drunk merchant toward the stairs much to his surprise. Her killing gaze directed at Stella fell short since Stella's back was to the stairs while she conversed with the celebrated gambler.

Chapter Ten

THE NIGHT WAS winding down. Just before closing, Kitty hit on the idea of playing slow, soft songs as a way to hint to the men to leave. The music also inspired more than a few to think of sleep and a soft pillow. They'd have no problem finding sleep, but a soft pillow might be more difficult. Otis stood by the door guiding the more drunk patrons out the door. Her fingers picked out Brahmn's *Lullaby*. She didn't expect anyone to know the name of the song. She almost thought she was alone until a familiar voice asked, "Isn't that *Brahmn's lullaby?*"

Inhaling deeply to calm herself, she continued to play, not daring to stop or turn around. "Yes," she answered in her husky male voice.

"Hmmn," Nick answered.

He sounded distracted, not focusing on her voice. Everyone was gone. It was time to help Otis clean up, but that involved walking past Nick and Stella.

Stella spoke, gaining Nick's attention. "So Nick, where are you putting up tonight?"

"Well," he paused and shot a disarming smile at her. "Hotel is full up. I was hoping to stretch out on your floor."

Making her way to the bar where Otis was gathering the dirty glasses, Stella's laugh boomed, startling Kitty.

"Yeah, sleep on the floor. I bet. Any of my girls would make a soft place for you to land, but I don't think that's what you are looking for? Is it?"

Kitty knew the madam raised a penciled-in eyebrow at the man without even looking.

Using the tray Otis handed her, she watched Nick and picked up the occasional glass. Odd, he'd refuse the flowers' eager offers. Could be if he had society matrons battling over him, he felt he was too good for saloon girls in a mining town.

"No offense, but I am tired." Nick started to explain, but stopped and shrugged his shoulders instead.

"No need to explain, I rather you didn't pick one of my girls to lavish your attention on. It only causes trouble for me. They were practically slugging it out for hair ribbons today. I shudder to think what they would do over you." Stella pretended to shiver, causing her large body to shake like custard. "I got a room next to Kit's you can have."

Kitty's head jerked up when she heard her name. Her hands tightened on the tray she held as she carried it into the kitchen. The room next to hers? Oh, great, she'd never get any sleep with only a thin wall separating the two of them.

Kit walked back into the room to run a rag over the tables, half-heartedly wiping. She was close enough to Stella and Nick to hear him ask, "Who's Kit?"

"Oh, that's right; you haven't met our newest piano player. Kit." Stella's voice was tired, but there was oddly enough an undertone of playfulness. "Kit, come here. There's someone I want to introduce you to."

She walked over to Stella, feeling how a man walking to the gallows must feel. She tugged her hat down a little bit more.

"Kit, this is Nick. You've heard us talking about him at dinner."

Nick interjected, "I hope it was all good."

"You rascal," Stella swatted Nick's hand. "You know we all love you."

"Nice to meet you again, Mr. Kennedy," Kit muttered with her eyes downcast.

Nick bent his knees a little in an effort to see the face underneath the oversized hat. "It's good to see you."

Stella snatched the hat off Kit's head and ruffled her curls. "Rose cut Kit's hair. Didn't she do a fine job?"

Stunned at Stella's actions, Kitty looked up in surprise, only to meet Nick's appreciative gaze.

"Rose did a nice job, as usual," Nick commented, as his long fingered hand reached for the tousled curls.

For a second, as she watched the hand with the winking diamond ring descend to her head. His touch landed as light as a kitten's breathe. She would almost think he wasn't fingering her hair if she didn't get a close-up view of his Egyptian cotton shirt, and then there were the hairs on his arms drawing her attention to where he'd rolled up his sleeves. Her senses drew in the essence of Nick similar to the sun-parched plains absorbing rain. Her nostrils flared. His bay rum cologne mingled with a lingering cheroot aroma. Underneath all was the earthy smell of sweat and—Kit sniffed the air again. It was hard to identify the final element making up the scent. Her eyes traveled up his powerful torso, past the beard-shadowed chin, the upward tipped lips, the strong nose, to a pair of knowing eyes. He knew she was sniffing him like a dog! Her eyes dropped immediately to the scarred floor.

"Kit, I believe we have met before, and um, let me see if I can remember where?" A mischievous light entered the gambler's eyes.

Crossing her fingers behind her back, she prayed for him not to say it.

"I know." His voice brightened at the captured memory.

Waiting for him to blurt out the details, Kit fisted her hands, causing her short fingernails to bite into her palms. Stella wouldn't be shocked. Neither would Otis or the girls. She sneaked a glance at the remaining listeners' avid expressions. Even tired and bedraggled, every woman looked a sight better than she did. It could be because they were actually dressed as women, well, fast women. The only thing Nick had ever seen her in was ill-fitting men's clothes and bubbles. She felt at a disadvantage. Why should she care what some footloose gambler thought?

"It was on the train," Nick continued. "You were escorting your beautiful sister, Harriet. By the way, how is Harriet?"

Salvation. He didn't mention the episode. Before she became too upset about Nick observing Harriet's charms, she remembered Harriet was beautiful. She told Harriet so several times. Before she could think of how her words might strike the waiting audience, she snapped, "Married."

"Well, that's to be expected since you were escorting her to her husband." Nick's voice was smooth, melodious, and carried a hint of laughter.

Nick grinned wider at Kit's remark, making her want to kick him. She would, too, if her boots fit. Who knows where a flying boot might land? Nick would probably laugh his fool head off. It definitely wasn't how she wanted to end their meeting. Grabbing up the rag she'd discarded on the table, she swiped at one table, then another. "Don't have time to be jawin'. I need to help Otis get things cleaned up." Without waiting for a reply, she swept into the kitchen with such vigor the swinging doors separating the two areas, swung wildly.

"Woo-wee," Daisy pronounced, looking in the direction of the kitchen. "Don't know what you did to set Kit off. He's always nice to me."

"Probably tired." Rose excused her new friend's behavior while escorting Daisy up the stairs. Iris and Lily followed, slower, perhaps hoping to hear the conversation between Stella and Nick. Kitty hid in the kitchen giving Nick time to reach his room, not meaning to be turning into an eavesdropper, not that she understood what she heard.

"Does Daisy know?" Nick asked.

"No, she doesn't, and it would best to keep it that way, from everyone." Stella put her hands on her ample hips as if ready to spar.

"Hey, Stella, it's me." Nick had one spread hand on his chest and an offended look on his face. "I can keep secrets. I kept yours all these years."

Grabbing a chair, Stella collapsed into it. "I know you can keep a secret. Gawd, I tried to leave my felonious husband. I'm unsure if we were ever truly married. The shabby parson who wed us was probably just another confidence man. I count myself fortunate you were here when my husband made his last appearance. The man is like a bad penny, keeps turning up when I least expect him. I'm sorry if I offended you. Seeing someone that naïve and innocent brings out the mother hen in me."

"You, a mother hen." Nick guffawed, pointing one finger at the tired woman. "More like a mother wolf." He cut off his next comment when he noticed the hard-eyed stare she directed his way.

"Humph," Stella huffed and crossed her arms. "I can be motherly. By the way, I'm not buying that we-met-on-the-train story. What's the real story?"

Kitty gasped, covering her mouth to make sure no one heard her.

"Well," Nick started, stopped, and looked off into the distance. "I don't believe it is any of your business. It's time to bid you adieu." He turned smartly on his heel and headed for the stairs, ignoring Stella's sputtering.

"Don't be thinking about getting up to no good," she yelled at the departing Nick.

Kitty hid in the kitchen a few more minutes, giving Nick time to reach his room. Stella made Nick sound like the Big Bad Wolf. He couldn't be bad. Why would people like him so much? No matter, she needed to get to her room so she could sleep.

Removing on her vest and kicking off the sloppy boots, but still attired in her piano player garb, Kitty lay stiff as a board on her bed, listening to the movement in the hall. For people heading to bed, there was a lot of noise in the hallway. Several flowers called out goodnights to Nick, sounding more like invitations. The sound of slow, measured boot steps stopped right in front of her door. He was out there. Kit could feel it. He might knock on the door. Then what would she do? Her memory supplied the tall, raven-haired, slightly rumpled male on the other side of the door. Men, like Nick were totally beyond her understanding. Back in Ohio, Teddy Merckely had constituted the epitome of masculine sophistication. She realized he fell short, very short in comparison. She blew the light out, in case Kennedy might want to talk. She definitely could pass on the man-to-man talks.

A dog howled long and loud at the moon. The lonely, solitary sound made her aware of how alone she was. Sure, she had Harriet, but her best friend was married and already growing away from her. Before the westward move, Harriet and she would escape their respective duties for a few moments of shared camaraderie. They would talk about their dreams and plans for the future. Now, Harriet lived inside her dream. It wasn't as if Harriet avoided her, but all the same, it was difficult to listen to how wonderful Adam was. In truth, he was a decent fellow and treated her well. Kitty wanted to dislike Adam. She wanted to monopolize Harriet's time and attention and not share her, a childish desire that made her ashamed of herself.

The dog stopped howling, leaving an open silence. Everyone in the world must be in bed. Kit imagined the pretentious mayor with his heavily waxed mustache asleep beside his plump wife with her lace-trimmed nightcap tied underneath her double chin. Stella was probably asleep in her too tight satin dress stretched on top of the bedspread instead of under it, probably passed out from too much liquor. Something was bothering that woman. Did the flowers, Lily, Rose, Daisy, and Iris sleep alone? Alternatively, did they crawl in bed with each other, so they might feel a warm body beside them? Perhaps Lily snuck a man friend up the back steps. If she slipped anyone in her room, Nick would be her choice. He would be almost any of the flowers' choice with the exception of Daisy.

The sound of a boot dropping to the floor on the other side of the wall signaled Nick hadn't slipped into anyone's bedroom. He was right next door. A couple of hard punches into the flat, mildewed pillow didn't make it any more comfortable. Kitty flipped to her back and put her hands behind her head.

A full moon beamed through the window cutting a swath into the shadows. Her eyes traveled around the room slowly cataloguing each item. A bowl and pitcher perched on a rickety dresser with one leg shorter than the others. The bowl had a chip in it, and the pitcher had a crack right at the lip. The other boot hit the floor. Kitty stared at the meager furnishings. As far as distracting her when she knew what was undressing next door, it failed miserably. Maybe it wouldn't be so bad if she hadn't already seen him naked, but she had.

The clatter of change, perhaps gold pieces meant he was emptying his pockets. A quiet shuffling, then a slight screech of a chair pulled across the wood floor followed. This was ridiculous. How could she sleep with Nick next door? Maybe she should pound on the wall and demand him to be quiet. The only problem was he wasn't noisy. Only someone who listened very carefully would even hear the slight sounds of disrobing. Clunk, something hit the floor. Kit knew. It was his belt with the large, ivory embellished buckle. That must have cost plenty, or maybe he won it.

Listening to a man, an extremely attractive male, undress, how bad was that. Plenty bad, she knew. Whom could she ask if she was a wanton? Did moving away from Ohio turn her into shameless hussy? She heard about women who loved the touch of men, not one man, but many men. The wanton women loved kissing, touching, rubbing of naked bodies against each other, even the making of babies. Missy Davis told her this, after admitting her sister, Peggy, was one of those women. It was probably the reason behind Peggy's long visit to her aunt in South Carolina. Missy made it sound like a bad thing to enjoy the touch of a man, but Kitty wondered.

A few boys back in Lancaster had tried to steal a kiss. She did her best to avoid their wet open mouths, which reminded her of leeches, heading her way. The mouths would land and attach themselves if she didn't move fast enough. Ahh, but then there was Teddy. When he started walking her home, her heart sped up and her hands sweated, which kept her busy trying unobtrusively to wipe her hands on her skirt, while keeping them free in case Teddy wanted to hold her hand. He did steal a kiss one night, more than one. His kisses were sloppy, rather like an excited puppy. She must have been in love, why else would she want to kiss Teddy or have him hold his body close to hers.

As for Teddy, his love ended fast after her aunt talked to him about her lack of dowry. She'd cried herself dry after Teddy stopped coming around. She wondered if she ever did love him. Could it be happening again? Well, this time it would be all one-sided masquerading as a man and all. Everyone believed her male disguise. Only Harriet, Stella, and Rose knew. She thought Otis looked at her funny as if he knew too. If Harriet was right, Nick also, not that it would matter if he did.

Thinking about him was useless. Even if she put her Sunday best on and wove a ribbon through her hair, Nick didn't have eyes for the likes of her. He went for society women. She heard him talk about them. They even fought over him at the opera house. Kitty wondered sleepily what an opera house was before closing her eyes.

NEXT DOOR, NICK stripped down to his drawers and started to strip them off, but changed his mind after looking at the darned cotton sheets. He was used to sleeping on silk sheets. This was quite a come down for him. Of course, some spoiled socialite usually spooned up beside him on the silk sheets, because they were her sheets. He often tiptoed out to avoid repeat performances or the shameless fishing for declarations of love. It made the price of sleeping on silk sheets high. He gently eased his long body onto the rickety bed. It wouldn't do if the bed broke. He'd have Iris and Lily pounding on the door, demanding to know what strumpet was in his room.

He didn't harbor any ill will toward Stella's flowers. He enjoyed their company outside the bedroom. He enjoyed teasing the beauties, except Daisy, who struck her as fragile. The majority of men who accompanied the girls upstairs viewed them as a commodity as much as the whiskey they knocked back. Daisy kept looking for that special someone to sweep her off her feet and carry her away. It could happen. She was still young enough and pretty enough.

The only reason he jaunted to Cariboo, besides avoiding the monotony of the social whirl in San Francisco, was to check up on Kit and Harriet. It would be hard to believe two more inept travelers existed. He grinned as he pictured Kit's macho swagger and punched his pillow before laying his head down. The ever-inventive Kit appeared to have added some padding in an appropriate spot to her disguise. A snort escaped him as he thought about Kit ignoring him most of the night. She was afraid, no doubt about it, afraid he might reveal their bathhouse encounter. Oddly, she thought her male disguise fooled him. He could tell her he knew, putting an end to all her role-playing, but it was such fun watching her flounder. Maybe he'd stay for the show instead of relieving miners of their gold nuggets or maybe he would do both.

A loud mattress squeak from Kit's room indicated she wasn't asleep either. Nick imagined Kitty's slender body mere feet from his with no more than a thin wooden wall separating them. In his mind's eye, he could see her rumpled curls and heavily lashed eyes staring up at him. Then there would be her graceful neck leading to her elegant shoulders, which would give way to a high neck muslin nightgown because no matter how he otherwise wished it, she was a nice girl. Nice girls didn't sleep in their birthday suits. A nice girl didn't attract attention with daring clothes or provocative words. Instead, she drew the eye with her stillness, sweetness, and innocence. Instead of expensive French perfume, she smelled of soap and sometimes apples. He thought he left his attraction to good girls behind when he left Indiana.

Maybe he felt protective of Kit since no one looked after her. Besides wanting to look after the plucky female, there was the incredible desire to bedevil her to see what she might do next.

"Kit," he called out, loud enough for her to hear. "Kit, I know you can hear me." A groan of the mattress indicated a vigorous rustling on Kit's part, but no answer. Nick smirked, knowing he had made Kit uncomfortable. He increased her discomfort. "Good night, darling."

Chapter Eleven

"GOOD NIGHT DARLING?" What was that supposed to mean? Kitty wondered as she flopped on her back. She exhaled slowly, knowing what it meant, but not wanting to admit it. Wasn't being wanted for assault enough? In addition, she was hiding out in a saloon. Never mind she strolled around town with an itchy wool sock down her pants for realism or she had to watch Adam and Harriet make cow eyes at each other. One more thing would send her over the edge. Unfortunately, the one thing resided next door stretched out on one of Stella's wobbly iron beds thinking up ways to torment her.

Maybe he hadn't called her darling. It sounded like a d-word or something like darling. Mmm, it could have been doggone, but that was a hard sounding word. Nick's word had sounded soft. A word might roll off a man's tongue without thought when cuddling. Maybe it was Marlin, but why would he call her a bird or a fish? Then again, he might have said darling. It was like the word dear. Lot of people used it, and it didn't mean anything. It certainly didn't mean 'I know you're a woman on the run disguised as a male.' Better yet, it could mean 'I know you're a woman, and I liked what I saw in the bathhouse, so much, so the two of us could take some time to get to know one another better.' She grinned at the absurd thought and turned on her side, finally giving into sleep.

The steely eyed gambler leaned over her flashing a grin, the most blatant invitation to sin she'd ever seen. As a preacher's daughter, there had been few opportunities to sin. Of course, she'd never really wanted to. She'd never encountered such a delicious temptation. Kit lifted her arms upward to embrace Nick as he settled on her bed. She inhaled, taking in the bay rum smell, along with the aroma of brandy and a spicy musk scent, exclusively Nick's own. His eyes sparked as he moved closer, causing her heart to race while a tiny fire sparked deep inside of her.

Boom! Her bed shook.

Not a fire, an explosion, Kitty's eyes flew open to her light-filled room, confused. Nick. She blinked. No Nick. She staggered to the window. Folks in the street looked northwest where a cloud of smoke darkened the horizon. A horse-drawn fire engine clanged by scaring horses, setting dogs to barking. The pedestrians regained the sidewalk and continued their strolling. A few of the men ran after the engine. What had happened? She must have said the words aloud.

"Too much dynamite is what happened."

Kitty turned slowly to see Nick, all spiffed up in a blue suit with a silvery diamond patterned waistcoat and bare feet.

"Didn't have time to put on my boots," he offered with an abashed grin. "Too worried you might think the world was coming to an end."

"No, I didn't," Kit offered slowly wondering what his presence in her room meant. Didn't she lock her door before going to bed?

Tugging on her piano player vest, she was grateful she hadn't given into the desire to change into her nightgown last night.

"Some impatient fool packed too much dynamite in a spot he wanted to blow. Blew the spot, himself, maybe his partner, and damn near took out a quarter of the mountain." Nick shook his head in disgust.

"I saw the fire engine go by. Maybe they can save him," Kitty offered, unsure how to deal with virile Nick in her room. Her eyes kept straying to his bare feet.

"That's not likely. They can't get the engine up to where the claim is. The engine is new, so they like to show it off whenever they can. When you heard the boom it was too late to do anything," Nick explained to the subdued Kit.

Nick growled in disgust. "All for nothing. The miners come with high hopes for getting rich. Some die from disease, some return home broke, obviously a few blow themselves to Kingdom Come, and very few actually get rich,"

Kitty lowered herself to sit on the edge of her bed. Here she thought she had it so bad. At least she was still in one piece, and she intended to keep it that way.

Nick sat down beside her, saying nothing. It was almost like her dream, she and Nick on her bed, except they were sitting instead of lying down and instead murmuring love words, their silence separated the two of them, caught in the contemplation of dead miners or so she thought. Their hands resting on the coverlet were about a half foot apart. Kitty wished he would hold her hand, but it would be an odd thing to do, especially with her masquerading as a man. What was he even doing in her room?

"Nick, how did you get in my room?" She turned her narrowed glance on the elegant gambler who leaned back on her mattress. He straightened upright before replying.

"It wasn't hard. None of the door locks will keep out a cool breeze. They're for show. The customers like them, though. Some of the married ones think their wives might sneak up the stairs and peer into every room. The joke is on them, because their wives are delighted to see them go." He chuckled at his own joke, but stopped when Kitty didn't join him.

"Why are their wives happy their husbands are—ah—associating with saloon girls?" a red-faced Kitty managed to stammer.

"Well, the men aren't good company. All they want to do is talk about politics, money, and religion and smoke cigars. The wives don't care to hear anymore while the flowers listen." Nick offered.

"Can't say I ever heard Rose or Daisy make a political comment before."

"They don't have to, all they have to do is listen and act fascinated. They can do fascinated. Haven't you ever had some sweet, young girl hang onto your words as if you hung the moon?" Nick asked with a devilish sparkle in his eyes.

"Of course not!" Kitty barked without thinking. The very idea of some girl staring at her in adoration was too ridiculous to contemplate until she noticed the sardonic raised eyebrow Nick did so well. Time to improvise.

"Well, there was Betty Lou Cooper. She used to love to watch me play the piano. It used to fascinate her she said. Are you telling me now, Nick, my one true fan was only pretending to like my piano playing?" Kitty teased.

There was never a Betty Lou Cooper. Barton Cooper, however, used to sneak into the church when she practiced the piano. Sometimes he tried to catch her in the cloakroom to steal a kiss. They were hard, pecking affairs usually ended up on her hair, neck, or even one time on her eye. She probably shouldn't have expected much since they both were only fourteen. The proper thing to do was to slap the opportunistic Barton, but it had felt good. Someone thought she was special. Unfortunately, shortly after the kissing incidents, his father's bull gored Barton while he was trying to lead the stupid animal to the stud pen. The last male she could remember who truly had liked her. She never counted Teddy despite her infatuation. He was too quick to marry elsewhere.

"That isn't what I said. If I hadn't heard you play I might agree, but you can make those ivories sing. You're as good as any I've heard, and I've heard a lot." Nick stared at their two hands, which were almost touching.

Kitty, embarrassed, pulled her hand away and pretended to adjust her cap until she realized she wasn't wearing one. Her hat was gone. Great, so was her disguise. Her eyes flickered around the room trying to spot the battered newsboy hat. It wasn't as if she had a large room.

"Forget the hat, Kit. You're inside. It's not as if you need it. Besides Rose does a good haircut."

"Did I hear my name?" Rose stuck her head in the door staring at Nick and Kitty sitting side by side on the bed. "Not interrupting anything, am I?" she purred.

"No, Nick was telling me about the dynamite," Kit offered to the slyly smiling Rose.

Nick stood up, adjusted his vest, and checked his cuff links before moving toward Rose and the door.

"I guess the coffee's ready, and I certainly could use a cup," he called out to the room at large.

Rose only moved partially out of the doorway, the better to whisper her sotto voice comment. "Couldn't settle for a sure bet, huh. Just had to go for the long shot. Think twice."

"Rose, I *do* believe you're threatening me." Nick spoke to the still smiling brown-haired woman.

"Try real hard Nick and see if you can remember ever being innocent. Then maybe you'll understand my objections."

"Whoa, honey. You got me all wrong. I'm actually trying to be helpful to the lad—a bit of chivalry and all."

Rose huffed in disbelief. "There ain't shar-var-ric bone in your body. I know your type. A gambler, not as nice looking as you, got me started on my fine career. I aim to make sure Kit doesn't have the same bad luck."

Nick threw back a searching glance over his shoulder. Kit pretended she didn't see or could hear them. She stood, grabbed her hat on the bed, exactly where Nick had been sitting. Fluffing up the hat, she drifted over to the faded mirror to place it on her head.

Nick's lips pulled tight, his hands fisted at his side. "Rose, I thought we were friends," Nick pitched his voice low. "I thought you knew me better. Now, I find out what you really think of me. I'm hurt."

"Get over it. You know as well as I do that there can't be no friendship between a man and a woman. It's all a sham until the man gets everything he wants off the woman and moves on."

Rose whirled in anger, causing a loud swish of her taffeta petticoats as she stomped off. Nick stood for second looking after her. "So what did you do to get her in such snit?" Kitty asked, as she gave her hat a final tug.

"Apparently being born male did it," Nick confided in a weary tone. He turned to head down the hallway.

"Wait, we can go together, can't we?" Kit hurried after Nick. Perhaps, she was being foolish, but she always saw men hanging around together chewing the fat. Oh, they were quick to accuse women of doing such a useless thing, when they were the main culprits.

"All right," the gambler offered with little enthusiasm.

Kitty almost declined the pitiful invite, but she could use some coffee. She tried to think up remarks one man might say to another to cheer a friend up after Rose's caustic remarks. "I figured Rose is upset at you because she's got her eye on you, a tall, good-looking man like you."

Nick stopped, turned, and looked at Kit for a second until she felt the tips of her ears turning red, then he laughed, loudly. It wasn't the thing to say to another man, but at least she'd cheered him up.

The hallway narrowed a little on the turn pressed the two of them closer together. The smart thing would have been to let Nick go first. Since she and Rose could fit through the turn okay, it never occurred to her it might be tight with a broad-shouldered individual like Nick. His arm brushed her arm despite he was holding himself in trying to make himself as small as possible, which made him look ridiculous. No more than a tiny brush sent a tingle through her. Once when she was ten she almost struck got by lightning. The bolt struck a tree not a foot from her, she felt the electricity flutter over her skin. She was sure the electricity stopped her heart for a moment, then, it started beating again much faster than before.

Nick's touch was as close to lightning as anything she'd ever felt. She didn't even want to think of anything else, like a kiss. A woman could pretty much die from too much lightning, but what a way to die. A smile graced her face at the thought.

"So, Kit, do you think I'm a good-looking man?" Nick teased, maybe prompted by her smile.

"What?" Startled out of her contemplation, she looked up at the grinning man.

"You said you thought Rose was so put out with me because I was a good-looking man. I asked if you thought so."

"Pshaw, I know what you're doing—fishing for compliments. You don't need to fish with me. There's women a plenty to whisper how striking your eyes are and what elegant hands you have." Kit parried his remark with finesse or at least she thought she did.

"Hmm, striking eyes and elegant hands. I must say I don't think I've ever had a woman compliment me on those features. They always saved their praise for other aspects of my person," Nick purred close to her ear.

They made the final turn in the dining room came into view. Daisy was sitting at the table laying out cards. Kit immediately called out to her friend and hurried to greet her—anything to get away from the impossibly attractive man beside her and all his naughty innuendoes. Maybe they weren't naughty. Maybe it was her own interpretation. She glanced at the exotically illustrated cards.

"What are those?"

"They're Tarot cards. They can tell people's future," Daisy said in pseudo-somber voice.

Lily sashayed in, giving Nick an obvious once over, before smiling. "What a girl likes to see when she gets up in the morning, six feet of lean, prime, US male." Lily tittered at her own comment before pouring herself a cup of coffee.

"When was the last time you've actually been awake in the morning?" Nick asked the lavish blonde, who displayed inordinate amount of bosom for non-working hours.

"All the time, sweetie. Morning starts right after twelve midnight." Lily dissolved into another spate of giggles.

Stella groaned as she entered the room, draped in a brilliant red and black robe trailing the ground. "Lord, Nick, as much as I like you. I can't abide Lily's giggling. Would you please quit being so engaging?"

Nick stood as the madam entered the room and moved toward her, stopping before her in an elaborate bow. "You know that I live only to please you."

"Huh, yeah, think you got me bamboozled too. Think again. I let you stay around because you're good for business. All the miners, merchants, and even the peace officers want to play a hand or two with you. I bet I'd make even more business if I opened up to the ladies so they could have a peek at you." Stella collapsed into a chair. Her blood-shot eyes and sluggish manner announced more clearly than words another night spent with the bottle.

Kit and Iris continued to watch Daisy lay out the cards. "See this one looks like a tower," Daisy explained.

"Daisy, you don't have those witchy cards again. I told you to get rid of them." Stella yelled, throwing a baleful glance toward the end of the table.

"Yes, I'm putting them up." Daisy replied and hurriedly wrapped up her cards and shoved them into her pocket before they were confiscated. Otis carried in a platter of fried ham taking the attention off Daisy for a moment.

"Otis," Stella began in a querulous voice, "didn't I tell you I wanted no witchcraft in the saloon."

"Yes, you did. Cookie put up all his hocus pocus bones," Otis said smoothly as he placed the platter in front of Stella.

"What hocus pocus bones?" Stella demanded.

Cookie, who'd poked his head out to carry in a second platter of biscuits, pulled it back. Kit, feeling sorry for the small foreigner, slipped into the kitchen and took the platter to carry into the dining room.

At least when they were talking about someone else they didn't have time to notice her. Rose slid in beside her and murmured, "Stella has a fear of anything magical or mysterious. I think it comes from her strong religious background."

"Religious background?" Kit squeaked, drawing all eyes to her.

"Did you say something, Kittrel?" Stella asked, her voice growing stronger and more resonant.

Great, she, Kitty, gets the full Stella, while the rest of them get the slightly hung over, whiny woman. Just for meanness, Stella had called her Kittrel in front of everyone. "Um, Rose was asking me about my religious background, ya see. It's Methodist, if you were wondering."

Rose arched a superior eyebrow and stared down at Nick who dug into his ham.

"By the way, the name is Kit, not Kittrel. If it was Kittrel I would have said so." Kit held her breath along with the other inhabitants of the table until Stella's hectic color began to fade a little.

She opened her mouth and laughed. "I like you, Kit Gruber. You're a regular bantam rooster."

Nick held up his coffee cup in salute to Kit's bravado.

Kit winked back, thinking of herself as an audacious, a manly man. Ignoring the fact by doing so, she was modeling herself on Nick.

Rose caught the wink and leaned over to whisper in Kit's ear. "What game are you playing?"

"No game." At least, she didn't think she was playing a game. Rose's partially opened mouth indicated she might say more, but she didn't choose to. The satisfied smirk on Kennedy's face confused Kit. How can you play if you don't know the rules? Apparently, Nick knew the rules. He'd probably created the rules for his own benefit.

The night started out like most at the saloon. Kit pawed through her sheet music she seldom used. Her music ritual allowed her to check out the room and to gauge the mood before selecting her first song. The family men came by first, for a whiskey and a visit. Lily was circling the edge of the room, ignoring any smelly saddle tramp who made the mistake of thinking she might spend time with him. She was looking for someone in particular, an established gentleman with money and a desire to spend it on her. Stella frowned at her from the other side of the room. Otis passed by Stella, carrying a case of whiskey.

The front door swung open letting the scent of night air. Daisy noticed the new arrival as soon as he walked in. "Hey, Kit, you're on your own for a while. There is a new fellow in town, and I like what I see. Time to make friendly." She sauntered in the direction of the awe-struck farm boy gazing around uncertainly. Kitty twisted around on her stool to see who managed to snag the melancholy Daisy's attention. The thin redheaded male looked bashful next to Daisy, definitely not an upstairs customer. A customer yelled out a request to get her playing again. Unaware, she'd stopped playing to peer at the newcomer; Kitty immediately started banging out a new tune for the demanding patron.

Nick flicked a look from his table, which she promptly ignored as she segued into another tune. She fought the urge to turn around and stare at the young man again. Something about him felt familiar. Her fingers danced across the ivories as her mind turned over memories. Red hair is very distinctive. Can't be many redheads, she thought when it hit her. George Breyer! Now she remembered George. He was a couple years younger than she was, probably why she hadn't remembered him immediately. He was a little shorter then, and, although it was hard to believe, even thinner. What was George doing here? As the night wore on, Kitty turned over in her mind the idea of talking to George. It would be nice to find out what was really going on at home, but on the other hand, maybe it wouldn't be so good.

Stella and Rose had seen through her disguise immediately. She was sure Otis had too, because he'd never let her carry anything heavy. The blasted gambler looked up and smiled as if he knew her thoughts. She was fairly sure he knew she was female.

A drunken miner started swearing after the indifferent Lily ignored him earlier and perked up when a mustached man with a derby strutted through the door. Punching the floor pedal down on the piano, Kitty played louder to cover up his ranting. No question about it, Lily was trouble. Most folks would have cut the fickle blonde loose before now, but Stella had some unlikely traits for saloon boss. Besides being horribly afraid of anything suggesting witchcraft or magic, she had a soft heart, perhaps not a good quality for a profitable business.

Kitty was looking around to see if the irate miner had left when she notice a shiny diamond-patterned waistcoat about her eye level.

"He left. The miner, I mean. Daisy is still conversing with the red-headed kid, and Iris is promenading around on the Pinkerton man's arm." Nick informed her, while leaning forward to turn the sheet music.

"Don't bother to turn the page. I know the songs by heart. Much easier that way." Kitty hid her smile when Nick looked astonished. Most folks didn't believe she could memorize a song right away. No doubt, some thought because she was female she wasn't smart. Nick didn't strike her as one of those men who considered women were little more than dumb animals. Wait, Nick didn't know she was a girl. Did he? "Did you think I couldn't memorize a song?"

"No," he stalled, stroking his chin, "I was thinking with a mind like yours you could be a killer gambler, especially paired with your choirboy face. You could be making ten times what you make pounding on piano."

"You're joshing me," she whispered, barely audible above the music. Her eyes shone at the thought of piles and piles of money sitting on a table in front of her. Of course, she'd have to take up smoking to be more convincing. She still had money left from her dowry, but the trip out here cost more than she expected. With George in town, she needed to be skedaddling sooner rather than later. Besides, the dowry wouldn't last forever; she needed some way to supplement it. "Could you teach me to play?"

The bourbon was relatively smooth for this part of the world, but it didn't prevent Nick from choking. A big ham-fisted miner pounded him on the back a few times, harder than necessary. He thanked the smirking miner who returned to his spot against the wall.

"You said you want me to teach you to play?" Nick managed to croak.

"Yes, I want to learn how to play cards. What did you think I meant?" Kitty shot a baffled look at the gambler, wondering if it was time to cut off his liquor, an issue Otis usually handled. Men tended to take him and his sawed off shotgun a bit more seriously.

"Ahh," Nick uttered and drew his hand over his face, "never mind." He looked around the room and pointed to a narrow rectangular mirror. "Tomorrow, I'll ask Stella to move the mirror above your piano. That way you can see everything behind you without turning around."

"Why would I want to?" Kit asked, bewildered by the turn of the conversation. Then she remembered the late piano player died from a knife in the back. "Oh, a mirror would be nice."

"That's what I thought, and it has the benefit of being close to the card tables." Nick added on reflection, attempting to lighten the moment.

"I should have known. Here I thought you cared about little old me," Kit laid on the Southern drawl on thick, "but all along it was about you and your winnings or lack thereof."

"As for winnings, I do all right. If I didn't care about you, I wouldn't have traveled up to this frozen mud hole."

Kitty stopped playing and turned to look at Nick. The gambler stared at the mirror over the bar. She had to ask, "You traveled to Cariboo to check up on me?"

"Start playing," he growled, holding his glass in front of him to hide his words from the any observant eavesdropper.

The boisterous sound of *Camptown Races* filled the room, two intoxicated patrons attempted to sing along, mutilating the words so badly, a glass became airborne, which set Stella in motion. Kitty waited a beat until she was sure all attention was on the singing duo. "Are you going to answer my question or not?"

"Not now. Later, after we close," Nick murmured softly and walked in the direction of the card tables.

If she weren't trying to hear his answer, she might have missed it. Came to Cariboo to see her? Couldn't be. It was more likely he came to Cariboo to see if Harriet actually married. There was a tiny part, a hidden part, wanting to believe Nick came for her. It might be likened to one of those romance novels her aunt refused to let her read, but Theresa Merckely, Teddy's sister, lent her some when she thought they'd be related. Of course, in the novels the women wore feminine clothing and didn't actually pretend to be men. Oh well, she'd find out her answer later tonight. All she had to do was keep playing for a few more hours. Wait. Speculate. Wait some more until Otis helped the last patron, a sodden, smelly miner, out the door.

The flowers mysteriously disappeared before closing time probably because they had no intention of helping to clean. Stella walked through the room pulling chairs upright. Nick started picking up empty bottles and placing them back in the original box. Glass bottles were so scarce in Cariboo the empty bottles were too valuable to toss. Whiskey arrived in oak casks. Otis later divided it into bottles and glasses. Kit started sweeping in the far corner. Jimmy appeared to toss sawdust on any wet spot. It was better not to speculate at the origin of the dampness.

The four of them working together pulled the place together quickly. The mop water was half ammonia to manage the sticky residue of spilt liquor. Later on, Stella sprinkled cinnamon sparingly around the saloon after mopping. She used to leave small bowls of toilette water around until some of the men complained they thought they stumbled into the ladies' sewing circle instead of a saloon.

"I'm heating up some water for you to bathe, like you asked," Otis called out to the bedraggled madam who had her foot on the first step.

She turned and smiled wearily at the barkeep. "You're a good man, probably one of the best I came across. Unfortunately, I'm too tired. Maybe you could use it."

Otis laughed at the suggestion and asked Kit. "Would you like a bath, young Kit? I imagine piano playing can be dirty work."

She laughed at Otis' joke, to make him happy. A bath sounded awfully good. She hadn't had a tub bath since—she looked in Nick's direction—the ill-fated bath in the bathhouse. Her heart sped up at the idea of bathing in the same room with Nick. Silly, there was only one tub in the bathing room. What was she thinking? Kitty chalked it up to be tired. "Sounds mighty good, Otis. I'll tote the buckets up."

"You go on up and start pumping in the cold water. I'll bring up the hot," Otis offered.

Chapter Twelve

KITTY SCAMPERED UP the stairs, not even bothering to look back at the watching gambler. The man had the audacity to stare at her, but to slow her ascent would indicate she knew he watched. Her shoulders tensed as she pretended not to feel the weight of his eyes on her.

"I can see you're not fooled," Otis commented as he poured steaming water into the buckets.

"Never was, well, maybe for a moment or two on the train. She's gotten better at it all. The walk, spitting, and scratching are authentic touches. So the padding." Nick chuckled and shook his head remembering her trying to sling up the carpetbag on the rack and failing miserably. Plumb pitiful excuse for a man. Harriet had to rescue her, saying a lot about how vulnerable she is. Obviously, they all knew it as well as he did.

Otis warned as he picked up the buckets, "All the same, keep in mind she's not a working girl. I can tell she's a decent sort, probably played piano at her local church."

"I used to be the decent sort to. Actually went to church on Sunday and heard her type play." Nick took the buckets from Otis.

"Used to." Otis muttered, still holding onto the bucket handles.

"What is it with you? I've been coming up to Cariboo for three years. I've brought you good Virginia tobacco, sometimes Havana cigars. I've done right by you and Stella. I've worked hard to keep all the flowers at arm's length, to avoid any tension among them. Yet,

Rose gives me the evil eye because I was talking to Kit this morning. Stella wanted to give me the talk earlier I could tell. Now, you."

"We're all attached to Kit and would hate to see her get hurt," Otis explained, then put the buckets on the floor. "Go ahead. Take them up before they get cold, but you mind your manners."

"Thanks, and I will." Nick picked up the buckets and carried them upstairs. He knocked on the closed bath door and stated the water was waiting in the hall before moving away from door before it opened.

Back in his own room, Nick addressed the ceiling. "When did I become a no-good scoundrel?" He pulled off his boots, removed his waistcoat, stiletto, and pistol before he stretched out on his bed. He thought about getting undressed, but wondered if Kit still wanted to talk after her bath. If he were lucky, she wouldn't even remember their earlier conversation. No, not a chance in hell of anyone who could memorize music the way she did would forget a thing. There was no backtracking on what he'd said so what was he going to say when she asked why had he traveled to Cariboo to check on her?

He'd tell her he wanted to make sure she and Harriet arrived okay, even though he hadn't been too worried about Harriet. He knew Adam Easton was a decent, hard-working sort and a surprisingly good match for the sunny German girl. Now as for a girl with no particular place to be or anyone to look after her who dressed as a male—she did need some looking after. He'd better not say anything to Kit along those lines. That would only get her dander up because she was under the impression she still had him fooled and was perfectly capable of taking care of herself.

The sound of splashing reminded him the object of his thoughts was bathing. Her curls were probably damp and her eyes closed to enjoy the bath experience, the way she'd look when he'd first walked into that bathhouse. Her long legs were no doubt resting on the rim of the porcelain claw footed tub. Perhaps she was thinking of him.

"This is sad. I am now hoping a woman disguised as a man is

thinking of me." Nick closed his eyes and tried to banish the images of Kit naked and bathing from his mind.

Not expecting to doze off, he woke up with a jerk. The lantern on the dresser cast a low glow over everything, indicating it was still night. Nick looked around the room wondering what woke him. It was Kit. She was still in the bath. As tired as she was, maybe she'd fallen asleep, even drowned. He'd heard about it happening once. The man was older and overweight. Still, the theory was he was unable to get out of the tub after slipping under water. Nick jumped from the bed and pulled the door open only to see a damp Kit leaving the bathroom wrapped in the oversized scarlet poppy robe.

KITTY DRAPED HER damp body with the robe she found in the bathing room. She'd forgotten little things like a towel and clean clothes when Otis mentioned a bath. Her work clothes were wet, since she'd washed them while she was bathing. The robe was a fortunate find, and she didn't expect anyone to be awake.

Too bad, she couldn't sneak into Rose's room to use her mirror to see how she looked. A rumpled, but delicious-looking, Nick stood in her way when she opened the door. His eyes, half closed, made him look sleepy. Perhaps, she woke him. Maybe he would think it was all a dream. If he remembered, she would make some joke about it.

He murmured something about talking when her only thought was getting into her room and locking the door. As soon as she pushed the door open, Nick rushed in like a stray. The only thing to do was to guide him back to his room. He must be sleepwalking.

Her lamp flared to life as Nick lit it. She'd never realized sleep-walkers could do so much while asleep. She moved slowly, trying not to startle him. With her hand on his arm, she guided him toward the door.

"It's time to go to bed, Nick. Let's go to your room." She guided the compliant Nick back to his room and led him to his bed without a word. She pushed him slightly until he collapsed onto the mattress. Her job completed, she turned to leave when Nick's hand manacled her wrist and pulled her onto him. Face to face, she had to admit Nick was very much awake.

"I've met some pushy females in my life. Never have I had one lead me to bed, then push me down on it." He grinned at her, dimples appearing in both cheeks.

"Well—I—that's not what I meant to do," Kitty's stammered explanation ended as soon as her lips met Nick's. She wasn't sure how it happened, but it continued to happen. His smooth, firm lips traveled over her face, across her eyebrows, her eyelids, leaving tiny kisses at each stop. A throaty, womanly contented growl permeated the room. Kitty realized, with chagrin, it was her treacherous throat that created the sound.

Nick spoke into the delicate skin where her neck and collarbone met. "What was it you were trying to say?" He licked her skin and gently blew on it, getting a shiver for his efforts.

"I was—uh—going to tell you—" She jumped from a playful bite on her shoulder. My goodness he made it hard to think. Sweat beaded her lip. The thin robe felt suffocating. Somewhere deep inside, an inner voice told her to leave, but she couldn't imagine why because everything felt so good. What was she saying? "Oh yeah, I'm not a man."

Nick drew back in mock surprise. "You're not a man?"

Kitty rewarded the grinning Nick with a pillow swat, which he batted away. "You knew, didn't you?"

"All the time, sweetheart." His eyes twinkled with humor. "The good news for you is I am a man." He placed his long fingered hands on her silk clad hips and bucked upward.

"Oh my." Kitty sighed as his hard body moved underneath her. She, who almost never giggled, chuckled at the absurdity of the situation. Maybe she was giddy. Before she could make a decision over what she should be doing, Nick was kissing her throat again. His hand slipped inside the robe opening. Resting near her breasts, his fingers left a fiery signature behind his caresses, making it difficult to breathe and think. A loud ahem, possibly a throat clearing, caught her ear. It didn't make sense. Nick was kissing her. That she knew. Shouldn't she feel some vibration if he cleared his throat. She didn't, that meant it wasn't he. Kitty looked at the door to check her hunch. Stella was standing there, looking none too pleased.

"Nick Kennedy, I am assuming you are underneath my poppy robe and my piano player?"

Kitty rolled off her would be lover so fast she landed on the floor. "Ouch."

Stella and Nick both spoke at the same time. "Are you hurt?"

"I guess I am okay." Kitty hung her head in embarrassment and contemplated crawling out of the room. "I'm sorry I disappointed you, Stella."

"Honey, I'm not mad at you. Putting Nick next to you is my fault. You being a youngster, you wouldn't be able to resist his charms." Stella patted her on the head like a wayward puppy.

"I'm not young. I'm nineteen." Kitty didn't know if she should be volunteering the information. It wasn't fair Nick got the blame when they were both participants.

"Nineteen's good," Nick said from his prone position on the bed.

"No, it's not good, you dog, you skirt chaser. I expected better from you." Stella fixed her basilisk gaze on Nick. She had cleared the saloon on occasions with the same glare.

"Stella, I understand if you don't want me to work here anymore." Kitty stood. Just when she was getting the routine down it was time to go. It might be for the best except for not having a clue where to head.

The irate redhead threw another venom-filled look at Nick and placed a plump arm around Kitty. "Honey, let's not talk about leaving. I can't lose you over a man. Piano players are hard to come by. As for men, there is entirely too many of their kind."

"Hey now!" Nick protested.

"I'll talk to you, later." Stella shepherded Kitty back into her room. "I know it will be hard, but try to get some sleep. I don't blame you, Kit. It would be like me trying to resist a chocolate bonbon." She swept a hand down her robust figure. "You can tell I've some problems resisting temptation, myself."

The large woman turned down the lantern and softly closed the door before heading next door to tangle with Nick.

Holding the door open a crack, Kitty witnessed it all.

"What do you think you were doing with my sweet, innocent piano player?" The angry woman crossed her arms and tapped her foot, which wasn't impressive since she was barefooted.

"I wish I knew. I wasn't planning to do anything. I was asleep, then I awoke suddenly convinced Kit had drowned in the tub." Nick explained, looking like he was dissecting the details in his own mind, searching for clues for his inexplicable behavior.

"What?" the disbelief was evident in Stella's voice.

"I ran out of the room, intent on saving Kit from drowning. Instead of drowning, she was damp, luscious, wrapped in a poor excuse of a dressing gown." A smile crossed Nick's face remembering how Kit had looked.

"Do I really want to hear the rest of this?" An expressive eyebrow told how she thought the story would end.

"I think you might because it is not what you think. I promised I'd talk to Kit after work about why I came to Cariboo. When I tried to talk to her, she became convinced I was sleepwalking and led me back to my room and put me to bed. I'm afraid that might have been when I slipped back to form. There is something about Kit, even in her male disguise. I like talking to her, teasing her, listening to her play the piano. It baffles me." Nick stopped his expression one of amazement.

Stella looked thoughtful. "Okay, why did you come to Cariboo if it wasn't to see my sassy self?"

"I came to check up on Harriet and Kit, mainly Kit, because I knew Adam would do right for Harriet. There is something about Kit. I worried about someone taking advantage of her. I even heard Harriet once talk of making a marriage for her once she arrived, when they thought I couldn't hear. That worried me too. I was afraid most men wouldn't appreciate her ingenuity, her pluck, or her sweetness."

"Well, that clears things up for me. Sleep tight."

Nick backed up and his door closed at the same time Otis padded down the hall holding a candle aloft. "I heard sounds, so I came to investigate. What are you doing up?"

"I was tucking the children in bed." Stella placed her hand into the crook of the barkeep's arm. "So pa, now the kids are asleep, maybe we can hit the hay."

A TEAMSTER CURSING at his wayward mule team awakened Kitty. The afternoon sunlight flooded her room. Odd she slept so late. Giving over to a luxurious stretch with her hands over head, she noticed the bright flowered robe. The silky robe slid open, revealing her nude body. She pulled the robe shut and glanced at the door to see if anyone witnessed the wanton display. Luckily, her door stood closed. Then she remembered the bath, the robe, and Nick.

Jackknifing into a seated position, Kit pondered her current situation. Nick knew, but he said he always knew. Not once did she fool him. All the looks, the touches, even the jokes were all for her, Kitty, the woman, not Kit the male. Harriet swore Nick knew all along. Just last night, he kissed her as if he had all night. Her fingers went to her lips, touching them as if she could still feel the lingering heat of Nick's mouth. The man could kiss. A man like that could be dangerous. She snorted to herself aware he was dangerous.

Harriet could put some perspective on the messed-up affair. Was it an affair? She didn't know what a few kisses meant, other than making her want more. Pulling on her pants and shirt, she was ready to go—quite a difference from the twenty minutes it usually took to work her way through petticoats and stockings. Fast was good, but she cast a lingering look at the discarded silk wrapper.

Running downstairs, she called out greetings to the flowers as she passed them. A startled Nick was lifting up his coffee cup as she shot by. Stella laughed behind her and shouted something about Nick losing his touch. Eastons was only a couple blocks away, and she managed to run the entire distance. Harriet met her at the back door.

"Kit, what's wrong?" Her eyes flickered over her tousled hair and haphazardly buttoned clothes.

"Can we talk?" Kitty gasped, grabbing the doorframe as she gulped air. Maybe she wasn't in as good of shape as she thought.

"Ya, come in." Harriet hauled in the still wheezing woman. "Adam, Kit's here. We are going upstairs."

Adam's tall frame came round the molasses barrels. He looked at Kit questioningly. "Hey, Kit, glad to see you. I guess I can spare my honey for a few minutes." He fixed an adoring glance on Harriet causing her to blush and giggle.

Harriet playfully smacked her husband before moving to the stairs. Kit waved to Adam before following.

Kit collapsed into one of the comfortable chairs, Adam constructed from an empty barrel. Harriet sat in its mate before saying. "Tell me all."

"It's Nick," she started, not sure what to say.

"I thought would be Nick, George, or Pinkerton man." Harriet nodded sagely as if she made perfect sense.

"What's this about George and the Pinkerton man?" Kitty remembered seeing George last night, and one of the flowers did say something about a Pinkerton man. She couldn't remember what.

"No, I say nothing until you tell about Nick." Harriet slapped a hand over her mouth to back up her words.

"Nick knows I'm not a male." Kitty watched Harriet's face to see if she was shocked.

"Is that all? He always knew. I told you." Harriet huffed in disgust.

"I know you told me, but I didn't believe you. Only now he knows I'm a woman." Kitty made prolonged eye contact to make her point.

"Oh," Harriet squeaked. "How was it?"

Kitty looked at the excited gleam in Harriet's eyes. "How was what?"

"You know." Harriet lowered her voice. "The mattress dance."

"Harriet Gruber!" she shouted, and then amended it in a quieter voice. "I mean Easton."

"Better." Harriet smiled slyly. "Why say he knows I am a woman?"

"He does, and we may have kissed once or twice or a dozen times, rolled around on top of the bed half dressed." Kitty concluded with an arched brow.

"You hussy! So how was it?" Harriet's vivid blue eyes were wide with curiosity.

"It was," she leaned her elbows on the table to whisper into her friend's ear, "heavenly."

Harriet clapped her hands together and laughed. "I knew it. You two from the start, sparks fly off you both. It was heaven for me too."

"It was heavenly for you too?" Kitty cocked her head and looked at her friend considering. An ugly feeling was starting to form in the pit of her stomach. "When did you kiss Nick?"

"Not Nick, you silly," Harriet squealed, taking a playful swat at Kit. "Adam."

"Oh!" Kitty hid her face in her hands. First, she thought Harriet kissed Nick, but worse, she was jealous.

Adam's bass voice floated up the stairs, "Did you call, sweet-heart?"

"No, dear heart, we're fine," Harriet called out. Both women waited until they heard his footsteps melt away before they continued.

"I can't believe you called him dear heart. I never thought the day would come when I'd hear you call someone dear heart." Kit shook her head in feigned disbelief.

"You're jealous," Harriet teased with a blush.

"Of course—not," she stumbled over the words thinking there might be some truth in them.

"Kitty, you got the same as me and Adam. You got Nick." She managed to grab one of Kit's fidgety hands.

"Not the same, Harriet, definitely not the same. We might share a few laughs, kisses, maybe even a hand of cards. The most either of us will have is a memory." She sighed at the picture her words painted. It was an honest one, but truth didn't mean she liked it.

"You are wrong about Nick," Harriet protested. "He is a good man. I spent time avoiding the hands of not so good men."

Kit wasn't going to point out to Harriet that not everyone got a happy ending. "Got anything left over from breakfast?"

"Goodness, we had lunch. How about a pork chop?" She bustled over to the warming oven before even waiting for an answer.

Between bites of the food Harriet handed her, Kitty managed to ask about George.

"He brought suitcase to pack up all the gold." Harriet's eyes twinkled as she relayed their townsman's naive remarks. They laughed together forgetting mere weeks before they were as gullible.

"Did he say anything about my aunt or me?" Kitty asked around the heart jumping into her throat.

"He said at first your aunt tried to interest the constable in looking for you. It didn't work. Then she hired a Pinkerton man to find you."

"No!" The image of the dapper man with the bowler hat from last night flashed in her mind. Pinkerton men were supposed to be good at getting their man, in her case, woman. He would arrest her and drag her away in chains. "I have to leave town right away."

"No, Pinkerton man will have followed my trail. I will tell him I do not see you after Lancaster. See, it will work." Harriet nodded encouragingly.

"I don't know. I need to plan. I need more money or at least a profession to make money. Nick was going to teach me to play poker. I could win some."

"Ask Nick for money if you need it. He'll give it to you. You can't learn poker in a night. You play piano, not cards."

"I'd never ask Nick for money, but you're right about the cards. I might lose what money I do have." Kitty sprang up, causing the chair to stutter on its four stubby legs. "I need to go, find out things, and make plans to leave."

"Katherine Hamilton, do not leave town without telling me." Harriet warned in her sternest voice, but Kit was already turning away without answering.

ROSE NARROWED HER eyes at the Pinkerton agent, refusing to be intimidated.

The man took a step closer as he spoke. "Have you ever heard of Katherine Hamilton?"

"No, I already told you no once," Rose insisted. "Is this Katherine Hamilton a soiled dove, a working girl?"

The Pinkerton agent frowned at the abrupt question and took another quick look at Rose's charms before answering.

"The information her aunt gave did not give any indication of her being a soiled dove. Although life on the run might include," he paused before emphasizing the next word, "*certain* hardships."

Rose's lips tightened. "I'll tell you again, I have not met any new ladies, fine or otherwise. I work in a saloon. Nice women do not come to a saloon. Because I work in a saloon, I am not invited to any church socials or sewing circles." She inhaled deeply and gave the Pinkerton man a contemptuous once over. "It amazes me how you would even waste time talking to me. You are well aware everything I said is true."

The man placed his bowler hat back on his head before turning away from the belligerent saloon girl. "Maybe you're right. Could be I talked to you because I enjoyed the view." He turned to walk away, turned back, and added. "It also could be you are hiding something, which in turn, makes me eager to find out what it is."

Rose snorted slightly to signal her dislike as he walked away. She turned and hurried toward the saloon. She hit the saloon doors at a run. "Where's Kit?"

Otis looked up from counting glasses. "I think he's in his room." He angled his bald dome in the direction of the stairs.

"Thanks." She galloped up the stairs past a startled Iris, who muttered under her breath.

Rose barreled through Kit's partially opened door. "Kit, you're still here, good!"

KITTY LOOKED AT the breathless Rose and knew fate had finally caught up with her. It was inevitable, but she hadn't expected it to happen so soon. She stepped away from the battered carpetbag open on the bed, her heart in her throat.

Sucking in air, Rose glanced pointedly at the carpetbag. "I was going to ask if you are the Katherine Hamilton the Pinkerton man is asking about, but the fact you're packing is evidence enough."

"No reason answering then." Kitty sighed as she stuffed all she owned into the small bag.

"Kit, look at me." Rose took Kit by the hands, turning her

slightly so she could see her eyes. "Running now would be a mistake. I know police officers, bounty hunters, even Pinkerton men. I've serviced enough of their type. Running would put him on your trail quicker than anything."

"What should I do then?"

"Stay calm, no one said anything about ever hearing of a Katherine Hamilton. Sit tight, wait for the Pinkerton man to leave before making any moves."

"What should I do after?" Kitty asked, glad she could share her dilemma.

"Well, I don't know. Maybe we should ask Stella. She's had a run-in or two with the law or we could always ask Nick. He has the ability to call in a lot of favors," Rose suggested with an arched eyebrow.

"Don't say anything to Nick," Kitty bit out the words.

"Why?" Rose wondered aloud. "Is this about last night?"

"Don't," Kit hissed through clenched teeth.

Rose cocked her dark head inquisitively and shrugged her shoulders. "If that's what you want."

"It is, but what should I do now." Kit drifted to the bed, pushing the small bag aside and sat down. She patted the spot beside her.

Rose crossed the room and perched on the bed, reaching for Kit's hand. "So what's the deal? What really happened to Aunt Eugenia?"

Kitty blinked twice to hold back tears. She looked at Rose, taking comfort in the concern she saw on her face. It didn't make sense to trust a woman she'd only known for weeks, but somehow it felt right. "Um, well, there was an accident. I must have knocked my aunt down. I don't remember. She didn't hit me when I first went to live with her after a while; her angry outbursts became more frequent. Often, they occurred while she held her buggy whip."

"I understand." Rose squeezed her. "You defended yourself?"

"She fell and hit her head. She laid there, all still. I thought she was dead at first. I ran for the doctor, even though she told me to get the constable, praying the whole time I hadn't hurt her bad."

"Did she die?" Rose asked her eyes wide with horror.

"No, actually she was okay, but she swore she'd throw me in jail even as I helped her up to sit in a chair. I knew then I had to get away before she talked to the sheriff." Kitty inhaled deeply before continuing.

"She asked you go yourself!" Rose's voice squeaked with surprise. "You really must be a good girl if your aunt thought you'd bring the law to arrest you."

"I was a good girl, but then I found the money she'd hid from me that was part of my dowry and ran," she hesitantly confessed.

"I would have done the same," Rose confided, "Why do think your aunt is still trying to find you? Obviously, she's okay. You took some money, but it really belonged to you anyway."

"Aunt Eugenia wants to see me suffer." Kitty sniffed and turned away from Rose to stare at the wall. "I thought if I ran far enough, it would end."

"It's only a matter of time. Outwait the old witch! Remember, she is looking for a sweet innocent girl in skirts, not some smelly male piano player. Besides, there might be more you inherited the old witch wants to make sure you never get."

"I do not smell. I'll have you know I took a bath last night." Kitty grinned as she swiped at her eyes.

"I know all about your bath and what happened afterwards." Rose teased.

"No!" Kit jumped up from the bed and spun to look at her Rose. "Does everyone know? How can I hold my head up? Maybe it would be better to leave now."

"Hey, I don't really know anything. I thought I heard something last night. It doesn't matter. I can forget it all. Just don't get spooked and run. It would be the worst thing you could do."

Kit paced the small confines of her room before turning to face her newest friend. "You're right. I shouldn't leave now. Tell me what you do know about last night. Be honest."

"There was quite a bit of racket last night or maybe I should say this morning. I heard Nick's voice and Stella's. It sounded like arguing coming from the direction of your hallway. This morning when I got up and came downstairs instead of Nick being his charming self he was grumpy. Otis commented he had been in good spirits until a certain piano player darted past him with hardly a word. It wasn't hard to put two and two together."

"What did you get when you put two and two together?" Kitty wondered aloud. What did other people see when they looked at her and Nick? Her eyes darted sideward to gauge if she spoke her last thought aloud. Rose wasn't surprised, but then again, she worked in a saloon. What would shock her?

Her friend smiled before she spoke. "Nick shows an unusual interest in you. In fact, none of the flowers could get his attention the way you did from the start. It's all starting to make sense. Nick knew all along you were female."

"Yes, he did. How did you figure out he knew?

"Trust me, a man like Nick wouldn't waste so much time talking to another man."

"Everybody loves Nick, men and women. What makes the way he treats me different?"

Kitty watched emotions shift across Rose's face before she answered. "Well," she started, then, stopped. "Nick is nice to almost everyone, male and female. There was one night when we had a drunk who tried to rough up Stella."

"What did Nick do?" Kitty asked in shock over anyone taking on the bold two-fisted owner. Stella was more likely to pull her one-shot derringer out of her garter than allow any alcohol soaked saddle tramp give her lip. Kit had seen her do it before, as well as coshing a belligerent patron over the head with an empty whisky bottle. It was surprising Nick had ever needed to step in.

"It's been a few months," Rose continued her story. "Gordie, one of the old-timers, finally hit gold. I was helping him celebrate if you know what I mean."

Kitty grunted an agreement to get her to continue, while wondering slightly if she actually knew what Rose meant. The image of Nick stretched across her, pinning her to bed, as his hands roamed her body producing delicious shivers everywhere they landed while his lips blazed a trail from her ear to her shoulder distracted her.

The thought made her move restlessly, wanting to unbutton the top button of her shirt.

"I remember when the man came into the saloon. He was a big one, reminded me of a prize bull with his thick neck and shoulders. Said he looking for something or someone. I thought at the time it must be trouble. There are always those kinds of men. They come in with the intention of butting heads together and bloodying noses for the fun of it."

"How did you know?" Kitty asked. The mysterious male world confounded her from taciturn Otis to grinning Nick to men bent on beating other men to a pulp for no obvious reason.

"It was in his swagger, challenging other men to take a chance at proving they were man enough to knock him down. He was a big man, over six feet tall, muscular, bald as a billiard ball and the six-shooter he wore on his hip was a bit of a discouragement too. It was Saturday night and crowded, but everywhere he walked a path opened up for him. Even the miners approaching sloppy drunkenness knew on an animal level that they didn't want to risk bumping into him. This all happened without a word, but the current was there, the feeling."

"How did you see all of this if you were upstairs, uh, entertaining?" Kit managed awkwardly, feeling the blush climb into her face.

A bark of laughter greeted her question. Rose shook her head as if trying to shake off the mental picture before speaking. "Kit, Gordie is ancient! He wanted a pretty girl by his side as he drank and bragged."

"Oh," she squeaked, while attempting to erase disturbing mental images.

"I guess I should have known what you'd think. All the good women always do. The men come because it is familiar. They feel comfortable here. Many times, I've listened to long drawn out stories of the sweethearts left behind. Sometimes, I think, some of them pretend I'm her, the one they left behind. All I have to do is be a patient female, sitting by their shoulder, smelling nice, and occasionally looking at them as if they set the moon, for which I often get a pouch of gold dust."

Kitty held her hands out in front of her, examining her cuticles before pushing them up. "I guess the men are lonely, something I never thought of, but it makes sense. Go on, what happened with the angry man."

"Well, Stella's got a sixth sense about trouble. She comes out of the stockroom to see what the problem is. When she sees him, instead of sashaying up to him as she normally would, she froze as if she'd seen something horrible. The man turns and sees her and calls out a name. It wasn't Stella. It was some long, flowery name like Emmeline. Stella didn't say anything. Just stood there, as far as I could tell, like a pillar of salt. Otis managed to lure the man away from Stella with an offer of a free drink. Stella immediately waded into the crowd once Otis got the man's attention. The man stood at the bar, throwing back whiskey after whiskey as if it were water. All the time, his eyes followed Stella. It was almost as if you could see a stream of fire coming from his eyes and touching her. It was obvious Stella felt it from her stiff movements and her false, loud laugh, a sound I've heard plenty of times. It was the sound of fear."

Caught up in the story, Kitty asked. "What happened then?"

"After downing almost a bottle of whiskey, the man lumbered after Stella. I was amazed he was still standing. He hollered out the name again, but this time he sounded more like an enraged bear.

Men scattered, deciding it would be a good time to leave the place. Nick was working a game near the back and saw the man grab Stella and whip her around like a broken doll. I was close enough to see her pale face. I knew she wouldn't put up a fight and take whatever the man did to her. That wasn't the Stella I knew. Nick jumped up from the card table and grabbed the man's arm, the one holding Stella. He shook off Nick as if he was a flea or something. Nick's no scrawny fellow."

"True," Kitty muttered under her breath. At Rose's sharp look, she motioned for her to continue.

"He didn't give up easy. He sidled back up to him and said a few words in his ear I couldn't hear. I expect he had his pearl handled derringer poked in the man's back because the mountain definitely wasn't moving until then. When he did, Nick escorted him out of town, and we haven't seen him since."

"Thank God for Nick!" Kit released the pent-up breath, she held almost the duration of the story with a whoosh. She knew the tale had a successful conclusion because Stella and Nick were both alive and whole. All the same, there were moments when she worried about Nick being hurt in the past. Then there was Stella. "What about the man? Who was he?"

"Don't know. I figure it was someone from Stella's past. She thanked Nick, climbed the stairs to her room, locked the door, and didn't come out for two days. My room isn't far from hers so I could hear muffled crying, the kind you do when you don't want anyone to hear you. I left her alone. If she wanted me to know, she'd tell me. It must have been someone from her past to cause that kind of pain." Rose finished her tale with a sigh.

Kitty eyed her wondering about the sigh, but didn't ask the cause, borrowing Rose's sentiment. If she wanted her to know, she'd tell her. The past had put them all together in this one place. She wondered about Nick's past. Everything always lead back to Nick.

Chapter Thirteen

POUNDING THE PIANO keys for all they were worth, Kit tried to pretend the Pinkerton man wasn't standing five feet away from her eyeballing everyone who entered the saloon. The shrill bark of Rose's laughter indicated she too was feeling the pressure. Daisy, listlessly walking between the tables, broke into an impromptu solo of *Jeanie with the Light Brown Hair*. Not liking the languid quality of the most vulnerable flower, especially with a room full of jackals, Kit switched songs.

Earlier a man with a silver-studded hatband had come in looking for Nick. Otis had pretended not to know who Nick was. The man apparently hadn't believed him. He came back. Kit saw him in the mirror. Her right hand ran up the keyboard in an agreed upon signal Nick had insisted on when he'd nailed the mirror up. What good was a mirror if it didn't keep the piano player safe?

It had only been up for a few days. In that time the only thing of note was the Pinkerton's man stocky body. She didn't have to see him in the mirror to know he was there. She could feel him, like some ill-tempered dog, waiting to bite the person who got too close. Kit was determined not to be that person.

Nick looked up from the game to see who merited the trio of chords. Spotting the stranger, he hailed him by name, drawing attention. Kitty swore under her breath at the man's stupidity. Nick might as well ask for trouble as the stranger strode toward him with his right hand buried in his jacket. The miners parted like the Red

Sea as the stranger approached the table. A card player jumped up in his haste to get away, spilling his beer and knocking over his chair. Experience kept a man alive in a freewheeling town. Experience also taught you to be wary of strangers, especially ones with their gun hand hidden.

"Stupid man," Kit hissed under her breath and involuntarily quit playing. Turning on her stool, she forgot about her plan to go unnoticed by the Pinkerton man as she watched Nick tilt back in his chair as if he didn't have a care in the world.

"Hello, Walt," Nick called out casually, but not overly friendly.

"Kennedy," Walt barked. "You know why I am here. I came for the money you stole from me."

Murmurs broke across the room like a wave lapping at the shore, considering an accusation of theft could result in being shot depending on who was being accused.

Stella hurried into the room with her small derringer tightly clutched in her hand. Otis was reaching underneath the bar for the shotgun he kept stored there. The Pinkerton man moved in closer, blocking Kitty's view.

"Gentleman." Stella elbowed her way through the crowd. "There will be no fighting in my establishment."

Nick grinned up at Stella, while keeping his eye on Walt, the way a person might watch a coiled snake, knowing it might strike at any moment. All Walt needed was the slightest move to give him reason to shoot. "Stella, you know I'm not a fighting man."

The brassy owner snorted in disbelief at Nick's claim. "So what is this ruckus all about?"

Kitty's gaze slid over to Rose, who clutched an empty whiskey bottle by its neck, and moved to Daisy slumped against the wall. Next, they alighted on Lily, who stood almost touching the Pinkerton man. Finally, her eyes settled on the red-faced stranger.

"It's about him," Walt said, pointing with his left hand in Nick's direction.

Otis swung the shotgun up and shot once at the ceiling showering him and the bar with plaster, causing most of the patrons to hit the floor. Stella swore while the Pinkerton man grinned as if he enjoyed the show. Pulling a bead on the stranger, Otis walked around the bar, keeping the gun barrel on Walt. "Pull your right hand out of your pocket where I can see it"

Walt, looking a little shaken, stared around at the people between him and the door. Making his decision, he slowly pulled his hand out of his jacket.

"I don't want a fight." He spoke to the angry barkeep who kept the shotgun trained on him.

"Ain't gonna be a fight," Otis grunted.

"I wanted a chance to win back my money," Walt explained, as if he didn't enter the saloon loaded for bear. The man had revenge stamped deep on his visage.

"Well," Nick drawled. "I would be glad to help you, but I don't have your money."

Taking a step toward Nick, Walt stopped when he heard the click of Otis cocking his shotgun. "You're lying. You didn't get in any big games between when you took my money and here."

Lifting one eyebrow questioningly, Nick spoke softly. "How would you know unless you were following me?"

KIT STOOD AND slid against the wall. No one noticed her as she worked her way up the stairs. The saddlebags were in Nick's room and full of money—obviously the stranger's money. It wouldn't do if found in Nick's room, especially with the stranger yelling about calling in the peace officers to search Nick's room. It would be best if the saddlebags weren't there. If they weren't there, the affair would end.

Once upstairs she headed for Nick's room. The saddlebags were where she remembered seeing them, surprising her. She remembered much more about the night than how incredible Nick had felt on top of her or how good he'd smelled. She'd accidentally kicked the bags and heard the gold coins hitting together. The best thing to do was to make them disappear. Grabbing the bags, she headed for her room to grab her newly acquired livery jacket and gloves. No real plan presented itself. All she knew was she needed to hide them.

Nick's horse, Duke, whinnied as she tiptoed past the saloon, stopping her. She could probably get much farther on a horse. After all, she and Duke had a relationship. She had been bringing the horse an apple every day. Untying the bridle from the hitching post, she mounted. Grateful, she could ride astride.

Loud voices in the saloon had her kicking her heels into Duke's sides. Letting loose a disturbed snort, the horse took off like a cannon, barely missing the man hidden in the shadows of the saloon. Obviously, Nick had made some fast getaways. They shot past some unsteady miners weaving their way down the sidewalk. Duke continued to run past shuttered buildings until they were on the edge of town. The half-moon shed meager light on the dirt path, a path she'd never even traveled in the light of day. Too bad, she didn't know where she was. The question was should she keep going or should she go back. A gunshot in the distance made the decision for her as the gelding lunged down the dark road.

Duke stretched out into a ground-eating gallop, taking the bit in his teeth since Kitty's hands were light on the reins. Trees threw out skeleton arms, and scrubby pines and occasional miner's shack squatted alongside the road. Peering into the darkness, Kit looked for a place to turn off and hide the troublesome saddlebags.

Unfortunately, no connecting path or a convenient turn-off was anywhere in sight. The sound of a rapidly approaching horse spurred her into sudden action. Kicking her heels into the already winded Duke, she managed to squeeze out a little more speed, shooting down the darkened path. It was probably only a miner returning back to his shack. Cold encouraged everyone to rush home instead of malingering on a deserted road. Kitty tried to reassure herself without any success.

Instead of half-drunk miners and family men out for a drink, the image of the Pinkerton man with his bowler hot on her trail was more likely. Maybe she'd given herself away somehow. She searched her memory for an occasion someone who might have called her Kitty by mistake. None came to mind. Harriet was the only one who knew her by name, and the Pinkerton man had never seen the two of them together. The sound of the additional horse's hooves alerted her there was more than one man trailing her, and they were getting closer.

Looking behind her, she could see her hoof prints in the frost-hardened dirt road. Her trail was obvious even in the moonlight. She had to get off the road, Kitty pulled the reins hard to the right, guiding Duke to an area littered with rocks, broken limbs, and a few patches of lichen that managed to survive the icy temperatures. Duke slowed as he picked his way through the shadows. The sound of running horses drew closer. Soon they would be on top of her. Slipping off Duke, she grabbed the bridle by the cheek strap, pulling him more into the shadows. She waited for the horses to draw nearer before she gently covered Duke's nostrils with her hands to prevent him from whinnying.

One rider shot by, causing Kitty to hold her breath sure the unknown rider could hear her. The second horse passed, causing Duke to shake her restraining hand off, and he snorted into the frosty air. Luckily, no response to Duke's comment. So far, so good, except she didn't have a clue what to do next.

Remounting, she let Duke pick his way delicately through the uneven terrain, whickering softly as if asking if this night traveling was necessary. The sound of his metal horseshoes hitting stone made Kitty cringe. It was so loud in the clear air. Surely, someone had heard it. To top it off, Duke stopped and refused to move another step. It was hard work trying to save Nick from a disgruntled gambler. Heaving a sigh, Kitty dismounted, prepared to lead the stubborn animal. Grabbing Duke's cheek strap she attempted to pull the animal forward. He didn't move.

Frustrated, she placed her hands on her hips and hissed at the horse, "I don't know what your problem is. Here I'll show you." Kitty took a giant step in the dark to demonstrate the way Duke needed to go.

"Help," Kitty yelped as she tumbled into a ravine. Hitting the bottom hard, she knocked herself out.

Coming to minutes later, she heard a low whinny. By narrowing her eyes, she could make the outline of Duke's head lowered over a dark gash, which must be a gully.

"Think you're pretty smart, huh?" Kitty muttered in the direction of the horse as she pushed herself up. There was something stuck to her cheek. She tried to rub it off, but it had already frozen. Breaking off a piece, she held it up to her nose. It was kind of jelly-like, but it smelled like copper. Blood? She must have hit her head on the way down or maybe it was the abrupt stop. Now why was she in this situation again? Oh yeah, Nick's mischievous grin formed in her mind. Managing to roll to all fours, she tried to stand up. Pain shot up her leg reminiscent of the time she stepped on the pitchfork barefooted, only worse.

Something was wrong. Dead wrong. Kitty hopped around on one leg, flailing her arms wildly, trying to find something to hold on to for balance. Finally, she found a rock face to lean against. She put the injured foot down gingerly to test it. A wave of intense pain shot through her. She felt like someone took a branding iron to her ankle. Great. She probably broke her ankle in her not so great escape. The truth was she hadn't escaped yet, especially if she didn't get to some place warm. Miners froze to death all the time in the unforgiving Canadian winter.

Needing to find a handhold on the rock wall, she peeled off her glove. A major sin in the north, but she didn't have much choice.

She needed to find a way out. Nick could take care of himself. Why did she do such an impulsive, stupid thing? She knew why even if she didn't want to admit it was something in his kisses. Then there was his voice, low, intimate calling her name.

"Kit, where are you?"

She could even hear it as if he was nearby. Amazing, Kitty shook her head, bemused until she heard the voice again.

"Kit."

Her imagination must be working overtime. Duke whickered loud and hard. She started to tell him to hush when she heard boot steps on the gravel. Freezing in place, Kitty strained to hear the approaching footsteps.

"Kitty, it's me, Nick. Where are you?"

Letting go of the breath she'd been holding, Kitty took another breath before calling out. "I'm over here in the hole. Be careful."

"I'm coming, sweetheart." He called back, his boot heels scrambling for purchase over the rocks.

He'd called her sweetheart. She sighed, and then she accidentally put her weight on the wrong foot. "Ouch!"

"What, honey?" Nick called out in a voice, which sounded a little closer.

"Hurry," Kitty managed through clenched teeth. He was there before she knew it. Deftly jumping into the hole and wrapping her in his arms, accidentally battering her already savaged ankle.

"Ouch, watch it," she complained.

"I didn't expect undying gratitude, but something like my hero might not be out of line," Nick commented laughingly.

"Thank you, Nick. I am grateful. I hurt my ankle when I fell into the hole." Kitty snuggled into Nick's shoulder appreciative of his warmth and inhaled deeply, enjoying the smell of worn leather and clean male.

Nick paced around the small hole with Kitty in his arms. He dragged his boot toe around the edge trying to find a way up or out.

"Well, darling, looks like I am going to have to toss you up," Nick acknowledged.

"What," Kitty squeaked. "Toss me where?"

"I looked, and there's no easy way out of here. It's up to you. Once you're up, I need you to tie the rope to the saddle horn on Duke's saddle and back him up. Once I get a hold of the rope, pull me up. Can you manage?"

Kitty had her doubts as she felt Nick's voice vibrate through the clothing separating the two of them. In the end, tossing was her only hope of getting out, and she imagined Nick was a good tosser. Naturally, he would be good at everything.

"Okay, are you ready?" Nick's voice rumbled against her ear.

"I guess. What do I need to do?" Kitty hoped she sounded braver than foolish, scared, and half-frozen. He moved closer to the rock face.

"I'm going to push you up the rock face. Grab on the ledge and I will boost you over. Can you do that?"

"I guess I'll have to if I don't want to freeze to death," Kitty agreed grudgingly, willing herself to do so.

"Good girl," Nick replied a hint of laughter in his voice.

He dropped a brief kiss on Kitty's hair before disengaging her arms from around his neck.

"Feel the wall," he ordered as he put his hands around her waist and lifted her up with a small grunt. Her face flushed as she realized Nick was struggling to lift her. It wasn't as if she was heavy, but she wasn't exactly petite either.

"Grab the lip."

The growled order had Kitty's hands skittering across the rock wall until she finally felt the edge. She put both hands on it and pulled herself up a little. "Got it," she huffed.

"Um," Nick managed while putting one hand on Kitty's posterior.

"Hey, watch where you are putting your hand!" Kitty squealed when his large hand covered her butt cheek.

"Honey, it's necessary to get you up."

Nick huffed as he pushed upward with both hands. The sudden boost had Kitty up over the lip of the hole. She grabbed for the trailing reins of Duke's bridle. Another shove from below pushed her all the way up.

"Don't remember you kicking up such a fuss last time I touched you," Nick grumbled more to himself than Kitty.

"I can hear you," Kitty hissed back. Pulling herself upright by holding onto the stirrup and moving her hands up the side of the sturdy horse she was able to stand with a minimum of pain.

"Don't forget I'm down here."

Kitty winced as she set her foot gingerly on the ground. "Keep your pants on. I'm getting the rope."

"It's tied onto the pommel," Nick instructed.

"I know. It was practically under my leg the whole ride here," Kitty grumbled. Why did Nick had to ruin a perfectly good moment by being such a know-it-all? Surprisingly, being out in sub-zero weather, inappropriately dressed with a banged up ankle was a good moment. What was she thinking? Of course, Nick came to her rescue, only to kiss her on the hair like a wayward little sister and bark orders like a domineering big brother. Not a good picture, but he did call her sweetheart and honey.

"What's taking you so long, I'm freezing my…"

"Quit yer bellyachin'." Kitty tied the rope to the saddle horn and threw it down the black hole.

"I thought you went off and left me," Nick complained as he grabbed the rope.

His head popped above the rim as she slowly backed up Duke. Pulling himself up, Nick swiped his hat off his head and shook it.

"We better head on back before frostbite sets in," Nick announced as he walked toward Duke and Kitty.

"Go back, when a stranger might kill you? Why do you think I took your bags and ran?" Kitty fisted her hands on her hips and glared at the stupid man. The moon chose the same moment to hide behind a cloud, ruining the power of her angry stare intended to incinerated Nick or at least slightly toasted him.

"Ah, Walt, don't worry about him. I've dealt with meaner hombres than him." Nick dismissed Kitty's concerns with a shrug and grabbed Duke's bridle.

"What are you doing?" Kitty hissed, still aware there might be someone listening nearby.

"Going back to Stella's to unthaw. If I'm lucky, Otis might have some coffee to compensate for fetching back a contrary piano player." Nick put his hands around Kitty's waist and plopped her in the saddle. "Swing your leg over."

"Contrary piano player, my foot," she grumbled as she followed orders. She barely caught herself to keep from squealing when Nick swung up behind her, heaved her up by her bottom and slipped into the saddle seat under her.

Attempting to sound unaffected, Kitty asked from her perch on Nick's thighs, "Where's your horse?"

"I'm riding it."

"No, really, how did you get out here?" Kitty craned her neck to see if she could see a horse shaped shadow without any luck.

"I rode Madeline, Stella's lazy mare. I am lucky she came this far. The second I dismounted, she turned toward home. I'm glad I found you and Duke. It would have been a mighty cold walk back."

"You're happy to get Duke back," Kitty grumbled as she flopped back against Nick's broad chest.

"And my saddle," Nick added. "Ouch, what was that for," he grunted as Kitty's elbow hit his ribs.

"You only came for your horse and saddle bags."

Nick wrapped one arm around Kitty drawing her closer to him before he whispered into her ear. "Sweetheart, I came for you." Kitty snuggled back into his arms and gave a little satisfied sigh. "Duke is smart enough to come back on his own, and I had no clue my saddlebags were even missing."

"Hey," Nick grunted from another forceful jab to his ribs. The lights of the saloon came into sight along with Stella standing on the porch.

Kit leaned against him, wondering why Duke had been outside the saloon. An expensive horse like him would not be out in the elements. Not only was he in standing in the cold, he was saddled as if ready for a quick pursuit. "Nick. Why was Duke saddled and stationed outside the saloon?"

He remained silent for a few moments as if he hadn't heard the question. He'd had to have as far as they still were from town. The only thing audible besides Duke's hooves was the crystalline sound of icicles cracking as the wind whistled through the trees.

"A gambler has to be prepared."

He knew. The man acted as cool as a cucumber tonight. Cracking jokes with Otis, flattering the flowers, and picking out a tune on the piano before sitting down to play poker. "You knew Walt would show up tonight."

Nick sighed, before answering, pushing Kitty slightly forward with the motion. "Not exactly Walt, but someone was trailing me. That's the downside of being a successful gambler. Someone is always willing to take it away from you."

It was exactly as she thought. Walt had been determined to steal the saddlebags. She'd saved him a fortune. "It was good I took your saddlebags and ran."

He snuggled his chin against her hair. "Mmm, I keep the money in the bank. The jingling you heard was probably the extra horseshoes I carry for Duke. I don't want any old clumsy shoes nailed on him. Most smithies use a heavier shoe, which would cause Duke to have one heavier hoof than the others. It would be hard on his legs, as well as the general ride."

She'd risked her life for horseshoes. Here she thought she was helping Nick. "I hurt my ankle for horseshoes?" Her voice grew louder as they approached town. "Horseshoes!"

Nick tightened his embrace, murmuring into her hair, "Very expensive horseshoes. Duke thanks you."

The silhouette of buildings surrounded them, most dark, but the saloons threw out rectangles of light onto the dark street. In one rectangle of light, Stella, Otis, and Rose stood on the walkway looking in their direction. A few men staggered past the trio. Kit hoped they lived close by. It wasn't that unusual to find men frozen to death from passing out in alleys or along the road on their way home.

Nick guided the horse to the saloon where the trio waited. Stella stepped off the porch and approached the couple. "I see you brought my piano player back. Thanks. I was getting rather fond of this one."

Nick placed his hands around Kit's waist to lift her down. "Stella, Kit managed to hurt her foot,"

"It's not like I tried to hurt my foot. I was doing it for you," Kit complained.

Nick added, "Might see if you can rustle her something up to eat. I think hunger is making her cantankerous."

Stella put an arm under Kit's shoulder to help her into the saloon and murmured. "Men, can't live with them, can't live without them."

Kit huffed her agreement.

Otis walked around the bar and returned to wiping glasses as he watched Stella help the lame Kit up the stairs. Nick followed a few steps behind, carrying his saddlebags slung over one shoulder and whistling. He stopped when he saw Otis and sauntered over to the bar.

Hooking one boot on the brass railing and dropping his bags, Nick leaned across the bar a little before speaking, making sure the two stragglers not quite out the door wouldn't overhear.

"Anything interesting happened after I left."

Otis picked up another glass to wipe it. "Depends on what you call interesting."

Nick grinned at the barkeep, flashing his famous smile. "Tell me what you saw with your unusually keen senses, and I'll decide what's interesting."

"Mmm, let me think." Otis stopped wiping the glass and rolled his eyes upward as if trying to retrieve a memory. "Those two miners you were playing cards with were disgruntled, knowing they couldn't win their money back."

A chuckle escaped Nick as he looked over his shoulder to track the slow-moving drunks staggering out the door.

Otis noticed the direction Nick was looking and called out, "Careful, Travis, watch out for the loose board on the porch. See ya tomorrow, Clarence."

They both waited until the door closed. Nick waited until he could see the men's silhouette against the window before resuming their conversation.

"What happened to Walt, the man with the fancy silver hat band?" Nick threw out the question casually as if he didn't care about the answer overly much while patting his jacket to find two cheroots and offered one to Otis. Striking a match, he lit his own and the barkeep's.

Otis inhaled on the cheroot to start it. He managed a half grin around the cigar. "Much obliged," he murmured after taking a few appreciative puffs. "I figure you would have met one of two men who took off down the road. Walt certainly was riding hell for leather on the only road leading out of town. Another man took off too. I couldn't rightly say if it was someone from the saloon or someone outside, maybe waiting for Walt, but they headed off in the same direction."

"You forget I was on Stella's overfed pet horse," Nick grumbled. "By the way, did she come back?"

Pulling the cheroot out of his mouth, Otis blew a perfect smoke ring, before speaking. "The mare made better time getting home than you."

"Then they must have been in front of me. That means neither was chasing me, but Kit." Shaking his head at the thought, Nick swore under his breath.

"Why? Kit is too quiet to rile up anyone," the barkeep added reflectively, tapping the ashes off his cheroot.

Snorting a little at the idea, Kit couldn't provoke anyone to anger; he drew on the cheroot to give himself time to think. "Wouldn't be after Kit, but the saddlebags." He gave the bags in question a slap to emphasize his point, which caused some jingling.

"What's in the saddlebags? A deed to the railroads?" Otis grinned a little at his attempt at humor.

"It's more what Walt thought was in the saddlebags. I won close to a thousand dollars off him. When I win a big amount of money, I always put it in the bank, but he wouldn't believe the truth even if I told him."

Otis grunted his agreement and wagged his head for Nick to continue.

"The man thinks I cheated him. Now he's convinced me should hand over my winnings at his say so. That's not going to happen." He pounded the bar with an open hand.

"Should say not. Strange he would follow you so far north."

"Yep, hearing you say so makes me wonder if Kit was right. Claims I don't take things seriously enough."

Instead of replying, Otis settled for a long, meditative hmmm.

Nick attempted a smoke ring, but his was a bit wobbly. "I wouldn't have considered Walt a danger back in San Francisco, but trailing me this far shows major desperation. I won't be returning his money, but maybe I could play a few hands with him and allow him to win other people's money."

Otis knocked the ashes off his cheroot in a nearby ashtray. "How do you make another guy win?"

"Sometimes, it's hard, but all I need is a couple players who aren't that good. Walt is a fair player, which probably caused him to be too self-assured he'd win. All I have to do is play well until the pot is up and then play poorly."

"What if one of the so-called bad players wins the pot?"

Nick grinned, then, exhaled a plume of smoke, before answering. "That's why they call it a game of chance."

Chapter Fourteen

VOICES DRIFTED INTO her dreams along with the smell of coffee and bacon. Kitty punched her flat pillow into a little more pleasing shape as she tried to return to her dream, something about wolves howling in the background, her ankle hurting, and Nick. Stella's voice became louder, angrier, making the possibility of returning to sleep impossible.

"You're paid up. I don't need your kind here, hurting my business," Stella declared.

Rose's voice was lower, impelling Kitty to sit up to catch the words. She recognized the timber and the cadence, but couldn't hear the words.

A male cleared his throat, blustered a little, obviously unhappy with whatever Rose said.

"Well, sir." Nick's baritone came in. "Don't let us keep you from pursuing this nefarious runaway girl. Could be you misread the trail."

"Well," the man drawled, "the only person to have left Lancaster near the time of the suspect's disappearance was Harriet Gruber. Odd, she came up with a boy. One I think that might be working here. It would help if I could talk to him."

They were talking about her. Kitty clutched the blanket to her chest as if it could protect her. What was she going to do? It was obvious the Pinkerton man was downstairs making trouble. Definitely, couldn't go downstairs, even disguised as Kit. Somehow, he would see through her disguise, she knew.

Nick's voice rang out again. "You're a smart man. Not the type to go chasing across the country after a slip of a girl. What was it you said she'd done?"

Here it comes. Kitty cringed. Now everyone will know.

"I'm not at liberty to say." The clipped tone of the words had Kitty imagining pursed lips and a disdainful expression.

"From what you tell me, or haven't told me, she doesn't sound like a bank robber, a regular desperado. So why are you trailing her to the ends of the earth?"

"It's my job. Some people work for a living." The Pinkerton inserted his jibe before his boot steps headed away, indicating the troublesome man had left. Nick's laughter, combined with Stella and Rose's, followed the Pinkerton man out of the saloon. Stella waited about a minute before hollering up the stairwell.

"He's gone. Might as well come down. I know you've been listening."

Red-faced, hair tousled, and sock footed, Kitty limped down the stairs, peering around the corner first to ascertain for herself that the coast was clear. Stella, Nick, and Rose stood in a clump looking her way. Feeling silly, she slid down the last two steps soundlessly. Might as well make a clean breast of it and hit the road before the Pinkerton man came back and started hurting business again.

"Um, I guess you want to know why the Pinkerton man is looking for me."

Stella waved her off as she headed toward the kitchen. "Makes no matter to me. That's why people go north—to leave the past behind."

Rose lifted an eyebrow as she proceeded to move around Kitty to reach the stairs. Of course, Rose didn't need to hear. She already knew the story. That just left Nick, who didn't make any effort to leave. Just her luck. She gave him a baleful glance, which caused him to wink.

"I'd like to hear this story." Nick pulled a chair out from the table and patted it.

"Of course, you would." Kit sighed and plopped into the chair. "Don't you consider yourself to be a nosy Ned?'

Her words surprised a large guffaw from Nick. "Here, I sent the Pinkerton man on his way with shame for a companion because he was chasing down some delicate flower of womanhood."

Kitty directed another glare his way. She was well aware she didn't look her best. Her little toe was working its way out the sock. Her prop sock hinting at her manhood felt out of place she noticed when looking down.

Nick's eyes followed the same path down her leg, causing him to chuckle again.

"You might want to take care of that. Gonna scare half the female populace, and the other half will be demanding a peek."

Turning her back to the grinning gambler, Kitty shook her pant leg hard until the offending sock fell out. Snatching it up, she turned to the stairwell to retreat until Nick's hand stopped her.

"Don't be in such a hurry. We need to talk."

Raising her eyebrows at the statement, she looked meaningfully at his large hand on her arm, but did not get her the results she'd desired. The hand still held her fast, along with his unsmiling stare. Kitty shook her arm, testing his strength. His grip tightened.

"Hey," she complained, pulling against his hold to no avail. Her struggles trapped her with the banister at her back and Nick in the front and one arm still pinioned. "I don't have time for this. A Pinkerton man is on my trail."

"Which is what we need to talk about," Nick managed to mutter as Kitty aimed a kick at his shin, unfortunately with her hurt ankle.

"Ouch," Kit complained, reaching down to rub her abused toes with her free hand.

"Try wearing boots next time," he offered. "Better yet, don't wear boots if you plan on kicking me."

"Let me go. I don't need to talk." She twisted slightly and slumped against the banister. "I need a better way to gain money than being a piano player. If it weren't for the room and board, there'd be no way I could survive without dipping into my dowry money. I might be able to land somewhere, but I need a skill to keep the money coming in."

Leaning over her, Nick placed a finger under her chin and tilted her face up. "Have it your way. We'll talk about money and ways to get it."

If anyone knew how to get money in this town without digging it out of the ground, it would have to be Nick. Maybe he could help. "Could you teach me to play cards? Daisy was going to, but I think you'd be the better teacher." Kitty asked, looking up from under her eyelashes.

"Hmm." Nick placed his other hand on Kitty's opposite arm and pulled her into standing position. "If I teach you how to play cards, you'll talk to me?"

"Yes, deal," Kitty affirmed a little uncertain, folding her freed arms under her breasts.

"Any particular game?"

Cocking her head to one side, she pretended to consider before answering, "Poker."

"Poker, it is." Nick grinned, placed a cheroot between his teeth, and patted down his pocket in search of a match.

Kitty cleared her throat noisily, catching his attention. "You're not going to light that thing, are you?" Her eyebrows arched waiting for his answer.

"Yep, what about it?" He continued to search for a match.

"The smoke." Kitty clamped her lips shut, wondering why she even have to explain such a thing.

"Kit, this is a saloon. That's what men do here, smoke, drink, gamble, and chew the fat, and if they have the money, sometimes they—"

"Stop there, I know what they do. I know this is a saloon. Every night I work in smoke—doesn't mean I like it." She placed both hands on her hips in a very feminine manner, despite her male attire, causing Nick to smirk.

"What?" Her jaw tightened as Nick's smile bloomed into a wide grin.

Nick pocketed his cheroot, tried to wipe the smile from his face. "It's not important."

Flouncing ahead, but still favoring her hurt foot, Kitty led the way toward the dining room. Nick shook his head, while murmuring under his breath, "Men in this town must be drunk or blind, probably both."

Otis rubbed wax into the wooden bar, as he eyed the determined piano player. "Glad to see the ankle isn't broken."

Nick shook his head. "A busted ankle might help keep her in place, but I doubt it. See you're keeping the bar slick."

"Nick, I thought you were going to teach me how to play," Kit called out when Nick started over to talk with Otis. "Afraid I might be good enough to beat you."

Laughing, Nick turned on his boot heel. "Talk big, little man, you don't even know how to play."

"Yeah, yeah, come teach me, gambling man."

"Okay, youngster, ready to learn?" He pulled a chair out from the table by tucking the toe of his boots under the chair trestle.

Narrowing her eyes, Kit arranged her face into what she thought was an inscrutable poker face. "I'm ready."

"Not with that face, you're not." Nick shuffled the cards looking down at his hands, not missing the outraged look Kit shot him. "Looks like you have a toothache."

Huffing, Kitty pulled out a chair and plopped into it, splaying her legs out like any man. "What type of face should I have?"

"Hmm," Nick shuffled the deck before answering. "A disinterested one as if you aren't interested in what's going on. You're thinking about something else—not the cards you're holding."

"Like what?" Kit asked, knowing by the way that Nick's eyebrow shot up at her question, she would regret asking.

"Well, you have to appear you don't care. Maybe you could think about kissing a certain person. Or maybe you might remember a certain bathhouse or maybe—"

"Stop it." Slamming her hands on the table for emphasis, she glared at the smirking man.

"I thought you wanted advice on what to think about to appear you weren't interested in the outcome of the game," Nick offered with a laugh.

"Sure, I could about you dropping your pants in the bathhouse and manage to keep a poker face." Kit darted a sideways look at Nick to gauge his response. His lips tightened a little. Good, she'd keep going. He deserved it. "Then there were the kisses. Nothing memorable. Yep, I've got all I need to keep the bland look on my face, all right."

Placing one palm on the table, Nick levered his long body upright, catching Kit's eye.

"What, what are you doing?" Kitty turned in her seat, to look at the looming Nick.

He leaned down, grabbed her arm and pulled her upright, flushed against his body. "Bland? You called my kisses bland?" Nick growled, "I'll show you bland."

His lips landed firmly on hers, causing Kit's knees to go liquid. Her arms found their way around his neck instinctively. She used the position to pull herself up on her toes the better to reach his lips. Nick traced the seam of her mouth with his tongue, forging ahead when she sighed. Kitty heard herself moan and flushed a little. Hard to imagine she was the same female who hightailed it out of Lancaster, Ohio. Things had changed. One of Nick's hands landed on her hip. Was it accidental? The same hand pulled her closer, answering her question.

Breathing in the scent of warm, aroused male, Kit snuggled closer, before whispering into Nick's ear. "Still, a little bland."

"You, little…"

Stella's entry into the room stopped Nick's comment.

"Not what I want my regulars to see, men pawing men. Even if one of those men isn't really male." Stella shook her head as she walked around the surprised couple.

Kitty scrambled out of Nick's arms so fast, she lost her balance and managed to catch herself on the table before falling. "Nick was… Nick was teaching me to play cards, poker."

"Yep," Stella acknowledged. "I've played a few hands of a similar game, myself."

Nick grinned unabashedly at Stella, his grin turned to a grimace as Kit kicked him in the shins.

"Ow!" Kit hopped around on one foot, glaring at Nick.

"I told you to put on boots," Nick added and laughed at Kit's infuriated expression.

"As much as I enjoy watching you children play the fool, I actually came down here for a little tip. Keep it down. The Pinkerton man is back, snooping. Unfortunately, Lily now thinks he is the love of her life and that's the way the sneaky bastard is going to play it."

Nick's smile vanished immediately. "Does Lily know about Kit?"

"Ha," Stella chuckled. "Lily doesn't notice anything, doesn't have anything unless it benefits Lily."

Kitty watched the interplay between the two, wondering what she should do.

"What now?" Nick said, expressing Kit's thoughts.

"Nothing. That's what. Any sudden move like leaving would look suspicious. I have to say you two groping each other in public might cause talk too. Can you keep it behind closed doors?" Stella turned with a click of her heel. A hand placed delicately over her carmine red lips muffled her laughter, a little.

"What am I going to do?" Kitty asked plaintively more to herself, than to Nick.

"I guess you'll sit tight, like Stella said. Maybe even learn to play poker." Wrapping one arm companionably around her shoulders, Nick pulled Kitty snug into his side.

"Stop, remember what Stella said." Kitty shrugged out of the loose embrace.

"Yep, I remember closed doors. So, let's go upstairs and close the doors," he purred into her ear.

"Oh!" The image of Nick's hand covering her breast rushed back, making breathing a little more challenging.

"So you can keep the weight off your sprained ankle," he added.

The seductive image disappeared with his practical explanation. "Oh." She sighed, a tiny bit disappointed. No, relieved, she should be relieved. Nick wasn't going to use his famous charm on her when she was in a vulnerable position. After all, she was still dressed as a man, by this time, a dirty man. How attractive could she be, when Iris spent every night bending low to give him a fine view of her cleavage?

"Did I hear a sad sigh?" Nick asked with chuckle as he scooped one arm under her legs, picked her up, and held her against his chest.

His movement startled her and caused her heart to speed up as he crossed to the back stairs. "What are you doing?"

Nick angled her body to make it up the narrow staircase without bumping her head or feet against the walls. "Obvious, I think."

Yes, the part where he carried her was self-evident. Was he truly making sure she didn't gain any more injuries or facilitating another opportunity to lay side-by-side exchanging kisses?

Nick gently laid Kitty on the bed. He plumped the pillow behind her head and half sat beside her with one long leg stretched out to balance his precarious perch on the narrow bed. "Sad?"

Kitty colored up as she searched for an excuse. She started smoothing down her clothes nervously, and her flailing hand hit Nick's nearby hip. Oh my, she couldn't believe she had touched him in so intimate a spot. For a second she stared at her small, pale hand resting on his dark wool trousers. She snatched it back, glancing up briefly, expecting Nick to be laughing at her, again, but he wasn't. Instead, his eyes stayed on hers, dark and glittering, reminiscent of a bull before charging.

If memory served her right, she ran like hell to escape the bull, but she chose not to run now. She watched as Nick's head came closer, slowly, giving her plenty of time to turn away. She didn't, too interested in what was happening as opposed to what ought not to. She started forgetting about all the things she ought not to be doing about the same time Nick dropped his pants in the bathhouse.

Nick's lips landed on hers like a butterfly alighting on a flower and were gone as quickly. Kitty's eyes flickered open only to see Nick's head moving away. What? He was stopping. The bed dipped a little as Nick pushed off it to stand. He was leaving? Stepping over to the closet, he located a folded blanket and flicked it open before covering her with it.

"Get some rest, Sunshine," he crooned as he turned to step into the hallway, pulling the door closed behind him.

He was gone. Kitty glared at the door a little before sinking back into her pillow. Just her luck, Nick was a gambler and a gentleman. He kissed her as if she was his little sister, but did most brothers kiss their sisters on the lips? She didn't think so, but he didn't actually stay for a second kiss.

So what did it mean? He covered her with a blanket—a brotherly action. Still, he carried her to bed, possibly lover like. On the same hand, a brother would carry his sister if he were strong enough. That didn't prove a thing. Then there was the way he looked at her, all intense and focused, not brother like. Who knows, maybe he was concentrating on getting clear of her, treating her rather like a horsefly.

Closing her eyes, she tried to talk herself into sleep. It didn't matter if Nick looked at her brother like or not.

Chapter Fifteen

N ICK SHOOK HIS head at the departing Kit. Everything was good between the two of them when he carried her up to bed. Give her a couple hours and she's stomping around muttering something about treating her like a little sister.

OTIS CHUCKLED SOFTLY to himself as he arranged the glasses behind the counter. Stella strolled into the room and cocked an eyebrow at the still bemused Nick staring at the staircase.

"Don't ask." Otis harrumphed and turned to lift a case of whiskey.

"No need." Stella guffawed as she approached Nick. "Woman troubles?"

"I wish," Nick growled. "If only it was simple. When a woman ties me up in knots, it's time to hit the road. Everyone knows one woman is as good as the next—Oomph!" Nick yelped as Stella's fist landed in his stomach, bending over double The woman could pack a punch. "Why did you punch me?"

The disgruntled madam landed a narrowed glare. "Think about it!"

Easing upward by resting one hand on a chair back and wrapping the other still wrapped around his injured midsection, Nick tried to speak, only to have Otis stop him.

"Think twice, boy, unless you want to get the left fist. Think hard."

Nick blinked, trying to get his thoughts oriented. What terrible thing had he done? "I guess it was the remark about one woman being the same as another woman."

Stella snorted, crossed her arms, and turned her back on him.

"Okay, I'm sorry. It's not as if you never heard the remark before. Even Benjamin Franklin said all cats are gray in the dark." Nick stretched out his hand to put it on Stella's shoulder, but snatched it back. Considering the mood she was in, she might separate it from his arm.

Twirling, Stella gave Nick the most set-down look she could manage being a good five inches shorter than him. "If Benjamin Franklin made such remark to me, despite him being a famous person and dead, I would still hit him."

"Stella, I didn't mean anything by it."

"Shut your mouth until I'm done talking."

Nick snapped his molars together instinctively. When was the last time a woman told him what to do? Had it been his mother? It was Kit. My how the mighty had fallen, told off by an innocent in male attire.

"Iffin ol' Mr. High and Mighty Franklin came in talking about cats I might let it go, but if he started calling Kit a cat, then I'm getting out the shotgun."

"Who's calling Kit a cat?" Nick blustered, balling up his fists.

"You are, you big dummy." Stella tapped him hard on his shoulders.

"I didn't mean Kit. She certainly isn't like any other woman I've ever met."

"I know, and I thought you knew. Still, when you start talking tomfoolery, it makes me wonder." Stella shifted her weight on feet encased in shiny red half boots. The constant balancing of her bulk caused her to turn her back on Otis and his frantic hand motions attempting to warn them of the man who came in.

Nick shot his hands through his hair. "Kit drives me crazy. I don't what to do with the woman."

"Kit wouldn't be short for Katherine Hamilton, would it?"

Stella and Nick both turned to find the Pinkerton man grinning at them.

"No, it's short for Kitten Lefaye, a new dancer they have over at the Roman Circus," Nick commented, without even blinking an eye. Sometimes, as a gambler you learned useful skills, bluffing, being one of them.

"A dancer, you say." The man reached up to touch the ends of his waxed mustache. "I may have to drop in and see her."

"You won't be disappointed. She does this number with fans. It is awfully nice, but you'll have to head down to San Francisco to see her," Nick said with a knowing smile. "The trip will be well worth it."

"So, if this Kitten Lefaye is such a hot number, why are you here?" The Pinkerton man inquired.

Both Stella and Otis laughed together as Nick tried to talk over their laughter.

"I'm a gambler. I win people's money. I have to go wherever there is money to win. It is always better if I play with people who aren't good at cards." Nick knew he was patronizing the investigator with his oversimplified explanation. He hoped it was enough to irritate him and send him on his way.

"Any chance of getting some food here?" the Pinkerton agent asked.

"None, especially since we are not open for another five hours," Stella gave the doors a plaintive look.

"I get the message," the man grumbled as he walked toward the door. "Tell Lily, I'll be back tonight."

Nick stroked his chin contemplatively. "I think the Pinkerton fellow needs some investigating. I'll check the path Kit took last night. Any of you see what type of mount the man rides?"

Stella placed her hands on her hips. "Don't go stirring up problems, Kennedy. Lily can distract Pinkerton. You go out guns blazin', and trouble will meet you."

"If it wasn't him chasing Kit the other night, I need to know who it was." Nick checked his derringer and placed it beside his Colt pistol on the bar. "Besides, what makes you think I'll go out with guns a blazing?"

Stella snorted her response.

Nick shoved the derringer back into the calf holster. "I'm not after the Pinkerton man. At least I don't think I am. I'm going to check the path and find out for certain if someone was after Kit or the saddlebags."

Stella gave Nick a measuring glance, "Do you think going out alone is wise?"

"C'mon, Stella. It's daylight. I need to make sure Kit is as safe as I can make her."

Otis interrupted the arguing pair, handing Nick a small sack.

"What's that?" Stella demanded.

"Ammunition," Otis answered and walked away.

"Ammunition?" Stella looked at the rapidly departing Otis, then Nick. "What is going on?"

"I need to take care of things. Someone has been trailing me for some reason. Figure it's the money, but you never know. Be back soon." Nick turned and headed for the door. Luckily, he only had to deal with Stella. Kit would have insisted on going with him.

The frost had melted under the afternoon sun, making it hard to find the hoof prints from the night before. Walking beside Duke, Nick stared at the ground, trying to find a clue. The first shot took his hat off. Grabbing the saddle horn, he swung into the saddle. As soon as he fit his foot into the stirrup, a bullet tore into his thigh. Wincing against the pain, he kicked Duke into action, searching for cover. There were no rock formations or large trees to hide behind. Nothing. A tumbled down shack hid the shooter, definitely not the way to head. A small group of scrubby pines beckoned in the distance.

Duke knew enough to run full out when bullets zinged past his head. Almost there and hopefully, out of rifle range. A buzz announced the bullet before it plunged into his shoulder, knocking him off Duke with one boot still hooked in the stirrup. This is how it ends. Nick swore. He hoped for a better ending than his horse dragging him as he bled to death.

Several more bullets whizzed by him before they stopped. With bullets no longer coming at them, Duke stopped as well and stood perfectly still. Thank goodness for a smart horse. Nick managed to work his foot free, all he had the strength left to do. He lay on the ground looking up at Duke who was gently blowing on him.

"Well, boy, this looks like the end for me, though I'd prefer not to die out on the road like an opossum."

Grabbing the stirrup, Nick managed to pull himself to a half standing position and to lurch alongside Duke as the horse walked slowly toward the trees. Once they reached the shelter, Nick released his grip on the saddle and tumbled to the ground. The sunlight beaming through the pine branches bounced off the icicles. He figured the sight would be his last memory on Earth.

DUKE GALLOPED INTO town riderless, stopping in front of The Gilded Lily saloon. Kitty grabbed the reins of the agitated horse and led him to the hitching post. "What's wrong, boy? Where's Nick?" She rested her hand on the saddle. It was slippery and wet. Turning her hand over, she looked at it. Blood. Nick's blood, she knew it. "Stella—Otis—Rose!" Kitty screamed, running into the saloon.

"What?" A frazzled Rose ran downstairs to meet Otis and Stella gathered around a babbling Kit. "Blood. It's Nick's blood. Duke came back alone." Kit trembled as Rose wrapped her arms around her.

"We'll go get him." Otis assured everyone. "I'll go over and get

Adam Easton since he has a wagon."

"I'll go with you," Kitty said as she tore out of Rose's embrace.

"No, Kit, not a good idea." Stella snagged her arm.

Kit whirled on Stella, screaming. "You don't want me to go because you think he's dead! He's not dead! I won't let him be dead!"

"We'll all go," Stella declared. "Rose, go see if you can hunt up that drunken doctor."

In a matter of minutes, they were on their way. Kitty spotted his crumpled form first and jumped off the wagon before Otis could even pull the horses to a stop. The men pushed her aside in their hurry to get him loaded. They couldn't stop her from scrambling up after him. She held Nick's head in her lap, hoping to spare him the bumpiness of the wagon ride. Adam steered carefully around the frost hardened ruts, but a wagon ride was never smooth.

Nick opened his eyes, causing Kitty's heart to turn over a little. She backhanded a tear threatening to fall.

He blinked and then gasped out, "I guess this means I'm not dead."

"Not dead. Thank God." Kitty hugged him hard.

"Ow. Not so hard. Gunshot." Nick groaned.

Stella turned from her perch on the wagon bench. "I'd watch the hugging, children, unless you want the wrong kind of attention. Gunshot wounds are a dime a dozen. Besides, people expect Nick to get shot."

"Hey," Nick complained.

"We're here," Otis announced.

Rose waited on the boardwalk, with the thankfully sober doctor. Adam lifted Nick from the wagon if he weighed no more than a five-pound sack of flour. The flowers followed Nick upstairs with Kit leading the way.

Nick managed to grin through his pain when Kit pushed the flowers out of the way to tend to him and directed his slurred words to the doctor. "Kit can be quite a powerful force when upset."

The doctor winked as if acknowledging the words, but was more interested in forcing laudanum down Nick's throat before removing the bullets.

Nick's eyelids flickered shut, as his arms flopped onto the mattress indicating the medicine had its desired effect.

Otis crowded into the small room, stroking his chin and muttered, "Damn, he's out. I never got to ask who shot at him."

Daisy volunteered her opinion from her place near the door. "I think it's the fellow with the silver hat band."

Otis worked his mouth as if he might have a chaw located in one cheek. "Could be. He struck me as a man who would get the drop on a fellow."

Stella folded her arms, watched the doctor, and listened to the discussion. "Don't count out the Pinkerton man. Something isn't right about him."

ROSE PUSHED AWAY from the wall, drawing attention. "Saw someone outside go after Kit, just a shadow, but it was on the outside, not the inside."

THE NEXT DAY stretched out long and aimlessly. Nick slept a heavy, drugged sleep. Kitty ought to know. She checked on him a dozen times since last night. She'd wanted to stay in the room with him, fearing he might die in the night. The result was she didn't get a whole lot of sleep sneaking in and out. She didn't stay, not because of what anyone might say, but rather what Nick might think. Was she making more out of this relationship than there really was?

Bypassing Nick's room, she headed downstairs. Lassitude appeared to be the word of the day. Various flowers draped themselves over furniture. Rose and Daisy carried on a rambling conversation, touching on everything, but saying nothing. Stella plucked a cigar from the humidor and sniffed it appreciatively.

Kit watched her as she rolled the cigar in her hands. "Stella, do you smoke?"

"I have, but I don't anymore. The smell of a well-made cigar brings back memories of my father and a friend." Stella replaced the cigar and closed the humidor. She turned facing the wall for a second.

Kitty thought her hand went up to her face, maybe to scratch it or wipe a tear away. Turning back, Stella smiled a bit too brightly before announcing, "Well, ladies, if you got nothing to do, we should be sprucing up our wardrobes. Appearances matter. Our customers don't want ladies in soiled or ripped dresses. They can find that at The Silver Spur. Remember the tone of the place. Ladies, go get your dresses."

Daisy and Rose headed for the stairs while Daisy grumbled. "You don't see Lily involved in our sewing circle."

"Don't envy her. I got a feeling Stella is getting ready to be shed of her. Besides, she's thinkin' her Pinkerton man is ready to propose." Rose grabbed the newel post to pull herself up the first stair. Kitty trailed behind them.

Surprise colored in Daisy's inquiry. "Do you think he will?"

"Why should he? He's an Easterner. He can have his pick of the women back home, not like out here where any woman will do."

Kitty followed more slowly not having any clothes to mend. She did have a copy of the novel *Robinson Crusoe*. Triple H gave it to Harriet thinking she might enjoy it a story of adventure complete with a half-naked native, she'd whispered behind a raised hand. Harriet took the book with a murmured reply, but her eyes met Kit's as her hand closed on the book. She knew Harriet could read English, but not well enough for reading a novel to be a pleasurable activity. Reading the novel and reporting the details to Harriet was no hardship. She was looking forward to it. Maybe she could discuss it with Nick. She opened the book to the first chapter.

I was born in the year 1632, in the city of York, of a good fami-
ly, though not of country, my father being a foreigner—

Her door flew open, interrupting her reading. Brandishing a dress, Rose spilled into the room and shook the cherry red satin dress in her direction while announcing, "Kit, this dress doesn't fit. Appears I grew. Come try it on. Maybe it will fit you."

What Kit really wanted to do was to find out what happen to Crusoe when he went to sea. The cheap fabric dripped black lace and had layers of ruffled underskirt. After a couple months of pants, any dress looked enticing. The freedom of being able to straddle a chair paled when combined with wrapping your breasts and wearing boots weighing two pounds each. Maybe she would try it on. After all, who would see her? Kitty reached for the dress. Rose surprised her by dancing out of reach.

"What? I thought you wanted me to try it on."

"I do, but I want to see it on you. None of this trying it on and not showing me." Rose wagged a finger in her direction to underscore her sentiments.

Sighing, Kitty lunged for the dress again. Rose allowed her to take it.

"Turn around so I can dress."

"Geesh, I knew you were shy, but…"

Kitty motioned for Rose to turn around and waited until she did. Ripping off her shirt and binding straps, she dropped the frothy dress over her head and batted around trying to get it to settle in the right place.

"Oh, for Pete's sake, let me help." Rose pulled Kitty's hands through the armholes while the skirt bunched around her pants.

The satin felt cool against Kitty's skin, quite a change from the wool worsted shirt she'd been wearing. "How do I look?"

"Mmm," Rose murmured with one hand against her cheek. "A little like a man in the circus sideshow. One side, he was a woman, the other a man. Only for you, the top half is female while the bottom half isn't."

Kitty looked down at her boots sticking out from the dress. "Oh, yeah." Sitting on the bed, she removed her boots, stood, and dropped her pants. Remembering the rogue wool sock, she reached under her dress and removed it too.

"Much better," Rose enthused, "but something is missing. Let's go to my room."

Kitty padded softly behind her. The room was pretty much like hers, with a yellow rose pitcher and bowl. Maybe Daisy had a similar set with daisies. In the corner stood a cheval mirror. Without thinking, she drew nearer to check out the dress. A thin girl in a loose satin dress with baggy socks and sun darkened face stared back at her.

"I look awful. People never suspected I'm female. I don't even look like a woman." Whirling away from the mirror, her gaze bounced about the room. There was Rose, and the look of pity in Rose's eyes might even be worse than the mirror.

"Ah, sweetie, don't take on so. All women have to fix ourselves up. I can fix you up. Do you want?"

Kitty watched her face to measure the sincerity of the offer. Maybe she meant it. Why not? She nodded her head slightly. Rose whooped with glee. Taking a leap in the direction of her dresser, she began to pull out stockings and garters, holding them up against the red dress and discarding them. Until she finally settled on a pair of black stockings and a pair of rose embellished garters.

"Of course, they would have roses on them," Kitty said.

"Put them on," Rose ordered from her position on the floor. Leaning under the bed, she made a couple of swipes, finally landing on her stomach with oomph.

Pulling on the hose, Kit watched her friend curiously before asking, "What are you doing?"

"Boots, Gladiola left boots." Rose emerged with a dusty pair of black half boots.

Taking the proffered shoes, she turned them in her hands, admiring the scallop top edges and decorative stitching. Tacked up or shortened skirts allowed the wearer to show off fancy boots. Better yet, they look like they might fit. Plopping down on the floor, Kit unbuckled one, then another and pulled them on.

"Woo-wee, you must be excited. Didn't even use a boot hook," Rose joked.

Grinning, Kit pushed herself up and stood on the tiny heels. She swayed a little as she tried to get her balance. Hard to believe she'd forgotten how to dress like a female. Taking a few tentative steps, she walked toward the window.

"Been walking long?" Rose teased. "Try shifting your weight from one hip to another it will help your balance and make your walk interesting," she advised with a laugh.

Looking at her laughing friend with narrowed eyes, she asked, "Do I want an interesting walk?"

"If you want Nick to see you as a woman, you definitely want an interesting walk. Let me help." Rose scrambled to her feet. "Let's do your dress up first, so your form is right."

The laces in the dress tighten as Rose tugged. It was almost like having a corset, but it was on the outside. Her spine straightened with the lacing. The result made it hard to breathe, but willowed her waist and pushed her breasts up high enough to threaten to spill out the low cut bodice. Aunt Eugenia had insisted she make all her dresses on the loose side as to not attract attention. It had worked. She'd be surprised if most of the men she'd known back in Ohio even knew she had a figure. The mistaken belief of a dowry and her thick hair had attracted her former beaus, not her shape.

Hair was the one obvious attribute that defined femininity, despite the fact women kept their hair up in public. Still, not having enough hair caused many women to use false hair or pads to make their tresses look fuller. Harriet had even mentioned the Matrimonial News insisted potential brides wear their hair down in case the potential grooms didn't want to offer for a wife with thin hair. At least, her hair was thick and wavy, even if it wasn't long anymore.

"You have such nice hair. Too bad you cut it," Rose remarked as she gave the dress lacing a final tug.

"It will grow when I need it to grow. Being a man is less work than being female."

Rose put her hands on Kitty's shoulders and pivoted her so they were face to face. "You aren't taking care of your skin. Look at those freckles."

"Men don't take care of their skin," Kitty answered.

Opening a jar, Rose applied cream to Kitty's abused skin. "This should help. I would also put some Spanish paper on your cheeks, kohl on your eyelids, and maybe some carmine on your lips."

Cosmetics. Her aunt would call her a harlot, a jezebel. Wait. Hadn't she already called her those things? It would be interesting to see what she would look like, but still. "Rose, what if someone recognizes me?" Her anxious question caused Rose to smirk.

"Even your momma won't know you when I get done. Oops, sorry, I forgot about yours being dead."

"Don't worry about it. What about your mother?" Kitty ventured, knowing so little about her new friend.

"Can't really say. I know where I left her," Rose offered while delving into her overflowing drawers and pulling out a black velvet ribbon. She tied it around Kitty's neck. "The way I figure it, she probably wouldn't welcome me back home with open arms."

"Oh." Kitty didn't know what else to say. She was sure her mother and father would welcome her home if they were alive. Aunt Eugenia was another subject entirely. Craning her neck, she tried to see around Rose and into the mirror.

"No peeking until I'm done," Rose cautioned as she laced a red ribbon through Kitty's short curls. "Almost there. Now a touch of cosmetics, not too much, we don't want to hide your fresh face."

"I thought it was a freckled face."

"It is, but still fresh. I even heard…" Rose paused for dramatic effect and lowered her voice to a whisper, "…some men like freckles."

"No!" Kitty played along, acting appropriately shocked.

With a final sweep of the rabbit's foot against her cheek, Rose smiled. "Gentleman, may I present our special entertainer for this evening, Mademoiselle Kitty. She has come all the way from Paris, France to sing for you." Stepping sideways, she allowed Kitty an unobstructed look into the mirror.

Blinking to check the image, Kitty stared. She could see Rose in the background so it had to be her, but it wasn't.

Rose's expectant face peered over her shoulder in the mirror. "Whadya think?"

"I don't know. It's like there is a totally different person in the mirror, not me."

"Maybe it's a different part you never let come out."

"That's for sure." She was sure there was no way she could let this aspect of herself come out in Lancaster. She wasn't sure where it could come out except here in Cariboo, where almost no one even knew she was a woman.

"Imagine all the miners who would come to have a look at you. Of course, Stella would have to come up with a flower name for you."

"How about Zinnia?" Kitty suggested, rather intrigued by the entire idea.

"That one hasn't been taken yet. Let's go show Stella." Rose grabbed her hand and tugged her out of the room.

The girls giggled as they made their way down the hallway past Nick's room.

"Ladies," Nick called out, "can I throw myself on your mercy?"

Chapter Sixteen

THEY BOTH STOPPED immediately. Kitty felt contrite. She'd forgotten about Nick for a few minutes, or did she? Wasn't the whole appeal of dressing like a woman, even a scarlet woman, more to gauge her attractiveness to a certain gambler? Laid up with a shoulder and thigh wounds, he could not move, according to doctor's orders. Kitty pushed the door opened to reveal a bare chested Nick sitting against the headboard.

The sight of so much succulent bare flesh made her swallow hard. Rose pushed her into the room with a snort.

"Ladies." Nick sketched an incongruous bow from his spot on the bed. "Welcome to my humble abode. Rose, who is this fetching creation?"

Kitty's mouth dropped open. He didn't know her? After all the time they spent together, plus the bathhouse and rolling around on the bed. A discarded pillow by the bed caught her eye. Grabbing it, she brandished it above Nick's head. "Maybe I need to knock some sense into you."

"Zinnia," Rose cried out, grasping Kitty's pillow holding hand. "Mr. Kennedy is already gunshot. No reason to hurt him more."

Kitty's shoulders slumped. Rose was right. He was hurt. Lowering the pillow, she looked into Nick's handsome face in time to see his smile vanish.

Did he recognize her? She wasn't sure. Gently, she placed her potential pillow weapon on the bed. "Sorry, sir. I don't know what came over me." Looking down at the toes of her new half boots, she almost missed his long slow wink, but not quite. "Nick Kennedy! You."

"C'mon, Zinnia. Let's go see Stella." Rose grabbed her and pulled her out of the room.

"Why'd you drag me out? I was ready to tell Nick what he could do with his tomfoolery?"

"Exactly why I did it." Rose shoved Kitty in the direction of the stairs. "You've spent so much time being a man you've completely forgotten how to be a female."

Holding on to the banister, Kitty carefully maneuvered her way down the stairs. She'd forgotten how difficult women's shoes could be to wear. Maybe she'd never known since all she'd ever had a chance to wear were low heel practical boots. "You know Nick was joshing me. He knew it was me all along. A big joke."

"A handsome man flirting with you isn't a joke. Women line up for a chance for Nick to notice them. You on the other hand try to swat him like a fly." Rose leaned forward to enunciate the last three words clearly.

Kitty turned to face Rose folding her hands in a prayer position in front of her chest. "Do you think he was flirting with me? Really?"

"Egad, you look like a hopeful virgin."

"I am a hopeful virgin," Kitty admitted.

Rose shook her head before answering. "Why am I not surprised?"

"Was he flirting?" She had to know. Her heart skipped a beat when she thought he might have been. Sure, he'd kissed her. Sure, they'd played and laughed together. Each incident, she put down as an oddity, something unusual that wouldn't happen again, no matter how much she wanted it to.

"Yes, he was flirting. Nick knew it was you. You look better in satin and lace, but it's not as if you turned into another person. Besides, Nick would know if Stella brought in a new girl."

Grabbing Rose's hands, Kitty begged. "Tell me what to do."

"Too late now. Didn't you ever flirt back in your hometown?"

"I remember when I was in school. If a fellow liked you, he might walk you home or offer to carry your books."

"Who carried your books?" Rose asked.

"More than one, but they came to a bad end. Daniel went to war and never came back. I was really too young for him to take me seriously. It was more of a case of me liking him and hoping someday he might care for me. There was Teddy Merckely who started courting me, but then threw me over for another." Kitty reached to wipe a non-existent tear away, but found her cheek dry. Usually talking about her never happening wedding caused her to tear up. Lately, Teddy didn't appear to be as good of a catch as he once had. Surprisingly, nothing hurt when she said his name.

"A girl who can't flirt manages to get a beau. How did that happen?" Rose wondered aloud.

"I wondered sometimes. I knew Teddy all my life. I used to beat him at marbles, but I don't think that did it." Kitty reached the bottom of the steps and turned to look at Rose.

"Go on, we'll show Stella how beautiful you are before we head back upstairs. Won't be nobody here since we aren't open yet.

The sound of Stella's raised voice helped pinpoint her location. "I've said it before. I can't help you. Go elsewhere. You aren't welcome here."

Kitty hesitated at the closed door, unsure if she should enter. Rose plowed into her from behind, pushing through the unlatched door.

The Pinkerton man looked up with an oily smile. "What do we have here?"

"Girls, this isn't the time." Stella stated as she turned, but catching a look at Kitty stopped her. Playing with her hair, Stella cast a sideways glance at the Pinkerton man who appeared interested, but not overly.

"New girl?" he asked with a lifted eyebrow.

"In a way," Rose offered, stepping out from behind Kitty. "She's my cousin from the next county over. She's only going to help out by serving drinks."

The Pinkerton man checked his watch and then looked up at Kitty. "Your name?"

"Zinnia, sir." Kitty tried for a higher voice than Kit's and ended up sounding like a cat with its tail caught under a rocking chair.

"Well, Zinnia, I look forward to seeing more of you." The Pinkerton man donned his derby hat and left.

Stella watched the man with both hands on her ample hips. "That won't happen. He will not be seeing Zinnia soon. We need Kit back, pronto. Go change."

Kitty slowly headed for the stairs reluctant to change back into her boy's clothes. What she really wanted to do was see how people might react to her in her saloon finery. She could hear Stella's angry tone. Rose was getting it. It wasn't her intentions to get Rose in trouble. It wasn't her intentions at all to even dress like a woman, but since she was. Maybe she could sneak over and show Harriet. They could both have a laugh about it. Grabbing a cloak from the peg, she whirled it around her. Kitty, knew she'd be back before the owner would miss it.

Slipping out the back door, Kitty turned left down the alley in the direction of the general store. Hurrying past a large stack of empty crates, a tingling feeling came over her as if someone walked over her grave, and then everything went black.

When she came to her handcuffed hands were roped to a saddle horn. The saddle horn was a tip off she was on a horse along with the swaying gait. Rope secured her cleverly worked half boots into the stirrups. This was not good, not by a long shot.

"I see you're conscious, Miss Katherine Hamilton."

The sound of her real name made her jerk. If she was a gambling person, she'd bet good money the voice belonged to the belligerent

Pinkerton man, Lily's potential bridegroom. The smug man astride a roan gelding confirmed her opinion. Kit looked at the horse she rode, an aging piebald from the livery stable.

"You are under arrest, and I am taking you back to Ohio for your court appearance," he affirmed with a smug smile.

"What about Lily?" It was a stupid thing to ask, but the first thing that came to mind. Lily would notice the absence of the Pinkerton man, but not her. Would anyone else notice they were both gone? Would Nick notice?

"Who?" The man looked slightly confused about the question.

"Lily at the Gilded Lily. That one."

"Her? The pretentious whore who thought she was better than the other whores. She was useful, but I've got all I wanted from her."

The callous words shocked Kitty. She said nothing, thinking maybe Lily inadvertently reaped what she sowed.

By evening, Kit's inner legs ached from the constant chafing of the saddle. Silk stockings did not make an effective barrier against the friction of her skin against leather. The gung-ho agent introduced himself as Henry Carlton and explained they would ride hard back to Lancaster to insure justice.

"I bet you bring in lots of outlaws," Kit cooed, modulating her voice the way Rose often did. Somehow, she managed to convey a sense of awe.

Carlton puffed out his chest. "I've assisted in the apprehension of several dangerous felons, mainly train robbers. You're my first solo assignment," he confided.

Searching her mind, she tried to recall how Rose flattered up her customers, making them think she only had eyes for them when her business forced her to have eyes for everyone. "You got me for sure, hunted me down like a dog would a defenseless rabbit."

Carlton bit his lip, looking unsure. Kitty wondered if maybe throwing in defenseless was a bit too much. The word slipped in, maybe because she felt helpless.

"Yep, I got you. Led me a pretty chase with your disguise, but I saw through it in the end," Carlton declared, tugging his derby hat down a bit to combat against the wind.

The wind chilled her body, raising goose bumps along her arms. What else could go wrong? Carlton pulled the horses to a stop.

"You're cold." Carlton dismounted his horse and pawed through his saddlebags, pulling out a jacket. "Here, put this on." He held the jacket out to Kitty.

She wiggled her cuffed hands meaningfully.

"Oh, right." Scurrying to her side, he untied the rope and unlocked the cuffs. He tried to help her wedge her stiff arms into jacket without any luck. "I think you'll need to get off the horse." He bent to loosen the ropes tying her feet into the stirrups.

"Gladly." Kitty swung her abused thigh over the saddle horn not carrying how much leg she exposed to Carlton. She slid down the horse's flank only to land unsteady on her half boot heels. Thank goodness, she had a horse to hold her up. Carlton held out the jacket. On her feet, she managed to pull on the loose wool jacket. It hung down past her thighs, guaranteeing the cold would start at her knees.

"Saddle up," Carlton barked.

"What?" Placing both hands on her hips, Kitty glared at the agent. "I just got off the horse. Now, you want me to get back on it. I could use some time to take care of some personal business."

"Personal business, what personal business? Is this some devious plan to escape?" Carlton rested his hand on the butt of his firearm.

"I have to use the facilities," Kitty yelled, aware her need to urinate might get her shot.

Red-faced, Carlton's hand slipped off the gun. "I'll have to go with you to insure you don't escape."

"What type of pervert, are you?" Kitty questioned as she hobbled off in the direction of a nearby group of bushes.

"Wait, I have to watch you in case…" His words trailed off as

Kitty reached some privacy.

She really did have to urinate, but as she squatted, she reviewed the possibility of escape. Several factors limited her, including not knowing the terrain, no transportation, and the fact the half boots had her walking like Grandma Coble when her rheumatism acted up. No escape. Walking slowly back to the horses and Carlton, Kitty wondered if Nick noticed her missing yet.

NICK WAITED IMPATIENTLY for Kitty to return. He wanted to get another look at her in her saloon finery. Her garish short dress would turn anyone's head, but he didn't like her tarted up like a saloon girl. He preferred her wet and naked reminiscent of their time in the bathhouse. Smiling, he sat up, tried to push a pillow behind his head, and waited for his confusing woman. His? Where did that thought come from?

Never mind, he reached for his pocket watch to check the time. It had been more than ninety minutes. Raised voices caught his attention.

Rose stuck her head in the door. "Seen Zinnia?"

Nick laughed before answering, "The better question would be have I seen Kitty?"

"Have you seen Kitty?" Rose put her hand on a hip to indicate her exasperation.

"No, I haven't, and I've been wondering why. I thought she'd come by before changing for work."

Crossing her arms, her brow wrinkled in thought. "I would have sworn she come to see you because you two…"

Nick sat up, raising both eyebrows in surprise. "We're what?"

"C'mon, despite the man clothes, you've been buzzing around her like a bee on a sunflower. It's been fun to watch you romancing a woman dressed like a man without looking like you are."

"So does everyone know? I imagine I look like ten kinds of a fool," Nick grumbled.

Rose laughed. "No worries, most people still think Kitty is a man. They aren't looking for what I'm looking for. I think it's sweet, but I will say this, Nick, Kitty is a nice girl. Break her heart and I'll break your nose."

"It's always a delight to talk to you. You're always so genteel." Nick commented.

"Ooh, fancy talk. I love it. I need to go find Kitty. Stella doesn't like her walking around in my old clothes." Rose reached for the doorknob. "Try to rest."

The noise below the stairs gradually increased, indicating The Gilded Lily had thrown open its doors for business. Turning his head, Nick tried to pick out the sound of piano playing. No music. Why not? Pushing himself off the bed, he ignored the sharp pain as his foot hit the floor. Hobbling to the door, he cracked it to listen for the sound of the piano. Still nothing. Something was wrong. Where was Kitty? Grabbing the cane Otis found for him, he debated on putting his boots on before going downstairs. He might need to go after Kitty so he had better be ready.

There was the usual crowd drinking and socializing. A few recognized Nick and called out for a hand of poker.

"Hey, Kennedy heard you were playing sick to get out of playing cards with me," an inebriated miner said.

"You're right." Nick commented as he worked his way through the room. Definitely no Kitty at the piano. Rose leaned against the bar tossing back a shot. Was she drinking? Stella insisted the girls not drink on the job. This demanded investigation. He worked in way through the room only answering half of the comments directed at him.

"Rose, is your drinking somehow related to our missing piano player?" Nick asked as he leaned on the bar, relieving the pain slightly in his gunshot leg.

"I kept pushing her. To dress as a woman, to show off for you, but I did something to make her run." Rose hung her head, missing the look Stella aimed her way.

Running a hand over his face, Nick looked up and asked, "How do you know she ran? Did you check her room?"

"No—Didn't realize she was gone until I started working."

"What about supper?" Nick mentally reviewed the order of Kitty's day. "Was she there?"

"No, but I assumed she was with you. She doesn't have to eat with all of us," Rose explained.

Nick calculated the time, ticking off the hours on his fingers. "It's been four hours since I last saw Kitty. Something's wrong. I know it." Slamming his fist on the bar, he startled several patrons who grabbed their drinks and moved away.

Otis sauntered up and lifted an eyebrow. "Got trouble?"

"I'm not sure yet. I'm heading over to Eastons."

Rose placed a restraining order on his arm. "They might be in bed. It's pretty late."

"Then they can get out of bed."

Catching Nick by the arm, Stella surveyed the crowd and asked, "It's Kit. Isn't it?"

Rose pushed her glass toward Otis for a refill. "Looks like she's gone. I thought she got scared and ran, but now I don't know."

Nick pried at Stella's fingers. "She didn't." he retorted, but he stilled to listen to Daisy, who eased up to the bar.

"Otis asked me to look into Kit's room, but everything is still there. She would have taken her stuff with her if she was running."

A gunslinger idled up to the bar during their discussion. He made the mistake of placing a hand on Rose's arm to get her attention, gaining a glare for his efforts. Stella added an arched eyebrow to send the man away with his puzzled frown and a grumble about unfriendly females.

Stella told Nick, "You just stand still a minute while I do some asking." She turned away as if to search for someone, moving casually from customer to customer asking if he had seen her missing piano player. Her slowness drove Nick crazy. The half-drunk patrons were quick to offer information. None of it was good, including details of dead cats found in the alley, coyote in the woods, and a loose milk cow.

"I didn't see yer boy. What I did sees might start a fire under Lily," a weasel-like man bragged.

Stella motioned for the man to continue.

"Done tole her what I seed. Da fancy man with his fancy hat Lily done looked right thru me ta spend time with." The small man put his thumbs under his suspenders and paused as if playing the crowd.

"Go on," Nick barked.

"I sees the fancy man pushin' another saloon gal onto a hoss." He finished with a dramatic brushing of his hands.

Stella reached out with her red tipped hand, grabbed the small man's shirt, and hauled him up to his toes. "Who was the girl?" She shook the little weasel for good measure.

"I dunno. Not yours. Just drunk as a bishop, couldn't even mount the hoss." He finished the last word on a yelp as Stella let him drop to the ground.

"Nick," Stella bellowed while walking in his direction. "That no good scalawag has Kit."

Otis grabbed his shotgun from under the counter and patrons ducked as he swung it around. A few scampered for the door while others dove under tables.

The drunk from his place on the floor called out. "He don't got your piano player. He got himself a fee-male."

Feeling like someone had him by the throat; Nick slammed his fist into the bar, startling the patrons who were starting to come out from the tables. They slid back under the meager shelter.

"The blasted Pinkerton fool," Stella mumbled while motioning for Otis to put the gun away.

Balancing awkwardly with his bad leg, Nick leaned down to grab the man's hand. The man shrunk away from him, but Nick managed to catch his arm and pull him upright.

"I didn't see a piano player. Told Stella," he babbled, twisting in Nick's grasp.

Nick shook him slightly to get his attention. "Listen, man, I'll let you go if you tell me what you know."

"I didn't see a boy. Was a fee-male," he whined, leaning in the direction of the door.

Nick gritted his teeth, "Describe her."

"White gal with short brown hair." The drunk cupped his hands on his chest. "Nice figure. Red dress.".

Opening his fisted hand, Nick allowed the drunk to fall to the floor. Ignoring the drunk's complaints, he headed for the stairs.

"What are you going to do?" Rose queried, running after him and grabbing his arm.

"I am going to get Kit back, of course." Nick replied.

Stella reminded, "The law is involved."

"It doesn't matter. I'm getting Kit back. Don't try to stop me." Nick shook off Rose's hand.

"Kennedy." The rejected gunslinger's voice cut through the pregnant silence. "I'll ride with you."

The man stood out since an empty space opened up from everyone inching away from him. Nick recognized the tall man. "Terrance, you can ride with me, but you'll have to keep up."

"You can't ride at night," Stella pointed out. "Get your supplies together and head out in the morning."

"Good thinking." Nick motioned to his old friend. "You got what you need?"

"Just got here, but I could stock up on some vittles if I could find someone to sell them to me."

Rose worked her way through the crowd to Terrance's side. She pulled his hand through her arm. "I know someone who will fill your vittles order even this late."

Nick continued slowly up the stairs, turning into Kit's room. He picked up her hairbrush fingering the short brown curly hair still caught in the bristles. Opening the chest drawers, he pulled out a ruffled nightgown and held it to his face.

How could Kitty be gone before he could declare his feelings? For a long time he'd known the gambling life was no longer for him. He thought a little farm might suit him. Even thought of breeding horses. After Rebecca, marriage held no appeal. Women did not inspire trust. Why marry? With Kit, they were friends. The jokes, the card playing, the conversations all added up to a level of friendship he'd never had with a woman. He grimaced touching her newsboy hat. What a gutsy female. Who else would have cut her hair, dressed like a boy, and headed to places unknown with her best friend? She took off with his saddlebags to protect him. He couldn't do any less for her. He would get her back. Life without Kit wasn't a life he wanted.

Feeling under her bed, he located her carpetbag. Opening it, he carefully placed in the nightgown, the boy's clothes, and the family photo. He found the Colt pistol hidden underneath the mattress, along with a bag of gold coins. Too bad, she didn't take the gun with her. It only confirmed his initial suspicions that her exit was forced. No way, she'd leave her money and her gun. My Lord, kidnapped, apprehended like a common criminal. The thought hit him harder than any roundhouse punch. Collapsing on the bed, he covered his face with his large hand and choked out a sob. What had he done?

Sitting up, he wiped away any suspect moisture. He knew what he had to do. A knock sounded, before Rose pushed the door open.

"You okay? Are you going to sleep in Kit's room?" Rose stood with her hands open and her reddened eyes watchful.

Nick picked up the flat pillow and inhaled. The faint smell of men's pomade lingered on the fabric. A reluctant smile curved his lips. He never thought he'd like the smell of men's hair pomade or it would remind him of the woman he loved. Loved? When did happen? He was too smart for love. He swore he'd never have the parson's mousetrap snap on him.

"Are you?" Rose asked with her furrowed brow. "I'd understand if you did."

Nick heard the words, but they made no sense to him. What was she talking about? He didn't have a clue. "Pardon?"

"I asked are you sleeping in Kit's room?" Rose tilted her head to give Nick a thorough look as if she was questioning his mental stability.

"No, I'm not sleeping. I got too much to do to get ready." He ignored Rose's protest as he hobbled out to find Terrance and see what type of supplies he'd secured.

Chapter Seventeen

D AWN PINKED THE horizon about the same time Nick swung his leg over the saddle. Terrance tied off the pack mule to his saddle horn before mounting his buckskin. A motley crowd of miners, saloon girls, and townspeople gathered around the two, shouting remarks and advice. Nick kicked Duke into motion, leaving the various directives behind them.

"Makes me feel a little like Lewis and Clark," Terrance quipped.

"We're nothing like Lewis and Clark. They explored unknown lands. We are rescuing a vulnerable female kidnapped by a nefarious sort," Nick growled.

"Really?" Terrance brightened. "Here I thought you were going to get Stella's piano player back."

"Never mind. Ride." Duke sprung into a trot at Nick's urging.

"You were never overly friendly, but now you're plain ornery." Terrance called out to Nick's rapidly departing back.

Pulling back on the reins, Nick slowed Duke to a walk. He should wait because Terrance was the tracker. Since only one road led out of town, not a lot of tracking could happen yet. He nudged Duke back to a trot. He needed to get there, be closer to Kit. Never had he felt so lost and helpless in his life. If he listened to Terrance's usual random comments, he might slug him. Flicking the reins hard, Duke responded by galloping down the straight path. Terrance could track him, Nick figured as he urged his horse on despite the pain in his thigh and shoulder.

Nick waited at the fork in the road for Terrance to catch up. Duke showed his impatience by stamping his front hooves. He was tempted to dismount and do the same until he heard voices. Terrance's, he expected, not a woman's. What now? He didn't have time or energy to deal with Terrance's shenanigans.

"What are you doing here?" he yelled as he spotted Rose aboard Stella's fat mare.

Terrance grabbed for Rose's horse bridle as if it would startle from the noise. "You got no call to be shouting at Rose."

Nick did a double take. Was this Terrance Ripley standing up for a saloon girl? He could tell by his narrowed eyes it was.

"Sorry, Rose, I'm upset as you can guess. You brought us news. Is Kitty back?" Nick asked, gentling his voice.

"No, Kitty isn't back, but your friend from San Francisco is, and he's trailing you. I thought you should know." Rose sat unmoving on her mount. "He's probably the sidewinder that shot you."

"Thanks. I'll keep it in mind," Nick answered. She was probably right, but now wasn't the time to worry about Walt. "Head back now, so you'll make it back before dark." He turned Duke's head back toward the path about the time Rose announced.

"I'm not going back. Kitty is about the closest thing I have to a friend." Rose's lips firmed into mulish expression.

Nick knew it was a fight he wouldn't win.

"Okay, but you got to keep up. I don't know how far they are ahead of us." Nick turned to look at Terrance. "Which way do you think they went?"

Leading his horse behind him, Terrance bent to get a better view of the hoof prints. Veering into the grass, he knelt examining the ground. "Found it. Good thing Archie at the livery rented the piebald with the split hoof to the Pinkerton agent. Makes it easier to track."

"Won't the horse come up lame with a split hoof?" Nick asked as he moved her horse closer.

"Archie put a bar shoe on to stabilize it, but still a good chance," Terrance answered, "if he keeps pushing the pace."

"That's what we'll hope for."

The three of them rode without talking for about five miles when they heard the sound of a wagon. The jingle of the harnesses indicated a wagon coming fast, they immediately moved to the side of the road to let the traveler pass. A pair of sizable draft horses emerged from the dust along with Adam and Harriet Easton.

Nick knew what déjà vu felt like. "What are you doing here?" he yelled as the team shuddered to a stop.

Harriet stared down Nick. "You would ask? Same reason as you."

Adam put an arm around his flustered wife. "I couldn't let my honey out on her own. There was no question of going to rescue her brother." He coughed on the last word and recovered. "It's what families do."

"Who's minding the store?"

"Triple H," they both chorused. "Hortensia used to work in her father's store back in Kansas."

"Okay." Giving up, Nick fought the urge to sigh. "We have to keep moving. Your job is to keep up."

"I brought supplies," Adam offered.

"Good," Nick barked.

"Guns and ammunition."

"Better," Nick agreed.

Harriet held onto her husband while asking, "There's not going to be a shoot-out?"

Terrance laughed. "No shoot out. We aren't an outlaw gang.

AFTER TWO DAYS on the trails, Kitty decided she might be open to an Indian attack, while Carlton acted as if he was bringing in Jesse James. Several times, he forced her horse off the path riding through stickers, tearing her skin and Rose's dress. The fool thought her outlaw gang would be hot on their trail to rescue her. Maybe he mistook her for Belle Starr. All she knew she was tired of his nonsense. She only hoped a train figured in his plan to deliver her to justice.

"Carlton, do you know the real story behind my flight?" Kitty queried, looking at the man holding himself stiffly in the saddle.

"I know what I need to know. Don't think to use your feminine wiles on me. I know your type," he answered, not even bothering to look her way.

"You mean innocent. That's my type." Kitty smiled, knowing the remark found its target.

"I said no feminine wiles." He shot her a pained look before kicking his horse into a gallop, which forced hers to run too since he had a lead rope.

Kitty flopped a bit in the saddle, before finding the stirrups. Thanks goodness, he gave up on tying her feet. Why did she have to rile up the Pinkerton man? There would be no knight on a white horse for her. She'd be lucky if anyone knew she was missing. Holding tightly to the saddle horn with her left hand, she lowered her face to her shoulder to wipe away a tear. She was back where she started, no hope and no future, no one to hold and call her own. Despites Carlton's fears, no gang would be rushing to her rescue.

The piebald started favoring his back leg, throwing Kitty forward every other step. Carlton's mutterings reached her ears as intended.

"I didn't do a thing to the horse. If you hadn't run him so hard and off the path, maybe he'd be okay," she snapped. Kitty had her fill of Henry Carlton, Pinkerton agent.

Carlton whirled around and backhanded Kitty almost knocking her from the horse.

Palming her struck cheek with her bound hands, she stared at the ashen Carlton. His eyes rounded with fear. Was he afraid she'd hit him back or report him to his superiors? Then she heard the snap of a twig breaking. It all made sense. Of course, anything that scared Carlton could be twice as bad for her.

"No one hits my woman," a familiar voice growled.

Nick! Nick's here! Kitty turned her head slightly and took in the stubble-covered face and bloodshot eyes glaring menacingly over the rifle stock.

"Don't shoot. Please." Carlton voice trembled.

"This is for daring to touch her." Nick lifted the barrel at the last minute and shot the derby off Carlton's head.

A man Kit had never seen before rode forward. "Enough, Kennedy."

Kit gave a quick, shocked glance behind the two men at Rose, Harriet, and Adam. She couldn't believe her eyes and couldn't even take the time to speak to them for what was going on.

"Whose side are you on, Terrance?" Nick questioned in a booming voice.

Terrance reached inside his duster and pulled out a star. "I happen to be on the law's side."

Carlton bristled up. "No two-bit sheriff is going to take my prisoner."

Rose looked up at Terrance adoringly. Terrance puffed out his chest under her scrutiny. "I'm a U.S. Marshal. Maybe you've heard of the organization?" All eyes were on Terrance, whose shoulders went back while his eyes reflected a steely determination. Carlton definitely took note. "What we have is a grave miscarriage of justice. A marshal would never hit a woman."

Carlton squirmed under Terrance's survey.

"The best thing to do," Terrance continued, "is to check out these charges against Kitty." Harriet gasped. Rose grabbed for Terrance's arm. Nick turned sharply with the rifle still in his hands. "Hear me out! If Kitty doesn't take care of it now, she'll always be on the run. From what I gather, these are made-up charges. Am I right?"

Both Kitty and Harriet nodded. Kitty told Nick, "I would like to clear myself so I can go on with my life."

"Okay." Terrance's eyes skimmed over the group, resting shortly on a puzzled Rose. "Who's going to Lancaster with me, Kitty, and Carlton?" A show of hands demonstrated the whole group would make the journey east.

Carlton slumped shoulders, straightened. "Wait a minute. We're not even in the United States."

"Sez who?" Rose asked, stepping closer to Carlton.

The Pinkerton man shook his head. "I know it took me more than a day to ride up here, and I wasn't tolling a whiny female behind me at the time."

Adam scampered off the wagon and stood, catching the Pinkerton agent's eye. "I ran freight for a couple of years on these roads. I know for a fact we just left Canada."

Carlton looked from Adam, to Rose, and then to Nick, who still held the rifle. His uncertainty, more likely, his resignation, registered.

With some fast maneuvering, Terrance and Nick sandwiched Kitty between them with a dispirited Carlton bringing up the rear. Kitty rode Carlton's horse while he rode the supply mule, and the lame horse followed behind the wagon. The small party startled when Nick called a halt. "Terrance, can I have a minute?"

At Terrance's nod, Nick helped Kitty and led her toward a copse of trees despite his limp. They were far away enough not to be heard, but still visible.

"Kitty," Nick looked into the eyes of the bedraggled beauty. "I don't know how to say this. I thought I'd die when I heard you were gone. I could not imagine life without you. Could you, would you, I mean…"

"Speak it plain, Nick." Kitty smiled at the sputtering man, liking his words, though she thought she knew what he might say next.

"Would you marry me?" He stiffened, waited for her response.

Kitty jumped into his arms, wrapping her arms around him tight while screeching in his ear.

"Is that a yes?" Nick managed to choke out.

"Of course, it's a yes. Does this mean you love me?"

"I do love you, darling." Nick dove in for a quick kiss, causing the watchers to cheer, all but Carlton.

"I love you." Kitty drew Nick's head down for a lingering, toes curling kiss that left her sighing for more. "Will you love me if I go to jail?" she asked, leaning against Nick's broad chest.

"It isn't going to happen. If need be, I'll hire the best lawyer money can buy. Let's go tell the others."

SACRAMENTO'S SILHOUETTE BECKONED to the weary travelers similar to a mirage. They checked into a hotel, while Carlton headed off to the telegraph station. He'd spent most of the trip threatening the whole of them with prosecution for interfering with his foresworn duty.

Nick reserved three suites of rooms for them, although he hoped not to end up sharing a room with Terrance and definitely not Carlton.

Harriet rolled her shoulders. "I need a bath."

People strolling through the lobby stared at the group, especially Kitty. A few women went so far to grab their skirts as they made a wide berth around her while complaining about the hotel allowing soil doves in its doors.

A bespectacled clerk came around the counter to grasp Rose's arm and reached for Kitty's too. "You need to leave. Go back to the saloon where you belong."

Nick turned at the low voiced threat, as did Terrance. The marshal took a threatening step in the clerk's direction. "You can remove your hand on your own, or I can remove it."

The clerk dropped his hand and took a step back, protesting,

"Um, we don't accept their kind here."

Adam fisted his hands. "Are you saying you don't allow happily married couples to stay here?"

The clerk gulped, gesturing to the three couples surrounding him. Terrance pushed back his duster displaying his gun and badge and gave an abrupt nod.

"So sorry," the clerk said, as he rushed back to safety behind the counter.

Terrance nodded. "Make sure baths are sent to the three suites immediately."

They headed up the stairs talking and laughing about the incident.

In the hall, Kitty dropped her voice to ask Nick, "If the clerk thinks we're married, where will I sleep?"

Nick winked. "You'll stay with your future husband. Are you shocked?"

She smiled up at Nick, who looked unusually sexy with his newly sprouted beard. "I will admit being shocked, though not at sharing the same bed. It's something I've been considering for a while. The fact I have a future husband is what really shocks me."

The room may not have deserved the name suite, but it looked very good after days on the trail. Nick walked to the window and pried it open, letting a breeze into the room. The room smelt stale as if closed up for a while.

Kitty turned in a circle, taking in the patterned wallpaper and brass bed. "You would think the clerk would be grateful to have the rooms in use, even with me dressed like this." She gestured to her bedraggled finery.

Nick walked slowly around her, his eyes flickering down her body.

Kitty put her hands over her face. "Don't look at me. I look terrible."

Putting his arms around her, he whispered into her hair. "You always looked good to me, even when you were pretending to be a boy. For a few seconds, I worried about myself, until I penetrated your disguise."

With her face pressed into his shirt, she still managed to protest. "No, you didn't. What gave me away?"

Using his two fingers, he lifted her chin to look into her eyes. "Your skin was too fine and clear, your eyebrows, delicate hands, you walk like a girl, and definitely no muscle. You couldn't lift your own carpetbag."

A knock sounded on the door, Nick crossed the room to allow in two young men carrying a hip tub. "Be right back with the water, sir," one said as they left.

True to his word, they were back in minutes. Kitty watched the servants fill up the tub. Nick placed an elbow in the water and pronounced it good. Along with the bath, several towels and a fresh bar of soap arrived. Would she have to disrobe in front of Nick? Better question was could she disrobe herself?

"Could you undo my laces?" She posed the question while looking over her shoulder at Nick.

He grinned as he stepped toward her. "Tell you what. I will undo your laces, but then I will have to leave. I'm not sure I could leave you alone long enough to bathe if I stay. I will have to lock you in to assure the good Pinkerton agent, I haven't allowed your felonious self to roam free through the city."

The sound of the tumblers falling into place assured her she was alone before dropping her dress. Easing into the tub, she wondered what she would wear. Nick did pack up her male disguise, but suddenly the freedom of pants was no longer desirable. What she needed was a decent dress, actually in her size. She lathered up her legs, imagining herself on Nick's arm dressed in female attire for a change. Ducking her head under water, she soaked her hair for shampooing.

Wrapped in one large towel and her hair wrapped turban-like in another, she prowled the room. Perhaps she should wash Rose's dress. Picking it up by the wide lace trim, she examined the various tears and trail dirt. There was no saving it. She'd have to suit up as Kit again. Taking the towel off her hair, she tousled her curls. Perching on the bed, she fell back on it. Soon, they'd finish what they started in her room at the Gilded Lily. She might not know all the intricacies of it, but her boy clothes would dampen Nick's ardor.

A knock sounded at the door. She hesitated remembering she couldn't open the door. Nick's beloved voice came from the other side.

"Kitty, it's me. I am going to open the door."

The door swung open, revealing Nick and a number of boxes. He carried some in, others he pushed in with his foot.

Curious, she drew closer, forgetting only a towel covered her. "What's in there?" She fingered one box, waiting for permission to open it. At his nod, she tore open the box to reveal a vivid flowered wrapper. Her eyes met his. "It's like Stella's."

"Similar." His smile broadened, causing his crow's feet to show. "It reminded me of how beautiful you looked in hers. I bought you clothes so you wouldn't have to be embarrassed by ignorant people again." His fingers reached out to touch the towel knotted at her breasts. "I have to say I like what you are wearing right now. You look every fetching."

Feeling attractive and playful, she danced away; leaving her towel in Nick's grasping hand. They both stared at one another. Using her hands, she tried to cover herself, but realized her small hands failed to do the job.

Nick took her hands, pulling them away from her body. "Don't. I want to look at you. You amaze me. I find it more amazing, I'm the only man who had sense enough to realize what a jewel you are."

His words made her forget her nudity. He managed to convey love through both his words and look. They stood there, staring at one another. It felt like a lifetime to her, wondering what would happen next. She knew what she wanted. Reaching up, she began unbuttoning his shirt.

Nick pulled his shirt out of pants. "I like the way your mind works. I bathed over at the bath house while I was out."

Smoothing her hands over his defined chest, she said, "I hope there was no Lolly offering to scrub your back."

"Jealous," he teased with a chuckle.

She pinched him, drawing an arched eyebrow and a teasing reply. "Okay, an old Chinese man ran the place. He didn't offer to scrub my back, either."

Placing a kiss on his chest, she murmured into his skin. "I'm glad. Otherwise, I'd have to hurt him."

Pulling back, Nick looked at Kitty, for one heartbeat, then two. Laughing, he scooped her up and tossed her on the bed. Diving onto the bed beside her, he embraced her. The two of them rolled around on the bed, laughing until someone pounded on the wall.

They stilled, looked at the offending wall, and laughed again. Shushing him, by placing a finger to her lips, her eyes twinkled, as she whispered, "We have to be very, very quiet as to not to disturb the other guests."

Nick sat up to remove his boots and waggled his eyebrows, making Kitty chuckle again. She covered her mouth with both hands trying to stifle her laughter, which made her laugh even harder. Nick stood up, gave her his back, and dropped his pants, which stopped her giggles.

She admired his tight backside wondering if all men were so handsome. She doubted it. He turned presenting evidence of his desire, explaining what she felt when they rolled around on the bed. Without thought, her hand lifted toward his cock.

Nick jumped back. "Whoa, now, sweetheart, I knew you'd be an enthusiastic lover, but I'd like your first time to last more than a few seconds." Placing a knee on the bed, he eased down, turning her to her back to run his fingers gently from her throat to her shoulders to the slope of her breasts. She sighed as her body softened to his touch.

"Happy?" he asked, as he drew his fingers up to her nipple.

Her eyes fluttered closed, as she sighed again. "I think I am more than happy. If this is happy, then I've never truly been happy before."

Leaning forward, he sprinkled tiny kisses down her neck, across her shoulders, trailing his lips to her breast. He stopped short of her nipple and looked at her. "Get ready to be happier." His lips molded around her nipple, her back arched off the bed, and she dug her heels into the mattress.

Lord have mercy. She never knew it could be like this. Why hadn't someone told her, but who would? Definitely not Aunt Eugenia, but Rose could have hinted. She drifted on a cloud of sensation as Nick paid homage to her other breast. She ran her fingers through his thick hair, holding his head to her chest. As a married woman, she could do this every night, even in the day too. Surprising folks ever got anything done, but she'd bet not every woman felt the way she did.

His fingers traced up her thighs, getting closer to the hidden maidenhead. Would she know when he broke it? "Nick, will I know when I am no longer a virgin?"

His eyes twinkled, as he bestowed a kiss on her nose. "One of the things I love about you is you're not afraid to speak your mind. I like to think you will know, especially if I do things right. Remember there might be a little pain, but it never lasts, and it doesn't ever happen again. Are you afraid?" His fingers stopped stroking her thighs.

Her gaze fell to his hand dark against her skin. Why did he stop? She looked up at his intent face, realizing he was waiting for her answer. "I'm afraid you'll stop."

Without thought, she rocked up, moving his fingers closer to her center until his fingers parted her nether lips. Her skin felt prickly, and her body ached, longed for something she couldn't quite determine.

"Nick," she breathed his name, hoping somehow he'd know what she'd need to ease the fire raging through her body.

"It's okay, sweetheart. I know what you need." He moved over her, placing his cock at her entrance.

In the sunlit room, she could see the tension in his face and feel the trembling in his body as he hovered over her. Perhaps she had the same effect on him as he had on her. His lips tenderly placed kisses on her brow, eyelids, nose, and finally her mouth. His tongue slipped in, tracing the roof of her mouth, tangling with her tongue.

Nick's sudden lunge filled her with a light twinge of pain. Was this it? She expected something more. Her body stretched around his, welcoming him. Sweat decorated Nick's forehead as he rested on his forearms.

"Are we done? I like the feel of you inside of me." Kitty hurried to add the last, uncertain if she might have offended him.

"Hell, no," he gasped before pulling out and plunging again several times. A warm feeling spread through her, reaching her toes and fingers, tugging them to curl. She sighed as he shuddered and collapsed onto her. He nuzzled her, before rolling to his back. "Kitty, I promise you the second time will be better."

Placing her hand on his sweaty chest, she gazed at him in confusion. "Better? I liked this time."

Pulling her body to spoon into his, he embraced her. "The more often we enjoy each other, the better we will get at pleasuring one another."

Resting against his chest, she spoke her thoughts aloud. "Just think, twenty, thirty years from now we'd be experts at making one another happy."

Nick chuckled. "It sounds good, but you are already expert in making me happy."

His words made her blissful, as she felt the pull of sleep tug at her.

A LIGHT TAP on the door awakened Kitty. Harriet's muffled voice came through the door. "We're heading out to supper. Do you want to go with us?"

She struggled to sit up, but found it difficult. Nick's muscular arm and leg thrown across her body pinned her in place. "Give us a few minutes."

Us. She liked the sound of it. Nick's eyes fluttered open, and he smiled at her. He rolled to look at the door before speaking. "Life intrudes. Might as well get something to eat." He placed a kiss on her nose before leaving the bed to dress.

Kitty followed and wished for a mirror to admire her smart walking ensemble Nick bought her. What is the use of new clothes when you can't see yourself? "How did you find clothes to fit me so well?" she marveled aloud.

"Didn't you notice me cataloguing your charms before I left?" Nick teased, while pulling on his boots.

"Hmm, I noticed, but I would have thought buying me clothing was the last thing on your mind." She perched the saucy hat atop her curls hoping she had the angle right. Obviously, due to a lack of a mirror, a man had furnished the rooms. Wait, there had to be one above the basin for the men to shave. Finding the mirror, she admired herself. Tilting her head one way, then another, she giggled. Kitty never thought of herself, as a vain woman, but then again she never had anything to be vain about. Perhaps, a hat, a man, especially the man, changed everything.

Nick's reflection in the mirror drew closer until he stood behind her, wrapping his arms around her. "She's magnificent, the woman in the mirror." He nodded, and then added, "But even she has to eat sometime.

Harriet and Adam met them in the hall with shining faces. Kitty wondered if their attitude reflected her own happy state, or perhaps they found a favorable way to spend the afternoon.

Harriet rushed to her side, to tug on her arm. "Kitty, Kitty, guess what?"

Before she could ask, Adam answered. "I think Pinkerton received a reply to his telegraph that didn't please him."

Nick hugged her close. "Probably something along the lines of Kitty not being dangerous."

The six of then went to dinner with Carlton trailing along, still insisting he had to take Katherine Hamilton to Lancaster, Ohio to hear for himself the warrant was withdrawn. The sullen Pinkerton man refused to join in the conversation, but sat with folded arms through the majority of the meal. As they sat around the table as they made their plans to travel east the next morning.

After what had been on heavenly night for Kitty, they made their way to the rail station, not that it eased any of Kitty's dread. They deposited the lame piebald and cow at the livery with money for their care. The group finally boarded the train in high spirits. No one doubted Kitty's innocence, except for Carlton. Attired in stylish women's clothes, Kitty resembled a wealthy banker's wife, while Rose joined her attired in conservative brown plaid traveling dress. Terrance even folded up his duster, looking less like a lawbreaker and more like a lawman.

"Did you always know I was a woman?" Kitty asked as they settled in for a ride.

"The bath house confirmed it, but I had my doubts early on. Too pretty to be a male," Nick commented while squeezing her hand.

"Why were you in Cariboo, Terrance?" Rose asked.

"I was following an outlaw," Terrance replied a little abruptly.

"I did kinda wonder why you showed up in Cariboo." Nick teased, figuring Terrance was holding back to keep Carlton from hearing. "I knew it wasn't because we were such good friends."

The trip went too fast considering Kitty might be getting closer and closer to jail. At the Saint Louis stop, Carlton insisted on stopping at the Pinkerton office. Terrance insisted on going with him. Carlton protested sure Kennedy would make a run for it, but Terrance, being the persuasive sort, convinced him it was better if they went together.

Kitty clenched her hands, worried about Carlton's certainty. The man wouldn't listen to anyone. If the law thought she was guilty, then, she was, which, would be unfortunate when she had a future with Nick.

"Hey, Kitty, I hear there is a bathhouse right beside the station. How about we…" Nick teased.

"There's Terrance," Rose said, pointing with one hand.

Kitty stood up, straining to see the tall man in the crowds of people. Terrance hurried forward as Carlton walked behind.

"What did you find out?" Nick reached for Kitty's hand.

"No warrant. It was withdrawn almost as soon as it was issued. If our man Carlton had checked in with the office occasionally he would know it," Terrance announced with a big grin.

"Woo-whee," Rose cheered.

Kitty leaned against Nick. "Should we turn back now?"

"Oh no, we haven't even made it to your new home, yet" Nick kissed the top of Kitty's head. "You'll have a lovely little farm in Kentucky. I looked at it last time I was through here. Will you miss Lancaster?"

Kitty thought about it. Would she miss Lancaster? "The only friend I had left in the place was Harriet. Now she's gone too, in a manner of speaking. I guess that would be a no, I won't miss it."

Nodding his understanding, Nick suggested, "I think we need to go see your Aunt Eugenia."

"Do we have to? The woman is a witch," Kitty pleaded.

Harriet joined the couple. "Think. You can show off your hand-some and wealthy husband like I am going to do."

Despite her reluctance, that was where she ended up. It was much too soon to be returning home as far as Kitty was concerned.

She stared up at the familiar porch. Had it only been two months since she was here last? It felt like a lifetime. She came to say her goodbyes to Eugenia since she had no desire to continue the relationship. She thought she could do it alone, but she found out she was no longer only part of a couple, but part of a gang.

She barely tapped on the door when Foster, the family doctor, threw it open.

"Katherine, you're back," he said and called back into the house. "Eugenia, she's back."

A smiling woman rushed out the door and embraced her while crying into her neck. "I'm so glad you're home." When she kissed her, Kitty backed out the woman's embrace, eyeing her suspiciously.

Foster laughed hard. "Eugenia, darling, she doesn't recognize you."

The smiling woman looked puzzled, then drew her eyebrows together and forced her lips into a frown.

"Aunt Eugenia." Kitty finally recognized her.

"Katherine, I want you to meet Foster..." Eugenia said while gesturing to the man on the porch.

"I know Foster." Kitty commented.

"My husband," Aunt Eugenia continued.

"Your husband?" Kitty looked back and forth between the two of them. "I understand now. You're in love."

Foster placed an arm around Eugenia. "Never underestimate the power of love."

Nick wrapped one arm around Kitty's waist, "I'll make sure she never does."

Epilogue

THE GROUP MOSEYED down the street. Adam slid up beside Nick. "That farm you're getting, do you think there might be some land to sell close by? My sweetie has a hankering to have a dairy farm, the closer to you the better."

Nick looked at the anxious man and his equally tense bride. "The place I have picked out has plenty of land. I'm willing to sell you some."

Adam and Harriet hugged in delight.

Adam slapped Nick on the back almost knocking him down. "We'll have to go back to Cariboo and sell the store, but give me your direction, and we'll be back as soon as possible."

Kitty turned to Rose. "What are your plans?"

Rose looked at her feet and kicked the ground some. "I guess I'll go with the Eastons back to work at the saloon."

Reaching for her friend's hand, she interlaced their fingers. "You could do that, or you could go with us and start a new life." She nudged Nick. "Couldn't Rose go with us to start a new life?

Nick looked startled, then grinned. "Yep, we can say your sisters."

Rose looked wistful for a moment, then crestfallen. "I couldn't do that. It wouldn't be right. I'd be a burden on a new couple."

Nick held up his index finger as if making a point. "Rose, I may be a gambler, but I always considered myself a man of honor. You looked after Kit very well, even to the point of trying to protect her from me when you thought my intentions were bad. The very least I can do is to help you get a new start. I also have a feeling you might not stay with us that long."

The three of them looked at Terrance knowingly. As if feeling their eyes, Terrance looked up. He touched his hat to the ladies, but motioned for Nick to step away from them. "As you guessed, I never caught up with the man I was trailing. I didn't want to go into any details in front of the women, but I believe he was trailing you, especially with the amount of money you win in your major stakes games. Name's Dover, and he's a no good hombre. He's terrorized folks, robbed others, even some rumors he may have killed one or two. I'm wondering now if he was after Walt. The way I figure it, one or the other of them is the one who took those shots at you. Maybe the two knew each other, or maybe there was bad blood between them. I think it might be best just to hang around you for a while in case he shows up." His eyes drifted over to Rose. "Official business, you understand. Might keep you bullet free for your wedding night."

Nick's eyes crinkled with mirth. The chances he was still being tracked were slim. Considering all the miles he'd traveled, it would cost a fortune to follow him. Eventually, it would end up being more than what he won that night in Frisco. "I'm thankful to have such a selfless friend who would put himself out for me."

Terrance winked. "You are a lucky man, in more ways than one."

Nick gazed at Kitty talking animatedly to Rose. His lips tilted up as his eyes warmed. "I'm a very lucky man, but it wasn't my good memory for cards, but my close observation of unusual travelers that did it."

THE END

Love or Deception

BY

MORGAN K. WYATT

2013

A Contemporary Romantic Suspense

Chapter One

"I LOVE YOU," Mark whispered into her hair as he slipped one long, muscular leg over hers. Amy snuggled closer to him, nuzzling his neck. Ah, she loved this time, right after a rousing lovemaking session when they were both sated and drowsy, drunk on the idea that in a world of mismatched couples, somehow they found each other. Mark's slight snore alerted her he'd dropped off to sleep. She should get up. There was so much to do before work. Instead, she stayed, breathing in the peace of the moment.

Hard to believe she was a bride. Not that she had anything against marriage. She just hadn't foreseen it happening to her. How could it? All she did was work at Theron under major security scrutiny. The only people she saw were other employees, with the majority being women. The confidentiality clause she'd signed forbade fraternization between employees. The company must have a reason for being so paranoid. Right now, she didn't care. All she wanted was her husband to awaken.

"Honey, do you remember our wedding?" Using her index and middle fingers, she made slow circles across his wide shoulders and around his muscular arm. The barbed wire tattoos encircling his biceps always surprised her, not that they didn't look good on his tanned skin. They did. No, it was that she never imagined herself as a woman with a big gorgeous husband who could easily be a male stripper or a porn star with his looks. Nope, she never expected to marry. Even if a part of her held out hope, she never expected anyone without a heavier eyeglass prescription than hers.

Mark held up one arm, stretched, and twisted it enough to make his bicep pop. He noticed her eyes following the play of muscles. His deliberate wink made her giggle a little. Geesh, just another sign she was way out of her depth. Truth told she never dated much, period. School, then work consumed her every waking moment.

He rolled to his side, facing her, and yawned before answering. "I do remember our wedding since I was there. Plus it was only two weeks ago."

"Yes." All that was true, but it wasn't what she wanted to hear. By mentioning the subject, he might tell her how wonderful it was or even describe it in detail. Did she expect him to gush about the meaningfulness of their vows? No way, she'd admit that she had issues bringing their wedding into focus. All she could see was a couple and minister on the beach with the sun setting in the background. With the shadows falling on them, it was hard to tell if the couple was even white, let alone if it was actually them. The sun was setting in the west, which worked since they married in Tahiti. Still, it had the same feeling of looking at a magazine ad for honeymoons.

The woman had on a short dress, and the groom wore a loose white shirt. That she could tell. They did have a whirlwind romance. Was it possible she was drunk when she married Mark? Was that why she couldn't remember anything very well? Her hope was, by mentioning the wedding, he might also confess how wildly in love he was with her. It might ease her fears about the two of them being an odd couple.

Her Aunt Remy raised her with a healthy self-esteem. Being worthy of her handsome husband wasn't an issue. It was more a case of like going with like. She'd heard enough comments when a couple showed with one partner being more attractive. When the woman was more beautiful, people assumed the man was rich and powerful. Charitable women might think he was charming and good in bed. Unfortunately, it never worked that way with the women. People seemed genuinely baffled and usually predicted a future break-up. Rather unfair if you asked her. Couldn't the woman have some great trait? Maybe she was smart, interesting, and a decent conversationalist, even reasonably good looking with a slender build and short blonde hair. Her nose crinkled once she realized she'd just described herself.

The curve between his shoulder and neck beckoned her to nuzzle.

The simple action reassured her that they were actually married and together. Everything happened so fast. A slow roll of her body had Amy looking up at her husband who pinned her to the mattress. "I think I know what my own Dr. Death needs." He wiggled his eyebrows and leered at her.

"MA'AM, MA'AM, COULD you take a look at this?" A man with a wrinkled jacket and mussed hair pushed Mark's appointment book into her hand. An appointment book, how quaint, when everyone else relied on cellphones and laptops for date keeping. She blinked twice wondering why the man with the short, abrupt-sounding name handed her the book. What was his name, Burt or Bark? She couldn't remember. Was it just yesterday, the day before, or even longer ago when she laid in bed enjoying the warmth of Mark snuggled up next to her? She lolled in the security of his embrace and now she was sitting alone in their living room, except for Bark and his partner.

"Ma'am, I need you to look at the book. Is this his? Does the writing looking familiar?" The detective stared at her as if dealing with a particularly recalcitrant child. He nudged the book as if she wasn't already aware that it was in her hand. It was Mark's day planner filled with his illegible scrawl. How could he be gone?

"Detective..." She hesitated unsure of his name, even more, unsure of what she was going to say. How did this all happen? It seemed like a fog encased her normally sharp mind. She was smart once. She couldn't remember anything clearly, but she had a vague memory of being intelligent. She even held down an important job of some sort.

A woman's shrill voice called her name. "Amy!" She turned in the direction of the voice as a woman hurried toward her all blues and greens and vivid red hair. She should be able to see better than this. Her glasses, she needed her glasses.

The woman reached her, hugging and enveloping her in a cloud of familiar scent. Something tugged at her memory. She knew this woman. A slight smile graced the woman's face, conveying both pity and solace simultaneously. Touching her face, she looked up at the woman in entreaty. "My glasses?"

"Amy," the woman stroked her back as she talked, "you quit wearing glasses after your Lasik surgery, remember? You said you wanted to look younger and flirty, not like the scientist you are."

Scientist. She was a scientist. Yes, that's right, but what did she study? Why was it so hard to remember anything? Maybe the woman knew Mark. Odd, she couldn't even remember that she no longer wore glasses, but she could remember Mark, the feel of him next to her, his smile, even his snorty little laugh that made him sound a bit like a pig, something she never mentioned, knowing it would make him self-conscious. She burst into tears, as a wave of desolation swept over her again like a hungry tide pulling her downward.

"Don't worry, Amy. Aunt Remy is here," the woman promised as she wrapped her arms around her and rocked her slightly as if she were a baby.

"Ma'am," the detective protested, "you're crushing the book. It could be evidence."

Remy pulled the book from Amy's unresisting fingers and handed it to the officer. "You'd think if it was so important you'd be dusting it for prints."

"Yes, ma'am." The disheveled man didn't answer her question, but managed a strained smile before taking the book. He walked over to his partner.

The two detectives spoke in hushed voices stirring Amy's curiosity. Her tears stopped as she sat up trying to hear them.

"Great another one who watches every police drama. They all think they are CSI experts. Did you find out anything, Maxfield?"

"Not much, the wife called the police stating her husband disappeared while she was in the shower. I don't know, Burt, it sounds peculiar."

Amy noticed Burt's measuring look and heard his comment. "She doesn't look like the type to off her husband." His partner huffed her disagreement. "Besides, I heard they were newlyweds."

Maxfield raised her eyebrows before commenting. "Newlyweds kill each other every day, especially if the will favors them. I heard Amy Newkirk is one of the top scientific minds in biological warfare. They call it something else, but that's what it really is. A woman who devises ways to kill off entire populations without a sound is not a delicate blossom."

Burt's head swiveled back to stare at Amy. "I don't think so. Those aren't movie tears. That woman's heart is broken right in two. Besides, what is the motive?"

Maxfield aimed a cuff at her partner's arm. "That's our job to find out before they call in the FBI."

Their conversation added to Amy's distress, restarting the tears she'd almost stopped and causing Remy to shout at the chattering detectives. "Will ya' all just shut up or move to a different room? She can hear every word you're saying. I can too, and I'm not liking it."

Wiping her nose with the offered tissue, Amy surveyed the room, trying to pull her thoughts together. The woman whispering to the detective with the short name said she worked on killing people. That couldn't be right. She'd know if she was a killer, wouldn't she? She looked up into Remy's concerned brown eyes. If she were a killer, would Remy hold her so tight? Did they think she killed Mark?

Blinking twice, she tried to clear her eyes of the vision-blocking tears. Everything still looked vague and blurry. Touching the bridge of her nose, she asked again, "My glasses?"

Remy jumped up surprisingly fast for such a large woman. "You stopped wearing them, but if you think you need them, I think I might know where a pair is, you being so organized and all."

Remy reappeared with a black case in her hands. Amy opened

the case to reveal a pair of plastic horn rimmed frame glasses. No wonder she stopped wearing them. Placing them on her nose, she peered through the lenses bringing everything into slightly better focus slowly as if adjusting a camera lens. There, she had it, mostly. The edges were a little fuzzy still. It was like one of those photos where the camera focused in on the center object and intentionally blurred the surroundings. Her eyes took in the plain walls stacked with boxes and one lone framed photo on the wall. Standing, she walked to the picture, which featured a grass shack perched on wooden stilts over water with palm trees in the background. No figures stood near the shack or even peered out its lone window. The photo gave her a sense of peace.

"That's probably from your honeymoon. In Bora Bora or was it Tahiti? You remember?" Remy nodded at her as if she should remember.

She shook her head no. "I don't remember anything. All I know is Mark is gone. My memory went with him. Those people," she pointed in the direction of the whispering detectives, "keep asking me questions I can't answer, and my head hurts."

"Oh, sweet darling, come sit down. Can I get you some aspirin? Maybe a glass of water? How about both?" Remy led Amy back to the couch, before bustling off to the kitchen. On her way back, her outspoken aunt, stopped in front of the detectives who conversed only a couple of meters away from the couch.

"What is wrong with you people? Can't you see my niece has been drugged? Why aren't you investigating that instead of having your heads up your asses? Standing over here making conjectures about how my niece might have killed her husband. Don't think I don't know how your lazy police minds work. Never wanting to do the legwork, just pin it on someone nearby, and call it a day."

"Ma'am," Burt said, only to have his partner interrupt.

"What makes you think she's drugged," Maxfield asked, opening her keypad on her cell to take notes.

"Did you even look at her eyes? Her pupils are dilated. She didn't know who I am, either. I practically raised her when my sister Cici ran off with some Marine. She stood and stared at a picture from her honeymoon and didn't recognize it. My gal is smart. She went to college on scholarships, has both a medical degree and a doctorate's in biochemistry. She's no party gal who does recreational drugs in case you were going to suggest that."

Amy fought the grin that tugged at her lips. True, she didn't remember much, but the sight and sounds of her Aunt Remy lighting into the detectives felt familiar.

Placing both hands on her hips, Remy continued chastising the two. "I mix up enough potions to recognize the signs of poison. Part of my business is to know when someone is hexed or poisoned."

Burt took an involuntary step back at Remy's revelation while his partner stood her ground.

"What do you know about Mark?" Maxfield asked.

Amy pretending not to eavesdrop picked up the discarded appointment book and flipped through it.

"Ah, Mark." Remy's smile could be heard in her voice. "I wish Amy could tell it. There was such joy in her voice when she told me about him. Suffice to say, she loves that man more than life itself. Your job is to go find him."

Remy turned and hurried over to her and flourished the glass in front of her face. "Drink it up with the aspirin, Sweet Pea."

Amy took the proffered tablets and sipped the water slowly listening to the detectives.

"She doesn't know anything about Mark," Burt commented. Maxfield mumbled her agreement.

"I suspect if Amy is as in love as her aunt declares, then all she would do is talk of her beloved, especially considering they are newlyweds. Keep in mind; this is a very smart woman, probably smarter than ninety percent of the population, so finding a boyfriend will not be easy for her. Especially if she wore those awful glasses."

Amy noticed the woman's shudder. She retrieved the glasses from her head to see if they were that terrible. Sturdy no nonsense dark frames surrounded sizable plastic lens. Obviously not that fashionable, but they served a purpose. If the glasses could talk, they could tell her all that she couldn't remember. No sudden influx of information came causing her to put the glasses on a nearby table. Her best bet would be to listen to what other people had to say and just maybe she might be able to piece together the missing parts.

"That means Amy knew very little about her new husband too." Burt stroked his scruffy beard. "Then we need to start there. Looking into who was or is Mark Schaeffer."

Maxfield shook her head. "Actually, we need to do a drug screen on Amy before it is out of her system, especially with all that water her loving Aunt Remy is pumping into her."

AVAILABLE AT ALL ONLINE RETAILERS

Author Notes

If you liked Escaping West, then you'll enjoy the re-release of The Rebel Hearts series in 2017.

Stop over at www.morgankwyatt.com to see what books are out, what contests are happening, and if I'll be making a personal appearance near you.

Make sure to sign up for the newsletter on the website too. It is a great way to get free stuff included stories, swags, books, and Amazon gift cards.

You can hang out with me at:

Facebook
www.Facebook.com/AuthorMorganKWyatt

Twitter
www.twitter.com/morgankwyatt

Pinterest
www.pinterest.com/morgankwyatt

Goodreads
goodreads.com/author/show/5826299.Morgan_K_Wyatt

Amazon
amazon.com/Morgan-K-Wyatt/e/B008EEC4EY